Until V
Again...
in Jannah

Laki Khan

ISBN: 978-1-9997820-0-9

Dedicated to
Maryah Isra Khan
Aamilah Isra Khan
&
Soyodun Nessa

ACKNOWLEDGEMENTS

There are so many people I want to thank, so please bear with me! First and foremost, my mum and dad and amazing grandma – thank you so very much for sharing the wonderful stories that you did about your village and my ancestors. Little did I know that these stories would later become the inspiration for *Until We Meet Again... in Jannah*. My beautiful sister and wonderful brothers – what can I say other than thank you for the unquestioning support in all I do, and thank you for always having my back. Next, I would like to thank RK, all of my family and friends, and everybody behind the scenes from editing, formatting, cover designers and bloggers for all your support – it means so very much. I want to thank my beautiful angels for allowing me to have those precious minutes, and sometimes even hours, to work on my book, and thank you for teaching me the meaning of love every single day. And lastly, to you, dear reader – thank you for picking up this book. I truly hope you enjoy the journey from within as much as I have.

Much love
Laki

Prologue

'When you find the one, you will know. It will just feel right! True love is not perfect – you love them, despite their imperfections.'

I have lost count of the number of times people have said this to me – mostly women who, perhaps, were testament to the overall impact of such a statement – words only spoken to discourage and fall upon deaf ears. These were women who tried to improve on a system of belief they did not belong to, or that did not resonate with theirs.

I have heard and read about the kind of love that can ignite an awakening of your soul, leaving you wanting more. However, in my case, it was emblematic that it arrived at the conclusion of compromise and loss. I was well aware that some people enter your life as a lesson and some as a blessing, and he was the latter. He taught me to stand when I had succumbed to falling. He became more myself than I could ever be; and whatever we had been moulded from, we were one of the same – alike – two souls destined to connect.

Like small particles of a shattered mirror, I lay broken, irreparable, oblivious to what lay ahead; in the predicament of fate and of what had been unwritten. Sometimes things just happen, incidents that are terrible and unplanned, and they have consequences. They often change you from within – for better or for worse remaining undecided and unaccomplished.

Ultimately the fact remained that I was a woman of ill fate: dishonoured, disdained and unworthy of him and his love.

Chapter 1 - Saira

It was almost midday. Complete with the magical riches of autumn, orange, brown and gold in the month of September 1996, and I peered out of the window to see a lady holding on to her daughter's hand tightly as they crossed the road, heading for pre-school. And, just like every other day, they were late again. The connection I felt with the little girl unsettled me because I wasn't sure why. It made me hyperventilate. Perhaps the girl reminded me of something, or someplace, where I had been obliviously happy, safe, secure and loved, until the course of destiny changed my existence in its entirety. It galvanised me to become the person I now was. Misty clouds had covered the entire lead-coloured sky, as the golden-brown leaves flew up and then back down again. Our first-floor London apartment was beautiful, so airy and light. In many ways it represented a new beginning, one with a profound purpose and a new love.

My body came to a momentary halt as I smiled and indulged in the familiar mixture of aromas: a little musk, soft amber, light lavender, a little sandalwood, and the freshness of the ocean with a hint of spice and, of course, a little of his very own body scent; it was mystifying. I could always smell him right before he appeared within my peripheral vision. It was a scent I had become so fond of that when I couldn't smell it I would long for it. In many ways he had become the representation of behaviour I was no longer able to express and words I could no longer speak. At once he wrapped his warm arms around me and I revelled in the safety of his embrace. 'Morning,' he said, brushing his cold cheek onto mine as I shrieked playfully. He was tall, lean built with a head full of short curly hair, and overtly handsome. There was a hidden solace, against that olive skin and, big golden-brown eyes that you could immerse yourself in till the end of time; and that smile that lightened his face like rays of sunshine.

'I will stand by you forever…' Those were words he had remained true to up until this moment, as if he were trying to replace the void in my heart and lessen the weight of my loss. His had become the shoulders that I instinctively reached out for; when I felt weak he gave me strength and when I felt fear he gave me courage. This was a bond, unbreakable beyond reason or explanation. We had been married nine months, and I could say with certainty that our bond was as special as they came – and one that was intricately complex.

'Where did you go so early,' I asked with curiosity.

'I went to see Kareem. He asked about you, and would like us both to go for dinner one of these days,' he replied with a smile. I became numb, but he looked into my eyes, threading his fingers through the tangles of my hair and reassuringly said, 'No pressure. I told him soon, whenever you're ready.' Kareem and Omar were good friends, and Kareem was my only acquaintance; I knew nobody else here. I didn't want to go. I had lost the courage to go anywhere, let alone for dinner. They had been business partners, only Kareem had given up working with Omar to become the sole carer for his father, who had unfortunately suffered a debilitating stroke a few months earlier. Kareem resembled Omar in many ways. Both were selfless and thought about others before considering their own needs. Although Omar was the owner of a successful real estate business, he chose to lead a life based on simplicity and was grateful for the smallest of blessings.

Just as I did every evening, I set the table for two, and today the flatbread had miraculously turned out round and fluffy as I had followed the steps of the method I had been taught. 'Saira, remember to press down well with the heel of your palm,' I recalled in remembered pain. A part of me felt guilty for not being able to move forward and was in constant battle at this most difficult time of day. I remembered when evening mealtimes used to give me so much joy that my stomach would ache from the discomfort of laughter. I reminisced about when Omar had held up the octagonal-shaped flatbread I had rolled; no matter how much I tried they were never circular. That evening the three of us had laughed so much that when I closed my eyes I could still hear the echo as if it were only yesterday. The irony being that now I had finally learnt to roll them round. Like the blink of an eye three had become two, and the pain shot through my internal being, pulling at the delicate cords of my heart so suddenly that I cried out. In trepidation his arms fastened around me in a protective embrace; and neither of us uttered a word as a ghastly silence ensued.

Today was the evening of Tara's party; Tara was his cousin, and was captivatingly beautiful. She was one of two children belonging to his paternal uncle and aunt, who we only saw at the very few family gatherings that we attended. I was secretly relieved at the little contact we maintained with them as they always mistreated him. The party was in honour of Tara's graduation. It would be a grand celebration and my instincts were almost warning a foreseeable calamity. I could see an uncomfortable grimace build up on Omar's face whilst he told me about this, and I knew that he was concerned more for me than himself. I pondered whether or not I would be able to handle the insults and the leading questions I knew inevitably I would be subjected to. Staring into his eyes over breakfast I smiled; he had taught me to silence the world so that I could hear myself. He taught me love while others had violated, so surely I could tolerate one evening for him.

'I've been meaning to give you this for a few days now, and today seems perfect,' he said softly, unwrapping a small sparkly silver box. I watched in the mirror as he adorned me with a golden bespoke pendant that sat almost perfectly around the nape of my neck. It was a very pretty, delicate chain with an oval-shaped pendant attached right in the middle. I carefully held up the pendant which read 'Saira and Omar till Jannah'. He whispered the words aloud.

'I love this,' I replied, now teary-eyed as we prepared to leave.

We were greeted at the door and they gestured for us to step inside. Just as I had expected she was embellished in her best attire, as if a trophy to be shown off; she looked absolutely beautiful. There were a lot of guests, and the inquisitively staring eyes dazed me almost to the verge of despair. The entire house sparkled with colourful lights, whilst a variety of food had been set up in a buffet style on a rectangular table that had been adorned with many intricately designed desserts; grandeur and opulence defined them. Omar greeted the ever-questioning onlookers with a subdued smile and not once did he leave my side.

As the evening progressed Chachi's unkindly glares became more and more difficult to tolerate. My throat felt parched and my palms became sweaty, as I took deep breaths and smiled at Omar. Chachi, Tara and their friends continued to stare and in response my nervous system appeared to heighten every sense within me, sending me into a panicked frenzy of emotions.

Later that evening Chachi walked over to me and smugly said, 'Saira, you're wearing a sari today, you look almost unrecognisable.'

She was joined by Tara. 'Oh Mum, I guess she has to follow the trends with her own life changes, or people may still mistake her as the maid.' This infuriated Omar. In response I held his hand and looked into his eyes, preventing his retaliation, and he knew my subliminal message was for him to remain silent.

Just as we attempted to walk away Chachi shouted, 'After all that we have done for you, and now you have rejected Tara for this orphan girl. What status does she have? She has turned you into what she is. Do you know how many men would line up to marry Tara?' Silence ensued in the entire party, and everybody's eyes were fixated upon us. I wanted the ground to open up and swallow me whole; why were they so mean?

Omar took my hand into his, walked over to Chachi, pulling me gently behind him, and spoke in a strong, calm voice. 'Your opinion makes no difference to me. I am just a man who loves my wife very much, and the sooner you accept that the better.' Nobody whispered a word while Chachi glared at us with hostility. Omar looked at me and said, 'We're leaving now, Saira,' as he led me out of the function and into the car, slamming the door shut.

'Omar!' I heard a familiar voice call out from behind our car. Much to my surprise the voice belonged to Tara who had the audacity to follow us out.

I stared, confused, as Omar glared at her unequivocally and said, 'Have you not caused enough grief already?'

'Does your wife know the truth?' Tara shouted back, which only baffled me further. Truth? Which truth was Tara referring to, I wondered.

'Tara, I am telling you for the last time, please move on with your life,' he said, clearly frustrated, and then climbed into the car. He was visibly angry as the cold reality of this evening had been on a greater scale than expected; I felt the build-up of aggression in the manner of his driving increase and he avoided eye contact with me.

'Omar, please say something,' I pleaded.

'What is left to say, Saira? This is why we never should have attended this function,' he said in a raised voice. I could almost feel the dejection and failure that was apparent in his voice. I wanted to comfort him only I surrendered to silence, water to his fire.

We sat close together, engrossed in the plethora of dark emotions in our apartment; it appeared neither of us had the courage to discuss the night's events. Only the word 'orphan' kept hovering in my mind. Almost as if it had awakened a storm that I had tried so hard to suppress, one that had resurfaced now, deep and strong, battling to stay afloat against the currents of the ocean. I looked over towards Omar, who sat hunched forward with his head between his hands, tense and preoccupied; the one thing I disliked was seeing him upset. I held him in my arms; only when I looked into his eyes I thought of Tara. I envisaged the way I had observed Tara looking at him; there was a longing in her eyes, a longing just for him, one that I could perhaps resonate with. I couldn't comprehend why my mind began asking a thousand questions. I was fully aware that Tara and both her parents had wished for her to marry Omar; however, did a minute part of Omar ever want to marry Tara? And had I interrupted an incomplete love that had been present between them? Would they have considered marriage had I been absent from Omar's life – and perhaps he would have been happier with her? I wondered if that was the truth that Tara had been referring to or perhaps this was a simple case of unrequited love. Although I knew very well that nothing about unrequited love was simple. These questions continued to inhabit my mind as I desperately sought clarity. Just then the sound of Omar's voice overpowered my thoughts as he asked me why I looked so perplexed. 'Can I ask you something?' I said.

He immediately sat up, his back straight, looked into my eyes and replied, 'Of course you can.'

'Do you regret any of what's happened with me and you? What I mean is, did I come between you and Tara?' I asked in the most non-confrontational way that I possibly could.

'What! Saira, what has got into you? Why would you even contemplate this sort of a question?' he exclaimed. He was correct – I was unable to comprehend myself why these thoughts had invaded my mind. He held up my teary face with both his hands and said, 'Saira, I have never regretted anything about you. Do you doubt my love for you?'

I took a step back, holding my hands over my mouth, breathed in and replied, 'No, I'm not doubting you or your sincerity, and the last thing I want is to hurt you, but I saw the way that Tara was looking at you. I just need to know if all those things had not happened, you would not have needed to take my hand in marriage, and maybe...' I trailed off, confused. A few moments passed and I felt the warmth emanating from his body onto mine as if he were trying to shield us both from this storm that was trying to capsize our lives.

'I just need to be alone for a little while, please. I need space to clear my head, I need to think.'

'I won't leave you alone in this state,' he said with an intense look in his eyes.

I held his hand a second time and pleaded again until he agreed to leave, informing me that he would be with Kareem.

It was twilight as I looked up at the bespoke grey canvas in admiration, a reflection of my internal being: empty, dark and dejected. I had failed miserably to suppress the numbing pain in my heart. I missed her with every bone in my body and with every breath that I took. I curled up into a foetal position, closed my eyes and began to reminisce. I wanted to reflect and to remember everything. I wanted to relive every last emotion and feel alive again. I wanted to feel her touch, her smell, her presence, and so I pictured her smiling angelic face. In my mind I travelled back in time to how my life had been back in my beloved village, beside my mother.

Chapter 2 – Jahed Pur

My eyes opened at 5.30 a.m. and I rose to the melodic calling of the Imam of our village mosque, who was calling the Adhan for the early morning dawn prayer. Everyone in our village adored his voice, including me. It was tranquil and harmonious as the sound of his voice echoed through the open valleys. Everybody in my village began their day with prayer at sunrise; it was a beautiful and serene start to the day.

I sighed in contentment as the breathtaking, heavenly black canvas above, painted with a million sparkles, now gave way to a new day. Beams of light had begun to shine through as I stood mesmerised beneath the scarlet of dawn. Ammu was already out in the back courtyard performing the ablution. I quickly joined her and she handed me the small kholosh containing warm water that she had kept aside for me, whilst she used water that was cold. A traditional urn made out of a thin metal that almost every household utilised to transport water to and from their house, be it water to drink or water to cook and clean with. Ammu had brought me a small one to play with as a little girl and ever since then I had remained fascinated by them. She thought of and fulfilled my every need even before I had expressed it. We prayed together, ate together, and in the evenings we would sit in our back courtyard where I would narrate the stories about the day I'd spent with my wonderful pre-schoolers.

There were just the two of us. My father had passed away a few years ago due to physical ailments and old age. We missed him dearly and not a single day went by when we did not think of him. I had just graduated from the first stage of my teaching English course, which now qualified me to teach pre-schoolers to read and write basic English. My entire community were proud; I had become the first female to teach English. Every time Ammu was around the villagers they would express just how happy they were with my achievement, which made her even more proud. I was overjoyed to say the least, as I wanted to promote education, success, achievement and employment for the womenfolk of my village, just as my father would have wanted me to.

Six thirty in the morning. Ammu and I sat together out in the back courtyard; our back and front courtyard had an extending roof made out of burnt clay called tali. This was very common in our village as it protected from the scorching heat of the Grishmo – summer – season as well as the heavy downpours that came in the Barsha – the magnificent season of monsoon. I adored this part of our house as it was almost perfect for our morning, afternoon and evening ginger tea and chat times, often spent in the company of Ammu and Sumayah. The air was fresh with a light breeze; I enjoyed this time of morning. I enjoyed watching and listening to the entire Gao come to life, as the melodic humming of the birds echoed through the mud-filled valleys, the children were up, and the women were heading down to the big pond that was shared by us and a few other families. The women of the house would take all their pots to be washed at this time so the morning tea could be brewed and food preparation for the day could commence. We had no running water in our village, hence the pond was the main source for cleaning, bathing, washing laundry, and even rearing fish, whilst water for drinking was collected from the water pumps and wells that had been randomly placed around the communal parts of the village. I heard the cockerels and roosters as they dawdled across the muddy ground pecking at seeds. The men were out in their lungis busy preparing the cattle to be taken to plough the fields, as farming and agriculture remained the profession and livelihood of the majority. Nearly every household in our village owned cattle, mainly to provide fresh milk and a means to bring goods such as rice back home from the fields, whereas chickens, ducks and pigeons were raised for fresh eggs and as a source of meat and poultry.

Life here was colourfully vibrant and happy. The air and food were fresh – almost every field grew fresh vegetables just ready to be added to the menu. People lived in beautiful houses built out of burnt clay, mud, tin and even brickwork, depending on their wealth and what materials they could afford, although most villagers were burdened with poverty. Our Bari consisted of three rooms and a bathroom; the structure was built of bricks with a roof made from tin. My father had worked very hard to build this house for us and everything about it reminded me of him: the colours, the very carefully chosen pieces of furniture. We were one of the few families fortunate enough to have an indoor bathroom, as usually only the rich and elite had that facility. There was an apparent division between the rich and the poor in our village and somehow we were categorised as working class. I slid into my – soft, cotton, patterned kaftan – providing ample comfort and coolness during the heat and humidity of the village air, and wrapped my scarf loosely around my face to escape the intensity of the heat. Just like every morning Ammu packed me some thinly cut pieces of papaya as a means to stay hydrated and to avoid the heat headaches. My satchel was already packed with materials I required for the day – some paper and coloured chalk – and I slung it across my body and set off.

'I'm going now, Assalamualaikum,' I shouted, which simply meant peace be with you, and hurried out. This was the way that we greeted and bid farewell to each other in our village.

I knew that Ammu's reply would be, 'Saira, don't forget to eat your lunch and return before nightfall.' Ammu always wanted me to return home before the darkness of the night loomed. Firstly because she was always worried for my safety, and secondly because in my village all the women would return home before it became dark – it was almost an unspoken rule that could never be broken unless the circumstances were exceptional – although most women did not even venture out of their kitchens let alone the house, and if they did it would only be in the event of a dire emergency. The sun was shining brightly and I knew it was going to be another hot and humid day. The mud on the ground was dry and I could see the dust scattering around me as I walked. The village school was ten minutes away and I was greeted by, and greeted back, almost everybody that I met on my way.

'Salam, Teacher,' I heard coming from behind me. It was a group of pre-schoolers looking adorable as they began skipping away in the direction of the school. This was a proud moment for me as only yesterday I had taught them to greet fellow villagers with 'Assalamualaikum', and amazingly they had been able to retain that information and implement it. I felt immense love and pride for this place, and for a second could not contemplate my life without it. Jahed Pur was the name of my village; it was situated on the southern banks of the Makunda River, one of the branches of the great River Surma. Jahed Pur was two kilometres in length and situated in the south-eastern part of Sylhet Town. The majority of my village heavily relied upon agriculture as a means of livelihood, the main crop produced being rice. Not everybody here had wealth, although they carried beautiful smiles on their faces as if they had everything in the world. It was a very close-knit community, full of laughter and joy, and seeing these children every morning warmed my heart and brought a feeling of satisfaction and contentment. Deep in my heart I knew that if my father had still been amongst us he would feel the same.

I welcomed and greeted my class in Bengali and then continued in English. We went through phonic sounds and simple welcome words of the English language. These children continued to fascinate me every day. They expressed a commitment to learn that I found inspiring and this made me teach them with even more dedication. We ended the day by singing the famous pre-school rhyme 'Goodbye everyone', which almost all the village children had been reciting for the past two weeks: 'Goodbye everyone, it's time for us to go home now… we say goodbye to all our friends and playmates too.' I waited for the children to leave one by one and then set off for home.

It was nearly afternoon and the sun was shining low and hot. I wondered how Ammu's day was going; she was a hard worker just as my father had been. Barefoot I walked along the riverbed. I sat down for a moment, dipping my toes in slightly, and closed my eyes, enjoying the light breeze and the coolness of the river. I looked up as my attention diverted to the sound of hurried footsteps, only to discover a group of women with what looked like bloodstained mouths from chewing pan, as if they were newborn vampires. They were heading towards the river. I continued to watch a lady fully immerse herself into the water, and, as expected, a few seconds later only her head remained visible and the sari that had been draped around her earlier was now floating in the river. This was how they bathed, which I always found mesmerising – often I asked Ammu how the sari used to float so quickly. Ammu just laughed in response, informing me that this was how life had been here for generations. This notion left me wondering whether or not these women were truly happy and content in their lives or perhaps I just wanted something more in mine. I found it uncomfortable to bathe in the river, thus Ammu and I always bathed in our bathroom, which most villagers found bemusing. Watching the children splashing away made me smile; some could swim, some new swimmers were learning using the thick branches of the banana tree that floated so perfectly to support them. I continued walking as the whiff of tobacco overtook the air; the elderly men of our village had gathered, taking shade beneath the tall towering betel nut trees, drinking tea from the makeshift tea stall and smoking tobacco from their hookas. As usual they raised one hand to greet me and I returned the gesture by waving back as the sweet aroma of frothy overcooked milk tickled my taste buds. I turned to watch one of the men throw a few biscuits into his piping tea and then slurp it down as if it were soup, which made me smile.

I reached home to discover Ammu was still at work. Although I was hungry I chose to wait for her return. I startled at the sound of a high-pitched scream and found myself being lifted up into the air and spun around the room. 'Saira, Saira, Saira, guess what?'

Screeching back in a state of dizziness I demanded Sumayah put me down at once. 'I can't guess anything until you put me down.' We ended up sprawled across the floor laughing so hard that we both complained of stitches. Only she would greet me in a manner this eccentric. She was my best friend, we had grown up together and shared everything from clothes to dolls to our innermost secrets. We saw each other every day, and could sit together for hours conversing, laughing, dreaming and even debating; most evenings the three of us would dine together. Sumayah was almost like the sister that I never had; in fact, most people upon first impression believed we were biological sisters. We sat out in the back courtyard near the narrow stream that ran through the back of our house. We sat for what felt like an eternity dipping our toes into the coolness of the water, and found it hilarious how damp frogs would jump in and out every so often as if they were stealing glances at the both of us. My stomach was still in stitches. 'Hey, so what did you want to tell me,' I asked, slightly out of breath. I soon discovered Sumayah's excitement was due to the fact that, just like every year, the elite and the exuberant as I called him had come to grace our village with his presence. Rahim Khan, who was one of the most eligible bachelors in our entire village for the prospect of marriage, was spending his vacation here at his grand house which was almost the size of a palace. He visited with family and friends for a month every year without fail. They appeared to be one of the wealthiest families in the village; they owned land, cars, a large house made out of brickwork and many servants. They resided somewhere in the United Kingdom, I never bothered to enquire where exactly, as we villagers referred to the entire United Kingdom as London. Every year that he visited, most of the girls in the village would secretly hope and pray that they would be the one he chose to ask for their hand in marriage. Unfortunately, Sumayah was in this majority. I mainly found him to be disrespectful and arrogant; there was nothing about him or London that I found alluring, and Sumayah of course thought I was strange for feeling this way.

'Saira, if I marry someone like him, I would be the happiest girl in the world. He has everything in life I could possibly want or need.'

'Sumayah, you don't know anything about him, apart from his wealthy, and that he prances around the village as if he owns it,' I reasoned with her.

'Saira, I am not educated like you, neither am I beautiful. What chance would I have with someone like him, I'm just being silly,' she replied, dejected.

'You are beautiful inside and out, and one day you will meet someone who will shower you with so much love that you will even forget me,' I placated her whilst placing my arm around her shoulder. We both giggled and sat in deep thought for a moment. I pondered and questioned many things, such as whether wealth could really bring happiness into one's life; surely that was a very skewed misconception. As for true love, I believed God had that one figured out too – everyone had a destiny and I was yet to embark upon mine. If I was completely honest, marriage was the last thing on my mind. I had just turned twenty-two years old. I had plans and goals that were yet unaccomplished, such as studying further and working, my ultimate goal being to set an example that would empower and provide opportunities for the women of my village and to inspire them to think beyond the limitations and confines of their own minds.

My attention quickly diverted to the sound of gentle footsteps coming towards the stream; Ammu had finally returned home. At once I took her bags and began to massage her fatigued feet with the mashed green roots of the water lily plant that we kept in our house, which seemed to ease her pain slightly. Ammu suffered arthritic pain and its severity appeared to be increasing on a daily basis. I had tried my utmost to convince her to give up work as I was now earning enough for the both of us; however, my efforts were to no avail. She was truly my inspiration in life; she had worked tremendously hard to build up her tailoring business, which she maintained with another lady from our village. Together they sewed baby clothes, shirts, dresses, and many other items that people requested. Ammu began this business after the devastating demise of my father; she wanted to teach me independence and to educate me, whilst instilling in me the qualities that would make me a good person. She always taught me to follow my heart and vowed to give me a life filled with opportunities, although this had proved to be a challenge at times as our village believed only boys should be educated and that girls should marry and become homemakers. Now that I was an adult, I wanted to tell Ammu and Abbu that they had given me every opportunity in life to prosper, and that everything I had achieved today was due to their love and nurture. I desperately wanted to hold my father's hand just one final time to express how much I loved him, and to thank him for giving me the life I lived today.

I thought back to when I had been a little girl, sitting tall up on my father's shoulders; together we would walk all around the village counting the numerous water lilies. Water lilies, or shada shapla, as we called them, were the national flower of my native land: Bangladesh. Abbu and I loved watching them floating around in the ponds, streams, lakes and rivers, especially in the monsoon season. I loved how the leaves opened up during the day and closed during the night. Abbu was a hard worker and was very passionate about developing our village and had been instrumental in achieving this goal. He encouraged the poorest families in our village to participate in the cultivation and growing of jute, in the wet and warm climate of Barsha. He then purchased handlooms and spinning wheels so that they could weave clothes, mats, and even bags to sell to nearby villages, which then became a source of livelihood for them. My Abbu was generous and kind and always smiling. One day Abbu was informed by our local Imam that the small mosque he lived in was collecting rainwater, which had seeped inside, soaking everything. The next day Abbu left very early in the morning; he walked to every house he physically could in our village and the nearby ones to raise funds just so he could rebuild our mosque. When he returned that evening, he was ecstatic. He picked me up and lifted me high into the air and said, 'You give me so much noor when you smile at me, Saira' When Abbu presented the funds to the Imam, who I always called Mesabji Chacha, he was so grateful that he kissed both Abbu's hands and cried out in joy. The next morning almost the entire village arrived to express their gratitude and respect to Abbu for this wonderful gesture.

Consequently, Abbu was asked to become the head of our village council, which he reluctantly agreed to. The village council comprised a few older men who were deemed to be wise in nature, fair and just, and experienced in matters of life in general. Every village was led by its council, which people utilised whenever they were unable to sort out their differences amicably, be it a quarrel between neighbours, between spouses, or even a situation that just required someone who was fair and just to provide a few peaceful resolutions. The main purpose was to maintain peace and harmony throughout the village and its occupants.

I thought about the time when a girl that Sumayah was acquainted with had been seen out in the fields with a boy from another village; this matter had been escalated to the attention of the village council. My Abbu, being the kind-hearted man that he was, sent away all the bystanders who wanted to defame and scrutinise this girl and even punish her, which was not uncommon. He turned around to the council members and said, 'A daughter is precious, just as is a son. They are our pride, honour and dignity and we must ensure we treat them with honour and love.' Surprisingly the council members surrendered to this and instead of rebuking and being punitive to this girl they treated her with respect, although her mistake was still seen as being undignified, and did not pertain to the societal constraints of our village. Later that evening this girl visited our house. She appeared very coy and subservient and wanted to thank Abbu for supporting her. I recalled the exact words that Ammu had said to her: 'All that love you have, you save it for your future husband.' I found myself wondering what she had meant.

My parents had an immensely profound faith in God, which shaped their principles and values in life and how they dealt with their trials and tribulations. I felt honoured that today those very principles and values had been instilled in me. I recalled a lady in our village who gave birth to her second child, only she considered this to be her misfortune and an omen, because she now had two daughters and her husband became adamant that he wanted to give the second daughter away. This mentality was common to the majority of people in our village; they felt daughters were mainly a burden, requiring dowry when it came to marrying them off. Whereas giving birth to a son was admirable as men were seen as the providers and the ones who would continue forward the family name, honour and traditions. This lady approached Abbu and asked where she could leave the abandoned child for someone to take in. I remember Abbu became very distressed by this; he held this child up in his arms and looked into her mother's eyes and said, 'Have you heard of the saying that lucky is the woman whose first born is a girl, and should a father who is blessed with two daughters raise them well with due love and care, then his journey to Jannah is made easier?' And he smiled at the child. Suddenly this lady began to wail uncontrollably, holding her baby close to her chest almost as if she was disgusted by the action she was about to undertake. I recall the sound of her crying hysterically and then repeatedly asking God to forgive her, as she pulled the child into the warmth of her chest almost in an act to placate her.

From that day onwards I observed that every time a woman had given birth to a daughter in our village, there was a celebration as opposed to a sense of mourning. I felt immensely proud that the villagers had stopped following lifelong traditions. That were mostly senseless cultural predispositions based on an extremely backward ideology. The villagers would often comment on and praise the way Abbu treated me – his only child and a daughter at that. Not once did Abbu enforce any choice or decision upon me, he had allowed me to make my own and was there to guide me through the good and bad choices. Vividly I recalled how every time I walked into a room, Abbu would give up his chair for me and would never eat a single meal without me by his side. I missed him dearly.

I continued to stare at the floating water lily almost like a frozen statue now, oblivious to the fact that Ammu had picked the flower out of the stream and placed it into my hands. The trickling sound of the stream reminded me that my physical being was here, sitting next to Ammu and Sumayah, whilst my mind was with Abbuji, may his soul rest in heavenly peace. The sky was dark now, covered in tiny bright shining stars. I felt Ammu's arm around my neck as she whispered, 'It's all right to miss Abbuji, Saira.' Even in my daze I was astonished at how Ammu always seemed to know my innermost thoughts, well before they had even entered my mind. I cuddled close to her like a small child, and we sat for a while thinking about Abbu in silence.

'Do you think we'll ever meet him again?' I asked.

'I pray that we meet again, in Jannah, and I know in my heart that we will all be together again,' she replied. Hearing this gave me a sense of hope, and something to strive for.

What could be better than dwelling in the astonishing gardens of Jannah, hand in hand with my father. Just then I realised Sumayah had vanished. Ammu informed me that she had to leave in a hurry, but she was unsure of what the emergency had been.

That evening we shared humorous stories about Abbu over dinner; we could talk about him for hours without fail. I noticed Ammu secretly wipe her face, failing in her attempt to conceal her sadness. A little chilly breeze overtook the night and just like every evening Ammu brewed ginger tea. We sat out in the front courtyard wrapped up in our favourite shawl. Most of the villagers were now in bed, as ploughing the fields was no easy feat. I felt the ginger cut deep into my throat as I told Ammu about my day, and how rapidly the children were adapting to the English language. Pleased to hear this she had even suggested that I start teaching the adults in the village, which I politely declined. The women would most likely attend class chewing betel nut with pan dripping from their mouths. Ammu found this amusing and soon we were giggling at the very thought of this spectacle.

The next morning I woke to the familiar melodic voice of Mesabji Chacha announcing the early morning call for dawn prayer, followed by the synchronised humming of birds. Ammu and I prayed together, as we did most mornings. I felt content beginning my day in this manner, with a strong sense of balance and direction. It was a chilly morning and we were both preparing to leave for work, ensuring to dress a little more warmly today.

I helped Ammu with the chores and responsibilities of the running of our house. I wanted to lighten her burden as much as I possibly could. I wiped clean our small patio bench, dusted the thin layers of fabric across the windows, swept the floors and then beat out the fluttering cobwebs that were hanging down the corners of the kitchen. Before she noticed I began to collect water from the pump outside. I managed to complete this task in three rounds using buckets, ensuring we had enough water in the kitchen and our bathroom to suffice for the entire day. Carrying water was strenuous and I disliked Ammu doing this. Almost immediately she noticed me catching my breath, and expressed her annoyance; in response I flashed a very cheeky smile, and soon she was smiling too.

Chapter 3 – Season of Bashonto

I commenced my journey towards the school, as the cattle were being prepared for another strenuous day in the fields, while tall roosters began dawdling around in search of food. This time of morning was very colourful; there was so much to see and hear as the villagers prepared for another day of hard graft. It was a chilly morning of the Bashonto season. This was Sumayah's and my favourite season and the most fun time of year. I could smell the moist jute in the air, so strong and reminiscent of Abbuji. Bashonto brought along the coolest of days and came just before the scorching heat of the monsoon rain. Although early mornings and nights were chilly, the days were golden, filled with light and warmth. Our entire village hummed with fairs, parades, and art festivals, as many villagers set up stalls with handicrafts. They participated in poetry, drama and traditional dance shows almost every evening; there was a feeling of happiness that captivated the air, and it was extremely contagious.

Sumayah and I loved watching the evening shows wrapped up together in woolly shawls and scarves, drinking Ammu's ginger tea. I decided to take the scenic route today and walk through the communal field. This was a piece of land that was shared by almost everybody in the village who took it upon themselves to cultivate and grow whatever they pleased, from spring onions to sweet potatoes. The purpose was to enable the poorer families who did not own their own land to be able to self-provide and in turn feed themselves and their families; it was truly a wonderful act of generosity, thought of and implemented by the village council. I was enchanted by the variety of fruit and vegetables in the field; it was beautifully vibrant and so full of colour, and we had everything in our village from juicy hog plums, litchi, pomelo, and jack fruit, to lime and bananas.

The presence of a lady dressed in a fluorescent yellow sari hand picking fresh lemons startled me at first sight. It was Khala, an aunt who lived close to us, who was also a dear friend to Ammu. Initially she gawped at me before saying, 'Saira, when will I get the chance to colour your milky skin and rosy lips with turmeric? We would all like to see how dark the henna appears on your hands.' She giggled. I made brief eye contact, smiled tentatively and continued walking. I knew that this was Khala's way of sending me a not-so-subtle message in relation to marriage, more specifically my marriage, as I was perceived to be a woman of age who must be married off immediately. Turmeric is applied to the face and hands of the bride to be and henna is applied as intricate patterns all over her hands and feet, according to the traditions of our village. An old wives' tale is that if the henna turns out to be very dark in colour then she will be loved deeply by her husband. These traditions, derived from village culture, were mainly implemented by the older generation. I was twenty-two years old; marriage was not a priority for me currently. This was typical of my village, always in a hurry to marry off females as if they were a burden so hard to bear, whereas males were granted superiority and power and were allowed to marry when their hearts desired. More importantly, men were encouraged to live, to excel and to think outside the parameters and the confines of their minds, and women were taught to bow down and submit to everyone except themselves. Had my father been alive this was one attitude he would have definitely challenged and changed.

School had been amazing; it seemed the children never ceased to fascinate me. We tried something different; I decided to walk with them through the communal field so that they could familiarise themselves with the fruits of Bangladesh that we saw on the way. I began to teach them the names of these fruits in English and, as eager as they were, they tried their best to use the correct pronunciation. Although, at times, pomelo became pamelo and litchi became leech, it was very cute. I noticed them suddenly become very excited and to my surprise the commotion had been caused by two ladies milking a cow, which they naturally found amusing. Sumayah and I loved the smell of fresh cow's milk; I was almost unable to separate her from my thoughts today. Quickly I diverted my attention back to the children and taught them how to say 'milking a cow'. However, it was apparent that they were still laughing at the entire process of milking. We walked back to the school from the field and I bid them goodbye, individually handing them over to their waiting parents.

It was early afternoon and I enjoyed the feel of the warm rays of sunshine beating down onto my bare feet. Sumayah and I were both looking forward to a Mela that was being hosted by our village that evening. At the Mela people would set up intimate stalls selling chutneys made from juicy, tangy, spicy hog plums. Traditional music would be playing in the background, entertaining the children. Most importantly, the older children of the village had planned to recite poetry and exhibit their art paintings, which I had helped to organise. It was a time of celebration, and happiness appeared to be floating in the air.

When I reached home I was almost unable to contain my excitement for the evening ahead. Ammu was already home, waiting for me and Sumayah so that we could all walk there together as planned. 'Ammu, where's Sumayah?' I asked as my eyes searched for her. We waited a short while prior to walking to the Mela. We arrived at the open courtyard and the food stalls brought an aroma just waiting to be devoured. All the villagers had congregated: men, women, children, and everybody was smiling. Hot tea with the inviting aroma of masala was being distributed, children were darting around and some of the older women were singing traditional Bengali songs while others watched, clapping their hands in encouragement. The ambience was truly heart-warming to the extent that Ammu and I stood in awe for a moment. I felt immensely proud to be a part of this community; more importantly I felt proud to name this as my village, my home and my native land. My peripheral search for Sumayah continued, as Ammu chatted to a group of ladies.

Just then I heard a deep male voice, which sounded like an attempt to sing the lyrics of a well-known Bengali song, with the hint of an English accent. Immediately I turned and to my surprise it was the sought-after Rahim Khan. He stood, staring in my direction provocatively. 'So, I hear you're Saira, the village poster girl,' he said mockingly.

I looked at him, smiled, and said, 'And I hear that you are the village playboy.' I found it amusing to watch his jaw drop wide open as he looked at his cousin standing next to him, who escorted him away at once, shamefaced. I began giggling to myself thinking about how Sumayah would have been hysterical with laughter, had she been here. Just then I felt the warmth of Sumayah's hand on my arm. Hugging her immediately, I asked, 'Where have you been all day? I thought we were coming here together.' She smiled, closed her eyes and held one ear with her hand, a gesture known as an apology expressed only to our loved ones. We both laughed as she led me to our favourite stall, the hog plum chutney stall. Tiny pieces of hog plum blended into a mixture of cumin seeds, fresh coriander, parsley, fresh red chillies and a little saffron.

We sat together devouring chutney, listening to the poetry readings, and then proudly admired the paintings as the students spoke a little about what they had created. With the adventures of the evening I almost forgot to tell Sumayah about my little encounter with her beloved, as I liked to refer to him. When I finally told her, just as predicted she was hysterical with laughter, causing Ammu and the other women to stare at us questioningly as if we were hiding a deep, dark secret. She continued laughing and said, 'Oh, I wish I could have seen his face when he realised you speak English – how funny.'

It'd been an amazing evening, and I sensed a flow of happiness piercing right through my heart. I looked up into the serene sky and smiled, thanking God. I was grateful to have been surrounded by such inspirational people, especially my mother. Immersed in my flow of happiness I had almost forgotten to enquire why Sumayah had to leave so suddenly last night.

The Mela had come to an end and all the stalls were being dismantled one by one. Most of the villagers appeared tired and had begun to disperse sporadically, ready to retire to bed. Ammu and I bid goodbye to Sumayah. 'Come round tomorrow,' I reminded her as we walked home.

I watched Ammu fall asleep almost instantly. Subconsciously something about Sumayah was bothering me, something I was unable to identify. To be precise I knew Sumayah all too well. The way she was laughing today, it was almost as if she had not allowed herself to laugh wholeheartedly. Or was my mind just conjuring up stories? Ammu always felt that I was a critical thinker, and that thinking deeply about every situation was not always a good thing – and she was correct. I closed my eyes, gradually drifting to sleep.

The next morning, Ammu and I left for work together, chatting on the way about the fun and frolics of the night before. I carried her bags into the tiny mud hut that was her office before I continued towards the school. As I watched the children walking in small groups chewing tantalising fresh sugar cane sticks – and looking adorable – I heard a familiar deep male voice call out my name from behind. To my shock it was Rahim Khan, who walked closer looking apologetic. He placed his hands up in the air in a defence gesture as if he were surrendering.

'Look, Saira, about yesterday. I'm sorry if my behaviour was disrespectful – that was not my intention.'

I smiled half-heartedly and assured him that I did not feel offended at all. In return he complimented the success of the Mela the previous night, mentioning especially how well I had organised it. I thanked him for both the compliments and the apology, and felt slightly guilty for branding him as arrogant and exuberant; after all, changed behaviour was the best form of apology. I smiled – this was now another story for Sumayah.

At school I decided the theme of learning for the day would be the Mela and my plan was to brainstorm a list of English phrases with the children, based on all the things they had seen, felt and heard there. They were very inquisitive and innovative, naming words such as song, dance, party, drawings; some even mentioned pan, which made me giggle. That evening I told Ammu about my class. She smiled and said she loved my way of teaching, as it emanated creativity and innovation.

The next few days were vibrant and adventurous. Pankaj, one of my students who lived with his mother Laxmi and father Rajesh, had invited us to join them in their annual celebration of Holi. They resided near the school opposite the river bed in conjoined mud houses with another few families. I adored participating in their fascinating festivals – Holi being my favourite. Holi is known as the 'festival of colour', a festival that marks the arrival of spring, fertility, love and the triumph of good over evil. I particularly enjoyed Rajesh's narration of the enduring love between Lord Krishna and Radha and the triumph of good over evil, right before the raucous chasing of one another with the coloured powder known as Gulal. It was early evening and we had reached Rajesh's courtyard along with most of the other villagers and the atmosphere was merry and splendid to say the least, and so full of colour as everybody immersed themselves in the joy of spring and celebration. There was a spectacular bonfire in the middle, and Laxmi was engrossed in the task of decorating a rather grand podium where they would place images of their gods. The devotees would then take turns swinging the podium as everybody rejoiced, singing special songs.

I stood with Khala and Ammu watching in awe. Pankaj sprayed red colour all over my face at which I shrieked with laughter and ran to gather some blue, yellow and red powders, colouring Pankaj in return, and then Laxmi followed by Ammu. Soon everybody was chasing each other with coloured powder, and some even began to throw coloured water over anyone who remained within arm's length. I watched as Khala scowled after a few children had poured red water over her hair, running away as she ran behind them. The magnificent festivities of the night were now coming to an end as everybody stood, wet, some red, some blue, some green, but still smiling. No matter how much I tried I couldn't comprehend the absence of Sumayah, as I knew she adored this festival just as much as I did. This only intensified my concern that Sumayah's avoidance was perhaps more suspicious than met the eye.

Ammu had been particularly busy with work, which kept her occupied most evenings. She had received a very large quantity of orders, gowns in particular, to be worn by a bridal party in a nearby village. Bashonto was also the season of weddings; it seemed like everybody was waiting for the blossom of spring to commence their new beginning. That evening, I sat out in our back courtyard, dipping my bare feet into the serene shallows of the running stream. This was the third consecutive day I had waited for Sumayah; however, she was nowhere to be seen. I was perplexed that she would miss a festival such as Holi, which was so unlike her. That night I lay in bed, convinced that Sumayah was concealing something from me and I was determined more than ever to unravel this mystery.

The next day, after school had ended, I decided to take a detour. Sumayah's house was very close to ours, but it was slightly smaller in size and built out of mud and burnt clay. I intended to confront her, determined to seek the reason behind her avoidance. I walked straight into the house and took a good look around, only to find an empty space. Just as I turned to leave, I saw Sumayah lying on the floor, silently staring up at the ceiling, completely oblivious to my presence. The first thought that crossed my mind was that she was unwell. Instinctively I ran towards her, and placed my hand on her forehead. She was startled to see me and sat up right away.

'Saira, what are you doing here?' she asked, not making eye contact with me. She seemed closed in, restless, as if she needed me to leave imminently.

'What am I doing here? I was worried about you. I haven't seen you for days. Why have you stopped coming round in the evening? Are you not well? Has something happened? You even missed Holi and you never do that,' I blurted out frantically with an angry undertone to my voice.

Sumayah became defensive at once, moving away from me and denying that there was anything abnormal about her behaviour. All the while she lurked away from the window, and then asked me to leave. I was even more confused now than before and pleaded with her to tell me what I had done wrong, why she wanted to end our friendship.

Sumayah finally made eye contact with me and said, 'Saira, you know you're my best friend, you're like a sister to me, but Abbuji has made it clear that if I continue to be friends with you then I won't get any proposals and will remain unmarried like you, and people will question his honour and dignity.' Her eyes were swimming, which made me tearful too. I stood speechless, unable to find the words to express any emotion. I gasped and hugged Sumayah. 'Abbuji thinks that you're a negative influence on me, and says everyone in the village is starting to gossip about why you're not married yet, and I'm not allowed to see you anymore. I'm sorry,' she cried.

I was devastated to say the least. Her words cut deep into my heart like a wound, but somehow I managed to maintain a neutral expression on my face – or at least I tried. I remembered how my Abbuji had worked so hard to change the mentality of this village so that women could have and pursue opportunities like the men here. The harsh reality was that it had remained of the same magnitude; the men were thought to be superior, the providers, whilst the women were merely an object for reproduction with no status or value. Although I felt upset and devalued, I decided I was not going to submit to this attitude. I composed myself, looked at Sumayah, and explained that she was doing the right thing and that she should listen to her father. I smiled at her, locking away my sadness, and bid her goodbye. I walked home alone unable to stop tears from rolling down my cheeks. I wanted to shout in retaliation at the turmoil inside. I wanted to question the entire village and demand answers right away.

Why was it deemed necessary for women to marry and reproduce? Was that our sole purpose and role in life?

Were women not allowed to make their own decisions based on their own intellect?

Had we become such a burden on mankind that an unmarried woman was thought of as disgraceful and an outcast, unless she surrendered to the superiority of men?

Why were women continuously taught and told that they must bow down to the authority of men?

Why were we continuously told that we can't?

The questions continued to manifest themselves in turn, increasing my anger and frustration all the more. I wanted to know why women were made to feel inferior, and given no choice but to conform to the cultural traditions of this village.

I stood in our front courtyard where Ammu's moving shadow was visible from outside. Taking care to wipe away all evidence of tears from my face I rearranged my hijab, making it neat. I was willing to go to any lengths to conceal this from Ammu. I figured she spent enough time worrying about me, and this additional stress would be totally unnecessary. Prior to entering I painted a smile on my face, attempting to bid farewell to the painful grimace and devastation I harboured inside.

'Ammu, I missed you.' I clung on to her in an embrace as she gave me that warm maternal smile and led me to our waiting dinner. Ammu chatted about the bridal gowns that she had created and how beautifully the colours complemented each other. I felt guilty for not being able to give her my undivided attention; after all, her hard work was for my benefit entirely.

In a state of emotional turmoil I began to peel a few litchis for our dessert. 'Saira, stop,' said Ammu. I was so distracted that I was unable to feel the sticky litchi juice dripping down my wrists and spilling all over my kameez. Ammu knew how much I detested the feel of litchi juice and she immediately began to wash my hands, giggling while I stared down at the sticky floor, expressionless. She looked at me ominously as if she could feel the worry and concern I must have been showing. I was angry at myself for being so transparent; Ammu could read me like a book.

'There you go – it's all silky and shiny now,' she said as she gently separated out the strands of my hair with her fingers, massaging it well with the strongly scented black seed oil. As always the massage relaxed me more than the intended result of the oil rejuvenating my hair. 'Saira, is everything all right?' she continued.

I reassured her saying I was tired and in dire need of sleep. That night I sat up thinking about Sumayah; I missed her terribly. I knew the cold reality was that I would have to forsake our friendship, to save her chastity from being questioned.

That moment I took an oath to sacrifice our years of friendship and sisterhood, for the sake of guarding Sumayah's honour from being painted by a tarnish that would forever remain immovable.

Chapter 4 – With Courage Comes Strength

The next day Ammu left before me. I walked to school in a daze of fatigue, although I was relieved that today was mostly singing songs with the children, which they loved. On my way back from school, I naturally thought of Sumayah; everywhere I walked in the village was reminiscent of her. When I reached home that day Ammu was still at work, so I sat beside the stream dipping my feet in to the tune of the running water. I recalled the umpteen times I had sat at this very spot with Sumayah, laughing, chatting, eating, and just enjoying each other's company. Her words echoed through my mind and I began to wonder. Had Sumayah's father been right, had people in the village been questioning my celibacy? I wondered whether they had mentioned this to Ammu. This notion concerned me; I did not want the villagers to disdain or blame my mother for something she had no control over. After all, it was my decision as to whether I wanted to take this enormous step in my life. Was I psychologically, emotionally and physically ready to surrender to a lifetime of commitment and responsibility? I knew that marriage was held in high regard in my faith and Nikkah – the wedding ceremony – considered to be an act of worship.

That evening Ammu and I were sitting together sipping ginger tea. I listened as she chatted, pausing and smiling at her every so often. 'Where's Sumayah,' she asked. Her question threw me as I was secretly avoiding this scenario. However, it seemed nothing escaped her observational skills.

'She's not been very well, and is resting mostly,' I replied hesitantly.

Ammu's confused expression made it obvious that she was not convinced. 'Saira, is everything okay?' she enquired, now with a worried undertone to her voice. I maintained my stance and continued to reassure her. I then searched for courage to broach the topic of marriage, failing miserably.

That night I lay in bed with the words on the tip of my tongue and then blurted it right out. 'Do you think I should think about getting married now?' The echo of those words seemed to surround me as my voice bounced back from every wall in our house.

Ammu sat up immediately and smiled, placing her soft hand on my head. She gently said, 'Is that what's been bothering you, dear?' I nodded in relief and asked her how she knew that my father was the one for her.

She smiled a dreamy smile and replied, 'We seemed to have this magnetic connection with each other from the moment we met, and I just followed my heart and my instincts and left the rest to God Almighty.' From what I had witnessed Ammu and Abbuji had had a beautiful loving relationship; neither had displayed superiority over the other, they were kind and had mutual respect for one another. They had even made the smallest of decisions together, standing side by side, unified through the good and the bad times. I decided that this was how marriage should be and this was what I would plan for: a relationship that was based on love, respect and mutual understanding, one that knew no boundaries, and with a bond so strong that it could withstand every trial and every tribulation.

I told Ammu that I would consider looking at potential suitors for the purpose of marriage; I wanted to prevent the gossip that had been gradually spreading from reaching her. Ammu always made me feel comfortable talking to her about even the most difficult subjects. She was delighted to say the least. She looked at me again and asked, 'Are you sure about this?' to ensure that I had thought this through carefully. I nodded; after all, the virtues of marriage did not include secluding oneself in a cardboard box. It was one of the most beautiful bonds of life and it was naturally the next chapter in mine. Searching for potential suitors was a speciality in itself in our village. The message would be spread far and wide by word of mouth, and people would bring potential grooms to Ammu's attention and the process of introductory meetings would follow. However, the Nikkah would only be concluded and solemnised when both the bride and groom and their families had given their full conscious consent.

A few weeks passed by, and I relished the beauty of my favourite season. The days were getting hotter and more humid, with the anticipation of heavy rainfall and mud slides to follow, although the villagers remained optimistic about being able to save their crops from withering away along with the monsoon rain. I continued to enjoy teaching as my children were now learning exceptionally well and never ceased to amaze me each and every day. I had a different story to narrate to Ammu every evening, which she enjoyed as much as I did narrating them.

During this time Ammu presented me with many photos with which she had been inundated by the people of our village, and it came as no surprise that they were very keen to marry me off. Only one person caught my attention: Hamid, who was seven years older than me, also a teacher by profession, and who resided in a village nearby. He had spent two years living out in Dubai where he taught English. However, he had now decided to marry and settle back here. Ammu and I met with him with the guidance and support of Mesabji Chacha. Hamid was invited to our house along with his parents for the introductory meeting. As tradition dictated

I draped a sari around me, attempting to look feminine and pretty. Although I was extremely nervous, I met with Hamid and asked him my pre-prepared set of questions, which he answered kindly, much to my satisfaction, mainly concerning my continuing to teach after marriage, which he accepted. I was so overtaken by his kind nature, level of maturity and love for teaching that I unconsciously turned a blind eye to everything else important. Sumayah's words were still etched in my mind and I thought about the scandal and rumours that were slowly spreading about me amongst the villagers. I was determined that this was something I would never allow to fall on my mother's ears.

A few days later, after much deliberation, I informed Ammu of my decision to accept this alliance. In my village, this was usually celebrated by handing out home-made sweets to every household, and that was exactly what followed. The union of marriage was celebrated in various ways depending on the customs and rituals of one's village, and your wealth and financial stability. The custom in my village was to have an intimate Nikkah followed by a public celebration which included the entire village, with food, food, and more food, accompanied by singing and dancing. The villagers would then all bid farewell to the bride and bless her with good tidings as she began the new journey in her life. The date of my Nikkah had been finalised for a few weeks' time and the arrangements had begun, although I felt indifferent to the entire process.

One afternoon, whilst on my return journey home, I stumbled into Sumayah who was carrying fresh vegetables that she had picked from the communal field to take back home. We both stood still on the path and a surge of happiness sparked through me. I had so many things I wanted to tell her. Unable to hold back I smiled, putting my arms out to her in the hope of a much-needed embrace; in return Sumayah flung her hands around my neck. 'Sumayah, I have so much to tell you,' I screeched. We walked together for a while, chatting about the smallest of things that had occurred in our lives since the last time we had met. I told her about my wedding, which sounded so strange when spoken out loud. We then chatted about Hamid; I told Sumayah everything I knew of him. Bewildered, she asked me how I had consented to marrying Hamid based on the very little information I had about him. I stood still, shocked, and stared at her in confusion and dismay.

'Saira, do you feel physically attracted to him?' This question unearthed a dilemma that perhaps I was trying to bury in the depths of my subconscious mind. I looked away in an attempt to disguise my anguish and distress, but she knew my innermost secrets. 'Answer my question, Saira,' she repeated.

'Well, is that the most important thing? What about a person's character?' I replied hesitantly.

Sumayah held my hand and said, 'Saira, I have known you a very long time and Wallahi, I swear to God, I love you as dear as a sister, but I am pleading with you do not sacrifice your life to something your heart does not accept. Please follow your heart and not your mind and stay true to your spirit.' She gently nudged my shoulder, giving me a knowing look, and walked away leaving me embroiled in a web of utter confusion. I sat near the footpath and watched her walk away into the distance until her shadow had become invisible and then a memory. Her words echoed in my mind, further increasing my frustration. What was Sumayah trying to tell me? How ironic that the person who had convinced me to contemplate the very idea of marriage was today the same person who was causing me to doubt my decision.

I thought about Hamid as I walked. It was true – I was unsure of whether or not I was physically attracted to him. Would it be immoral and unethical to marry a person I did not find attractive? The internal debate only intensified, producing more questions in my mind, most of which I was unable to answer. I watched a tired-looking lady walking with her children and as usual she held out an umbrella, allowing her son to walk in the shade as she and her daughter walked in the searing heat. They came to sit near me, and the lady brought out sugar cane sticks and water, allowing her son to eat and drink first while her thirsty daughter waited patiently, holding her muddy marbles, and only came forward when her mother instructed. Childhood was where it all began. I could recall as a little girl being told umpteen times how we must wait for the boys to take the lead, be it playing a game in school, or waiting in line for sweets at the local shop. The fact remained that it was ingrained within us to feel subordinate, and inferior. This was testament to the lifestyle that was led by the women of my village.

I finally reached home to the sweet smell of fresh jalebis, which was one of Ammu's special home-made delicacies: a dessert she made during times of celebration such as Eid and, of course, weddings. Our house was filled with an aroma of sweetness, reminiscent of a time of celebration and joy. I stood still and silent behind Ammu, merging into her shadow. She turned around, almost scalding me with the heat from the sizzling pan in her hand, and quickly hurried me out of the way. Ammu then placed an appetising plate of jalebis in front of me, gesturing with the other hand for me to eat. I placed a piece in my mouth, devouring the juicy sweetness that tickled my taste buds, while the turmoil in my heart grew stronger, reminding me of the storm brewing in my mind. I felt ashamed; how could I be so cruel and take away this happiness? Ever since I had consented to the alliance, she had immersed herself in making arrangements and preparing for my Nikkah. She sat next to me and I smiled in an attempt to conceal my dilemma.

'Saira.'

'Yes, Ammu,' I replied.

'I'm just going to clean up the kitchen and then I need to show you something,' she said. I nodded and placed another jalebi in my mouth. I sat out in the back courtyard dipping my feet into the coolness of the stream. This was my favourite place in the entire village, so beautiful and serene. I enjoyed sitting here, connecting to nature and reflecting. This was also the place where I did all my thinking, and today especially I needed perspective. I wished for Sumayah to be by my side, so she could explain what she had meant earlier. Perhaps she was implying that I was not ready to take on the responsibility of marriage.

I heard Ammu call out for me. I lifted my feet out of the water and immediately began walking towards her voice. 'Close your eyes,' she instructed as I entered the house. She held my hand, guiding me to sit down. I heard rustling sounds as if she were unearthing treasure that had been hidden away. I waited anxiously, attempting to peek, although Ammu placed her hand over my eyes just in time. 'Right, now open your eyes,' she said with a joyous dreamy note to her voice, which I seldom heard. I opened my eyes and to my astonishment she was holding up a gown against herself. My eyes were now wide open, appreciating the sheer beauty of this dress that shone before me. I gasped as I touched the layers of raw silk fabric that fell all the way to the floor. The dress was an off-white, milky ivory colour. The arms were long and made from a lace with intricate, delicate, and elegant patterns. The bodice was of an Italian silk covered in net lace filled with many shining diamanté stones coloured gold and bronze, resembling an antique piece of artwork. I was enthralled by the sheer beauty of this gown, which in a strange way reflected the expression on Ammu's face, fascinating me all the more.

As she looked at the gown I knew she was smiling internally, reminiscing about Abbuji. She walked me right in front of the mirror and held the dress against me, standing close. We both gazed at the shiny reflection of the stones against the light in the mirror. 'Ammu, this is absolutely gorgeous, it is so beautiful,' I squeaked in excitement.

'It is, just like you, my dear,' she replied. We sat down, still holding the gown, and, as she took my hand in hers, her voice began to break a little. I knew she was feeling sentimental. She looked at me and said, 'Saira, your father gifted me this dress when we married, and I wore it during my Nikkah. After you came into our lives we both decided that for your Nikkah we would ask you to wear this same dress – but only if that is what you want, dear.' She smiled and explained that my father had wanted her to wear white as it symbolised purity and a new beginning, and then added that wearing this gown would be like having a piece of Abbuji with me. Her words touched my heart so intensely that I began to feel goosebumps all over my body; this was a beautiful gesture. I felt proud to have parents who I held in such high esteem; how thoughtful of Ammu to safeguard her wedding dress all these years just so I could feel and be a part of the love they had shared between them.

'This is awesome,' I gasped.

'Does that mean you will wear it?'

She giggled as I nodded in agreement and said, 'It would be an honour.'

The excitement of the evening made it extremely difficult for me to wind down for much-needed sleep. I sat up slowly and quietly as Ammu slept. My body was wounded with fatigue while my mind was full of worry. I thought about the occurrences of the day, starting with my conversation with Sumayah and then about Ammu, and then the gown. My head and heart began to ache with the weight of this burden I carried. How could I disclose my dilemma and anguish to Ammu? How selfish would it be of me to want to destroy the happiness I had witnessed on her face today? I thought about Abbuji and how much love they'd had for each other. My interpretation of marriage was that it was a partnership based on love, trust, respect, mutual understanding, growth, communication, and the constant pursuit of keeping all of those things alive. This was what I had witnessed in my parents' marriage, and perhaps this was what I was in search of.

The next morning, I woke up feeling tired and overburdened with a mind full of racing thoughts. I prayed with Ammu and left for school. I taught the children how to say names of fruits in English as a continuation from my last class. At the end of the session one of the children asked me a question that left me feeling nonplussed: 'Teacher, after your wedding, who will teach us? You will be in the kitchen cooking like my Ammu does.'

I stood and stared at him in silence until he tugged at my hand, bringing my attention back to his question. I locked away my emotions, touched his worried, angelic face, and said, 'Don't you worry. There is another teacher who will teach you many different things, and who is much more fun – you will be laughing every single day, I promise,' I reassured him, and he smiled.

That afternoon I reached home and took comfort in sitting in my usual place. I felt so disconnected that I hadn't realised my sandals were almost floating away into the stream. My Nikkah was now only a few days away and worry had now given way to panic that was brewing like a storm inside me. I had captured the little boy's angelic face in my mind, and many questions now surfaced that had been triggered by his. Although he was a small child, even he had observed the ritualistic behaviour of life in our village and reached the conclusion that women refrained from work outside the home after marriage, in order to shoulder the responsibility of the smooth running of the household and more importantly to bear and raise children. I wondered if that was the life I wanted to subject myself to. Was I really and truly physically, emotionally and psychologically ready to commit myself to Hamid and surrender all my goals in life for a responsibility I somehow felt obliged to undertake, due to the societal traditions of my village? My mind flew back to Sumayah; it felt as if my thoughts were clearing like a dark cloudy sky slowly turning pale blue and bright. I had come to the realisation that I was not physically attracted to Hamid, although this was something I was prepared to work on, and this will gave way to a new determination, almost like a light that shone the brightest in darkness.

Just then I heard Ammu's voice. 'Saira, are you in the back?'

'I'm coming,' I said, loud enough for her to hear me. I quickly dried my feet on the muddy ground and hurried inside. Ammu was carrying a load of bags and appeared exhausted, so I offered her some water to drink.

'Saira, let's eat first, and then I have a few things to show you,' she said. I sat through dinner silently cursing myself at the mere thought of how I had even contemplated disappointing her – the most precious person in my life. I quietly sat beside her after clearing the dishes, and Ammu began unpacking items that appeared to be to do with my Nikkah.

'Look at this, Saira,' she gushed, as she held up a beautiful bronze-coloured necklace covered with shiny stones that reflected beautifully against the light. I held it up in my hand as the beauty of it continued to captivate me. Ammu informed me she had travelled to Sylhet Town, where they had many antique jewellery stores, just so she could purchase a matching necklace for me to wear with my perfect gown. She looked at me with pride and joy and said, 'Saira, this is going to be one of the most prominent days of your life, and I want you to enjoy it and look like the princess that you are.' I began to choke on my own tears as she buried me deep into her chest in a maternal embrace. I was filled with panic and I needed to somehow stay composed; I gave a weak smile.

In that moment I surrendered my physical being, my mind and my soul to Hamid, with whom I would very soon be forming the most intricate bond in life. Whether this was a compromise or a sacrifice I remained unaware; however, I silently took an oath of determination to make this work no matter how difficult the struggle ahead may be.

Just as planned, my Nikkah took place. I was adorned with sweet-smelling fresh marigolds that had been intricately tied to both my wrists, ankles and around my forehead in the form of a crown. There was an intimate ceremony, followed by a gathering in our courtyard for the entire village to attend, where food and traditional Mitai were served on cut-out banana leaves to everyone in attendance. I held my mother's hand one final time against the beat of my heart as I bid her a devastating farewell, forsaking the heaven that lay beneath her feet, before handing her over to the custody and care of the villagers. Although this broke my heart, I felt assured she would be safe as I made my journey to begin this new chapter with Hamid and his family in a neighbouring village, completely and utterly unaware of what was to ensue.

Chapter 5 – The Shadow of Fear

It was Friday morning, the day when all the men in the village attended Friday Jummah prayer at the local mosque, Hamid being one of them. It was my third month here in my marital home as a newly wedded bride, and I sat plucking the first of the three slaughtered chickens in front of me in preparation for the feast hosted every Friday lunchtime for extended family. I was not familiar with plucking chickens, as with many things here – things that did not resonate or appeared nonsensical no matter how many times I ruminated over them. One of these was my husband, who appeared to hibernate during the day and would roam the village at night, as if in search of something he clearly knew he would never attain.

‘These need to be cooked and ready for serving by two o’clock,’ said my authoritarian mother-in-law Amma, sourly. I scurried into the kitchen, gathering whatever pieces of firewood I could muster, and placed them deep inside the stove. Then I returned to my uncompleted task of plucking chickens. I detested the feel of the rubbery skin against mine, but I ploughed on bravely. I dissected the three chickens, ensuring they were in small pieces according to Amma’s instructions. I then macerated them in a large pot with some onions, a little salt, a little oil, and a little more water; Amma shouted if I used any more than two teaspoons of oil, often accusing me of using too much and increasing the household expenses. I then carefully added Amma’s selection of spices along with crushed garlic and ginger, ensuring the flavours blended well. I just remembered to garnish it with the aromatic fresh coriander as Amma had told me; she was extremely pernickety.

I still had the mundane task of making a dozen samosas. In a hot pan I added the soft white coconut pulp that I had grated earlier into small thin pieces and began to cook it in its own sweetness until the mixture had turned a golden brown. Kamla, the lovely young girl who worked in the house and was my helping hand, began to roll out the dough in thin circles, and I quickly placed small portions of the coconut mixture inside them, folding them in half and then pinching the sides into half-moon shapes. I panicked at the thought of not having enough samosas so Kamla helped, enabling me to complete the task in the nick of time. I then prepared and set out the finest cutlery the family owned and headed upstairs to wipe off the accumulation of beads of sweat that now decorated my face.

They did this every Friday. I knew it would be an extremely long and exhausting day; I would be expected to serve food, followed by tea and snacks, and then the vital task of cleaning after everyone had dispersed one by one would await me. All this while my taskmistress stood over me imposing her authority. I failed to understand the traditions of this family, which had no correlation with mine. Some things baffled me, such as the men being served the entire meal that had been prepared while the women would eat only after they had finished, and only what was left over, if anything. One Friday, while I was cleaning, I watched curiously as Hamid took out a plate of rice and chicken that he had apparently kept aside for me, without the knowledge of anybody else. He would have been penalised for expressing even an inkling of humanity or affection towards his spouse.

I entered our room as quietly as I could; as expected, Hamid lay fast asleep amongst the plastic flowers that had been used to adorn the newly wedded bed. Reclusive was the word that best described him and, as for our relationship, I was dumbfounded. I was perplexed, unable to comprehend the change I had witnessed the very evening Hamid had brought me here as his newly wedded wife. I remember coming back to an empty house with him and his parents, minus the wedding procession, fancy lights or decoration. The house was dark and unwelcoming, and I was left alone on the first night of our marriage. Secretly I was grateful for this, although I did wonder where Hamid had disappeared to. The suspense continued when I later discovered his nocturnal behaviour; he spent his nights loitering around the village and slept during the day. I often wondered whether or not this had been his lifestyle out in Dubai, although I couldn't muster the courage to ask about it as we had failed to even establish a bond of friendship let alone lay the foundations of a solid marriage. I felt guilty, mostly about my poor mother, who I had only seen the once when she had visited me the previous month for the first time. Miraculously, that day Hamid became once again the lovely gentlemen he had portrayed during our introductory meeting, and suddenly his parents became loving and kindly spoken, together creating the most perfect ambience and harmonious matrimonial home I could have wished for. That day Ammu was convinced that all was well, so I took care to maintain the facade and hide what was in fact my horrid reality.

I continued living submissively in that mysterious house, although I questioned many things, such as, why did Hamid marry me? And what was the mystery behind this charade of hosting luncheons when they were all living in complete misery, or at least that was what I had gathered from my short period of living there? Hamid appeared to be detached from his parents in every sense possible. My father-in-law spent his days sleeping and his waking hours smoking tobacco from his brass hookah. However, Amma appeared completely oblivious to the behaviour of her son and husband, dictating every last task and decision in the house from the breakfast menu down to how many onions would be required before the next monthly visit to the local bazaar. She was a woman spent, taxed in every way, and on a mission to change the inevitable, it seemed.

I looked away as Hamid turned over in my direction, eyes half open now, and we both heard the chatter of the guests who had begun to arrive one by one. 'Saira, can you begin with the snacks first,' called out Amma. As usual Hamid said nothing; he just stared into my eyes for a second and then looked away. For that second it almost felt as if there was something he desperately wanted to tell me; only an unknown dark force prevented him, a force that perhaps, if revealed, would provide the sense within this nonsensical household.

I went downstairs adorned in a pretty sari and matching bangles, as wearing anything else would be deemed unladylike. It was traditional to greet the extended family members, consisting of aunts and uncles, in this manner. They were extremely backward in many ways, believing that women should bow down to the dictatorship of men and have no voice at all. 'Assalamualaikum,' I said politely, and they all stared back, evaluating me. They expected me to serve them while they sat and watched me pander to their every need.

The previous Friday, I had clearly overheard them whispering something about 'the previous one', and 'if there had been any news', only they discontinued the whispered conversations whenever I was around. They engaged in whispered conversations with one another often, which left me wondering about what the mystery was. I had become so confused following this that I even approached Kamla.

However, when I asked her, a terrified look appeared on her face and she squeezed my hand so hard that it hurt. 'Please don't ask me this ever again, both of us will be in danger,' she said. Danger! I thought out loud; clearly she must have been exaggerating. Admittedly this family was extremely odd and reclusive; however, I did not feel that they posed any threat or danger, or at least that was what I thought.

I served everybody snacks; the huge number of coconut samosas that I had fried earlier had begun to repulse me now. The abhorrent luncheon continued as I served them the main meal, and silently watched them devour it all without so much as a thank you or even an inkling of gratitude. It almost felt as if Amma needed the approval of these people to create the image of herself that she aspired to, and the only way that she was able to achieve this was through hosting these grand gatherings. Perhaps it was an attempt to conceal something deep and dark on a much larger scale. Every so often the ladies would stare at me then break away whenever I stared back, and then talk amongst themselves as if evaluating and critiquing a conspiracy known only to them. As I stood sweltering in the intense heat like the melting wax of a candle, I cursed myself first and then my surroundings.

All the guests had finished lunch and gathered out in the open courtyard, some in the shade beneath the towering betel nut trees, and some of the women lounging on the small, humid kitchen floor. Kamla and I sat down for lunch, as I knew it would soon be time to serve tea followed by more savouries. I offered Hamid lunch as he entered the kitchen; however, as I expected he declined, leaving the house as the guests condemned his behaviour. It almost appeared that he was the ugly duckling of the family, and that there was something more to him than met the eye.

There was hardly any food left over for Kamla and I, so I gave her the last of the chicken and she smiled. I collected water to brew the tea; thirty cups of tea required several pots, something I had learnt the hard way a few weeks before when Amma shouted at the sight of half-filled cups. I went to gather a few more pieces of firewood, which was piled up in a shaded corner of the back courtyard, and I heard a very hushed whisper: 'Have you asked Saira about it? It's been a few months – she should have been pregnant by now.' I was now on full alert, my nerves tingling, and I peered round to discover Amma talking to one of Hamid's aunts. They very quickly walked away as Kamla followed outside with the kholosh. This baffled me to such an extent that I was unable to comprehend what I had just witnessed. Why would this question even arise at a gathering such as this? Pregnant? Surely if Hamid wanted children he would have spoken to me about it. Surely he understood that in order to reproduce, a certain level of intimacy was required? I couldn't stop thinking about it.

I began serving the women tea with their savoury snacks as each one stared at me. It was now late afternoon and much to my relief the luncheon was finally coming to an end, and I began to bid them all farewell individually. I watched as one of the ladies said to Amma, 'Maybe next week you will share some Mitai.' In response Amma just laughed uncomfortably, attempting to disregard the comment in its entirety.

'Everything needs to be cleaned, Saira,' said Amma with a scowl across her face as she disappeared into her room for her late afternoon nap. I sat down to rest my exhausted feet and sore hands, while I tried to connect the dots of all the strange happenings. Only none of it connected, nothing appeared to fit or make sense.

I heard Kamla piling up the pots, so I walked over to her, sat her down and told her about what I had witnessed. 'Kamla, I know you know something. Tell me, please, what does all this mean?' I demanded.

'I don't know anything,' she said, petrified.

'Please, Kamla, you have to help me, what's going on here?' I pleaded with tears streaming down my face.

'Okay, but you must promise never to mention my name,' she said quietly.

This revelation was one I could not have prepared for in a million years; it shook the ground beneath my feet, it was cruel and callous and premeditated in every way possible. I stood, shell-shocked and broken, as Kamla informed me that I was in fact Hamid's third wife, and that his parents had insisted he remarry a young girl so she could produce an heir, which the other wives had been incapable of. Amma in particular found this to be shameful and a disgrace, and was continually taunted by the extended family members; the luncheons were her way to stay integrated and to remove the tarnish. Hamid had been an only child and Amma's ultimate goal was for him to produce an heir for their family; I had been specifically selected for the completion of this task. I felt betrayed and disgusted in every way possible by this cold reality, but when I turned around to ask Kamla where the other two wives were, she had disappeared. I felt as if I was in a state of mourning, as if I had lost a piece of my identity and integrity. Did I not matter? Had my feelings and emotions been reduced to this level of inhumanity, I questioned, as I cleaned the kitchen.

I sat on the cool muddy ground beside the stove lost in deep thought as I reflected on when I had mentioned to Hamid about teaching in the nearby school. His response had been, 'You're still a new bride, Saira.' I figured what he had meant was that that would defeat the purpose of my being here. A sudden fury overtook me, mainly at myself and then at Hamid; why had he deceived me so callously? I decided I would no longer submit to this anguish no matter what the consequences.

I walked upstairs to find Hamid preparing to leave for his nightly adventures. 'I need to talk with you,' I told him.

'It will have to wait, Saira, I am on my way out,' he replied in another attempt to brush me off.

'No, it cannot. How dare you deceive me like this?' I said sternly in a raised voice. He stood up to look me in the eye, now giving me his undivided attention. 'How dare you conceal from me that this is your third marriage. I have been nothing but good to you and your family, and you forget to mention that I have been selected as an object to reproduce an heir for you and your family,' I blurted out. Crying uncontrollably, I sat on the floor, dejected.

'Saira, you must understand I never wanted any of this, but they just don't get it,' he said with a look of disgust on his face.

'Who are you blaming? You're a grown man, and you have made this decision consciously,' I told him.

'That's just it, I'm not a man, and they will continue making me remarry until I prove that I am,' he said facetiously. This confused me further, and I continued to question him until he gave me the answers I demanded; but I was unable to bear the truth. He revealed that he was infertile, and that Amma was in denial of this even though it had been investigated and medically diagnosed. Amma remarried him a second and a third time in her attempt to prove these findings to be incorrect – and to conceal the truth and appease their ever-questioning judgemental relatives. She believed that this truth would bring shame and dishonour to the family and lower their status drastically within the community. 'She will continue doing this to me for as long as she can,' he said with repulsion. I sat speechless, feeling numb and sad for both me and Hamid. I had held him responsible for my plight, when his had been much worse. Everything now began to make sense: this house, Amma and her behaviour, the luncheons and the relatives. Even Hamid's behaviour towards me, I figured, was his way of trying to protect me from this reality. 'I'm deeply sorry, Saira,' he said with sadness.

'Hamid, where are your other wives?' I asked. He looked away in disgust, so I repeated my question.

'Saira, Amma made everyone believe that they were infertile and so they were punished by stoning,' he said, defeated, and I gasped in utter devastation. I could not help but cry out at the brutality of these people.

'Hamid, you must tell everyone the truth – you can't continue living in this way, this is no life,' I said as he turned away. 'Hamid,' I shouted, now standing tall right behind him, but he just stood still and said nothing, which only intensified my frustration further. 'Hamid,' I shouted a second time, shaking his arm vigorously.

He turned, wide eyed with rage, and looked at me intently. 'Whether you like it or not, there is nothing that can be done, so it is better that you accept things for what they are and carry on the way that you have been,' he shouted back.

'No, I won't, I will go and tell everyone the truth right away,' I said and headed for the door. He grabbed my arm from behind and violently swung me around to face him, slamming the door shut. 'You're hurting me, Hamid, let me go,' I protested as his grip on my arm tightened with a strength that was difficult to break away from. 'I won't live like this,' I yelled; he continued holding my wrist so tightly it began to sting.

'What will you do? You can shout and scream as much as you like. You are my wife and nobody will come to your rescue here,' he warned, red-eyed with rage.

'Argh, Hamid you're hurting me,' I pleaded. He yanked me closer to him and looked me in the eye with fury as I squealed in pain, then threw me to the floor with a thud that echoed so loud my ears hurt. 'What kind of a monster are you?' I cried out.

'I am the one that you married,' he screamed into my face, 'and I can do a lot more, so don't provoke me, take this as a warning,' he shouted, pointing into my face as I sat sprawled across the floor grimacing in pain.

'You think you will get away with this? I am leaving right now.' I stood up, heading towards the door. He grabbed my arm a second time, cutting into the same wound and I shrieked in agony. This time he threw me as far as he could across the room where I landed on the dresser.

'Don't you dare ever try to leave this house. Even if you do, Amma will find you, and the consequences… well, you can imagine, can't you? You're an intelligent woman, so I suggest you continue the way that you have been,' he shouted at the top of his voice and left the room, slamming the door behind. I cried out in pain, struggling to even breathe. I could barely move my wounded body, as I sat in darkness condemned by betrayal and deceit. This was the real Hamid, the man I had married and would have to endure for the rest of my life.

I woke the next morning flinching at the very thought of Hamid, and breathed a sigh of relief at the sight of his empty pillow. My arm was red and bruised, as was my leg, making it difficult to move. I'd heard the stories well enough to know that this was something that was considered to be an act of love. A man who is at the peak of his love for his wife often expresses this love by beating her. Not only was it something to be proud of, it was something that was passed on through ancestors and family traditions. Only my father rejected this notion and the people who practised it. Little did I know it still existed and that I would become its victim.

I managed to make my way downstairs and into the kitchen; the sun was already up and I knew Amma would be, too. In anticipation I began preparing the tea, ensuring my sleeves were rolled down to my wrist. Kamla walked into the kitchen and greeted me. 'Saira,' she said, at which I flinched. 'What's wrong?' she asked. 'Why do you look so worried?' She was standing right next to me.

'It's nothing, Kamla, I am just a little tired,' I snapped. Kamla continued to stare at me with a knowing look, as if to say that she knew this was history repeating itself. I wanted to cry and tell her everything, only I knew this cold reality was not one that I could escape.

'How long will I have to wait for a cup of tea this morning? All you two do is eat and sleep and walk around like princesses. You're useless, the pair of you,' shouted Amma upon entering the kitchen. In a state of panic I moved away from Kamla and began to pour tea frantically, as she served the breakfast snacks. 'When your highness is ready,' Amma sneered in return, leaving the kitchen with the tray of tea and snacks. I sat near the stove, dejected, almost in tears as I rolled up my sleeves to begin rinsing the pots for lunch preparation.

'Saira,' Kamla gasped, pointing down at my arms as she noticed the red bruising.

'Kamla, it's nothing.' I flinched in fear and immediately put my arms behind me. She brought both my hands forward and touched the red bruises as I looked into her eyes, which must have told her everything.

‘Does it hurt?’ she asked, and we both cried together.

‘Yes, it does, a lot,’ I admitted as she massaged my arm gently.

‘Did he do that?’ she asked, and I nodded in between muted cries of fear.

Kamla took it upon herself to take care of me, in an attempt to mend my heart which had been shattered into a thousand pieces. She massaged oil onto my bruises, prepared lunch and even swept, cleaned and washed, allowing me to recover from the barbarity of the previous night. When Amma had taken herself upstairs for her afternoon nap, Kamla sat with me near the stove and confessed that she had observed the same bruising on Hamid’s previous wives. Sometimes they appeared as redness on their arms, cheeks and even forehead; it seemed Hamid was no angel in all of this. The only difference was that those women had lived in complete isolation and fear of the consequences and of what society would say.

‘Saira, I warned you, this is how these people are. You must remain quiet or this will happen to you time and time again.’ Kamla tried to pacify me.

‘Kamla, this is injustice, they can’t get away with this,’ I explained to her.

‘Saira, we are women, this is how it is for us. Even if you try to leave, they will find you and bring you back here,’ she stated prior to walking out of the kitchen. Those words became the deciding factor; the words that made me realise that this is not how it is for us. The words that determined that one day I would leave, never to return. Although I was hurt and scared, I decided I would not succumb to this injustice; if not today then tomorrow I would find a way, no matter what it took. I continued sitting on the coolness of the muddy ground, thinking of my mother who would be devastated to learn my plight. My bruised leg made it difficult to move around the house and I needed to go upstairs and face Hamid; I knew he would have returned at daybreak. I felt scared and frail, although internally strong as my father had taught me to be. I knew I needed to prove to Hamid that I would not live in fear of him; although my fear was overwhelming.

Slowly I crept upstairs and into the room and as predicted Hamid lay fast asleep. Quietly I grabbed a change of clothes and headed for the door just as Hamid sat up, making me flinch and tremble at the very thought of him coming close to me. 'Saira,' he called out, much to my surprise, as I stood still as a statue, barely breathing, with my back turned towards him. Within a few seconds he was standing directly in front of me caressing my frightened face; my heart skipped a beat. I immediately took a step back, moving away from him, but he came closer as I continued moving backwards in desperate search of safety and stumbled, nearly falling. Hamid grabbed me by the hand. He held my face as I struggled to breathe and caressed my hair. 'Saira, you look terrified,' he sneered. My entire body struggled for air as I stood, fearful. 'Look, don't be afraid,' he continued as I gasped for air and tried to move away from him. But he followed and was in my face again. 'Saira, I apologise for yesterday. However, as your husband I do have some rights over you. I am allowed to touch you now and again,' he said, laughing and touching my cold cheekbones. I was repulsed by the feel of his hand on my skin; he had violated me like no other, and the sight of him revolted me.

I somehow managed to stay composed and said nothing; this was how I needed to remain until I had devised an escape plan. 'Please don't be frightened of me. As long as there is never a repeat of yesterday then this lovely pattern on your arm will never reappear,' he said happily, touching the redness of my bruises. I moved away at once taking deep breaths. 'We just need to find a way to live together amicably. I am sure we can teach one another to do that right – after all, we are teachers,' he continued. I maintained my closed posture and said nothing.

Much to my relief, dusk was taking its course across the bright skies, and Hamid left for his nightly adventures. Immediately I breathed out a sigh of relief and sprawled out across the floor, crying out in dismay. The only person who was able to console me was someplace far away and out of reach. I missed my mother terribly and ached to feel the warmth of her hand once again.

'Saira, Saira, where are you? You wretched woman, Saira,' I heard Amma shout out in annoyance at the top of her lungs in a high-pitched voice. At once I wiped my face clean and made my way back downstairs. Amma stood tall and angry under the small kitchen doorframe and I stood behind her, timid and fragile.

'I'm sorry, Amma, I couldn't hear you,' I told her in a quiet voice.

'You couldn't hear me, what were you doing, sleeping? What happened to the oil?' she continued to shout. I stood still, diminished by her obscene behaviour towards me. 'What did you do with the oil? How many times have I told you to only use a few spoonfuls at a time, and now it's finished. Will your mother pay for it? Do you know how expensive it is to manage this house?' she demanded. To hear my mother's name from her in this manner enraged me, and Kamla nudged my shoulder reminding me to stay quiet. I clenched my hands and closed my eyes in surrender. Amma continued to mutter a few more obscene words and then walked off with the lantern she was holding. Electrical power cuts were very common in the villages; it seemed Amma needed some oil to fill the lantern, even though I had reminded her a few days earlier that we were down to the last few drops.

That night I cried uncontrollably as Kamla sat close, consoling me as best she could by constantly reminding me to say nothing in retaliation. I spent the next few days mostly in sullen submission, trying my best to keep out of Hamid's way and attending to Amma as she required. All the while I felt detached, as if I had become a bystander watching this oppression. Although my body was weak, my mind was strong and I had decided I would not stand by. I would retaliate, and I would leave at the earliest opportunity. My days were spent with Kamla who gave me much love and care, and my nights were spent thinking of my mother, father and Sumayah.

I gradually adapted to avoiding Hamid almost like the plague, and would leave the room at sunrise just as he would enter. One morning he caught me off guard when he returned just before I was able to leave. 'Saira, what a lovely surprise,' he said, taking me by the hand. I squirmed, loosening the grip of his hand upon mine and managed to set myself free. 'You're doing very well, I have taught you well.' He laughed as I left the room, breathing heavily. I despised the sight of him and this house. Quickly I composed myself and collected the firewood from the back courtyard; the scarlet sky reminded me of my home. Kamla joined me as we began to brew tea and prepare breakfast in preparation for Amma to descend. Just like every day, together we prepared snacks of Amma's choice and poured piping hot tea into two small cups and waited for her.

The early morning sunshine was now beating down, but surprisingly, there was no sign of Amma, which was extremely unusual. 'Kamla, where is Amma today?' I asked.

'I don't know, Saira, she is usually up and about by now,' she replied. My father-in-law had been visiting relatives in another village and would be away a few more days, which left me pondering as to why Amma had not been for her breakfast. She was not one to go without food, especially breakfast. After much deliberation, Kamla and I decided to go up to Amma's room to enquire.

Kamla knocked timidly. 'Amma, Amma, are you there?' she called out. 'Amma are you there?' She knocked again as we waited. 'Amma,' she called out a third time.

'What is it?' Amma's angry voice came through the door.

Kamla and I entered the room to discover Amma lying in the dark holding her head in her hands. 'Amma, we were worried… as you didn't come downstairs for your breakfast. Is everything all right?' Kamla asked hesitantly.

At once Amma stood up. 'How can it be all right when I have to look at you both? Have you come to check if I were dead?' she said scornfully, screwing up her face as she looked at us.

'No, Amma, we were worried about you,' Kamla explained.

Amma frowned and replied, 'Looking at you both is making it worse.' And she lay back down again holding her head, cursing us and then herself, it seemed.

'Amma, what's the matter?' I enquired politely.

'Can't you see what the matter is? My head is going to explode and on top of that I have you two wretches to look at,' she shouted. I had heard that Amma suffered terrible migraines, which lasted for days at a time, but this was the first one I had witnessed.

'Can we get you anything?' Kamla asked.

'How about you bring me breakfast here – the pair of you are good for nothing.' Amma scowled.

We placed her breakfast in her room, allowing her some time to recover. 'She is always like this when she has a migraine,' Kamla stated upon our return to the kitchen, as if to pacify me more than anything, although I knew there was no excuse for her behaviour – or Hamid's for that matter. I said nothing and smiled at Kamla for her kind efforts to maintain my sanity. There was hardly any housework that day, as Hamid was sleeping and Amma was left to rest. It was peaceful sitting with Kamla as she shared stories with me of her upbringing. She had no parents and was raised by a maternal aunt who could no longer support her due to financial constraints; therefore, she was handed over to Hamid's family as a maid. This was the devastating plight of so many other young girls who had no one apart from keepers such as these. I was fortunate to have had such wonderful parents who gave me the life I had lived; only today they would be devastated to see me this dejected. I only noticed the sky become the grey of dusk when I heard Hamid leave; my heart skipped a beat and then returned to normal.

'Kamla, it's almost night and Amma hasn't left her room yet,' I said to her.

'Shall we go and check on her?' she asked. Together we went up to her room once again. 'Amma, how are you feeling?' Kamla asked, entering the room as I followed behind.

'You leave me for dead the entire day, and now you're asking.' She frowned.

'Are you feeling better, Amma,' I asked.

'Don't just stand there – go and get my balm,' she shouted.

I stood staring at her, unsure of what exactly she was asking for, until Kamla said, 'Sure, Amma, I will just get it for you.' I followed Kamla into another room where she picked out a small pot from a medicine cabinet. 'Oh no, what will we do now? She will not allow us to get away with this,' she cried out.

I panicked. 'What's wrong, Kamla?'

'Saira, the balm is finished and it's the only thing that helps with her migraines. What will we do now?' she continued anxiously.

'Don't worry, we can just go and collect some more,' I reassured her.

'No, Saira, there is nobody around to collect it. She will be hysterical,' Kamla cried.

I tried to pacify her. 'We will go and explain to Amma.' Panic stricken, we returned to Amma's room. The dryness of my throat overtook me and I couldn't speak.

'Well, did you get the balm? Do you want to kill me with this migraine?' she demanded. We both stared at her silently. Kamla had been correct that Amma would be hysterical.

'Amma, the balm… it's, it's, it's…' Kamla stuttered.

'It's what? Get on with it.' She scowled.

'Amma, the balm is finished,' I told her in a strained voice.

'Well, don't just stand there and look at me – go and collect some more from the doctor's hut. Do you want to kill me with this migraine today?' she shouted.

'We will do that right away, Amma,' said Kamla and grabbed my hand, swiftly pulling me downstairs as quickly as she could move. 'Saira, we get to go out,' Kamla screeched.

'Are you sure the both of us should go?' I said.

'Saira, we will never have this opportunity again. Come on, let's breathe the open village air and nobody will see us because it's dark,' she said, tempting me all the more. Leaving this house for a short while sounded just like the relief I needed right now. Kamla wrapped a large shawl around her and then handed me one. I smiled, placing the shawl over my head and upper body: the perfect garment to conceal our identities, it seemed. Although I was hesitant, the thought of being out in the open village air enthralled me and I followed Kamla's lead almost in exhilaration. The doctor's hut was a tiny mud house situated near the end of the local bazaar near the large bamboo bridge. It was extremely popular amongst the villagers. Kamla and I walked the long distance as I revelled in being out in the open air after such a long time. There were many people who I did not recognise, but it reminded me of my village, my home.

I walked warily, concerned that Hamid would see us, and hid my face with my shawl. It was chilly, and grey areas of fog were beginning to appear; Kamla joined her hand with mine, both of us smiling as if we had escaped from long captivity. 'Are we nearly there yet, Kamla?' I enquired. We had almost reached the end of the village and I could hear the sound of water and the crashing of waves. It seemed we had also left the villagers behind as there was no one else around.

'Nearly, Saira,' she said. I was intrigued. It seemed as if we were walking to an empty space and I wondered where this doctor's hut was situated. I was perplexed at the sensation of grass and muddy ground as opposed to dust beneath my feet. I continued to follow her lead in the darkness as quietly as possible. Kamla halted abruptly. 'Here we are,' she said. She stood pointing to the long bamboo bridge, the only link between this village and my own, and told me to go and never return, bidding me a tearful goodbye.

Shock took over my entire body. 'Kamla, what do you mean?' I asked her, trembling.

'Go, Saira, go. You will never get another opportunity like this,' she insisted, grasping my hand.

'Kamla – go where? I can't leave you here like this, I won't go,' I shouted.

'Saira, please, they won't allow you to live in peace. Go back to your mother and never return here – go before someone sees you,' she pleaded.

'No, Kamla. I can't leave you here, they will blame you,' I cried.

'Don't worry about me. I will tell them that you ran off. Now go,' she repeated.

'No, Kamla, please,' I protested.

'Saira, you're not like the others. You're strong and clever and beautiful and you deserve a better life than this. Now please, for my sake, just go,' she begged. I held Kamla as we both cried together. It seemed she had planned this and wanted my freedom even more than I. 'Now go, Saira, before anyone sees us,' she told me firmly.

'Kamla, thank you so much, I will never forget you,' I said as she let go of my trembling hand.

I looked at her innocent face one final time as she hurried me to leave, saying fearfully, 'Be careful, Saira. Amma will never give up looking for you.'

With my heart beating wildly, I stepped towards the bridge as Kamla vanished into the darkness of the night. Beneath the bridge lay a river, deep and wide. I began to follow Kamla's instructions; I knew I had to escape this abhorrence that circumstances had led me to. Barefoot I stepped onto the bridge, which had been made by the people of the local villages. It was about sixty feet in length and four feet wide. This was a bridge I would never have even contemplated crossing had my mind been clear – the fear of falling into the river sent shivers deep into my spine. I took a step forward and shrieked as the bamboo stick beneath my foot rolled over, causing me to lose my balance and let go of my shawl, which fell into the river beneath. The night was cold and black and I was surrounded by a thick fog preventing me from seeing anything in front or around. The only thing I could hear was the roaring sound of the waves beneath me, crashing into each other. I trembled with fear, feeling disgusted and ashamed – with myself, mainly – as I continued taking faltering steps until I was standing right in the middle of the bridge, shell-shocked. I closed my eyes as my breathing shuddered, but I knew I needed to cross this bridge and honour Kamla's sacrifice; I knew all too well the consequences that would be awaiting her.

Just then I was startled by a light which shone directly into my face, causing me to scream in fear. The cloudy grey fog shaded all visibility, so I could see only the shadow of a man holding what appeared to be a torch; I continued to tremble. Then suddenly I heard a soft, reassuring voice. 'Don't be afraid, I won't hurt you.' I stared at the bright light in astonishment, breathing so heavily that my pounding heart began to hurt. My initial thought was that perhaps it was Hamid, only this man was at the opposite end of the bridge. He then held out his hand. 'Take my hand, you're shaking, and the wind is strong,' he said.

'I just want to stay here,' I shouted, breathing raggedly.

'You're going to fall into the water. Take my hand – it's going to be all right,' he said, coming closer to me holding out his hand. There was something alluring about his words, encouraging me to put my trust in him and to take hold of his hand. He spoke with an integrity that was hypnotising. The grip of his hand on mine felt warm, momentarily allowing me to feel safe and secure. 'I'm going to help you walk slowly off this bridge. I promise I won't hurt you,' he said. I shrieked as the bamboo beneath my feet rolled over once more, causing me to stumble, and in response the grip of his hand on mine tightened.

Keeping me close he began taking small steps. 'The wind is causing the sticks to sway so tread carefully. I've got you, and I won't let you go,' he said softly. The wind was howling and blew stronger as I continued to follow his lead one step at a time until we reached the ground beyond the bridge. I began shivering uncontrollably. 'Here, take this.' He wrapped a woolly shawl securely around my shoulders shielding me from the gust of cold wind. 'Are you okay?' he asked.

'Yes,' I stuttered.

'Where's your house?' he asked. I pointed in the direction of the village entrance and he began to walk beside me. We walked side by side in silence; I was still unable to see his face. All I gathered was that he was tall, softly spoken – and a complete stranger who had been sent as my saviour on this frightening night. We reached the village entrance and after a pause he asked again, 'Which way is your house?' I pointed in the direction of the distant lights that were just visible. 'Don't be afraid, I'm going to watch you just to make sure you're safe. You keep walking until you reach home,' he instructed. I held out the billowing shawl towards him. 'You keep that,' he said, wrapping me up again tightly.

I took a step forward just as he had instructed and began walking; the echo of his presence surrounded me with a force almost as strong as the storm. I glanced back and to my surprise the light from his torch was still visible. A surreal feeling overtook me and I suddenly felt a sense of clarity run through every crevice of my body and mind. I had always believed in Tawakkul: having reliance, trust and faith in God. Once again this trust had been confirmed and I felt stronger, strong enough to deal with the consequences of my actions that were yet to come. It was almost as if this bewildering encounter had revived an innate strength to enable me to overcome the conflict I was going to have to face. I was thankful firstly to Kamla and then to this unknown gentleman. That was the deciding moment: I vowed not to become the definition of myself that society wanted for me, but the definition of myself that I wanted to be, although I knew that this would have many consequences. I would remain strong. I would never give up and I would never submit.

I reached our courtyard, and on the other side of the doorway was my beloved mother. I was fearful – firstly about what explanation I would give her about why I had returned home alone in this manner in the middle of the night. How would I explain the reality of my short-lived marriage to Hamid, while I myself was still struggling to comprehend how I had fallen prey to such abuse? I was hurt and brutalised by this cruel deception. But I felt honoured by Kamla's sacrifice and pitied Hamid for enacting this cruel charade, and hoped that one day he would finally accept his situation. I also knew very well that his mother was a cunning, stubborn lady who would go to any extreme to preserve her honour and dignity. A part of me felt guilty, knowing that I had left Kamla all alone to face this wrath, while another part felt relieved at the thought that I had been rescued from the fate of his previous wives. 'They were stoned,' I whispered in despair, and I wondered where and how they were now or even if they were alive; it did not bear thinking about. Those poor women had been subjected to this very same deception and much more. I was grateful to have escaped. I knew that my journey was far from over and that it would be a path filled with many roses, but picking out each thorn would prove to be more painful than ever.

With enormous fear in my heart I knocked on the door. 'Ammu, are you there,' I called out. The door swung wide open and my beloved mother stood in the dark with half-open eyes. She looked startled to find me here at this time of night, and then I guess her maternal instincts took over and she figured out that something was wrong; something terrible and untoward had happened.

'Saira, my baby! What are you doing here at this time of night?' she asked, ushering me indoors and wrapping me up in blanket after blanket to warm my freezing body.

'I'm so sorry, Ammu, please forgive me,' I said hysterically as my face flooded with tears. Ammu frantically began to comfort me, pulling me close to her chest and stroking my hair.

'Whatever it is we will deal with it together,' she reassured me, 'everything is going to be okay, I promise.'

'I'm so sorry, Ammuji, I have made a mess out of everything,' I said, looking at her worried face.

'Oh, Saira, dear, you're not making any sense, and you haven't made a mess out of anything,' she assured me.

'Ammu, you will be so disappointed with me. I'm sorry, I never meant to hurt you, please believe me,' I continued to plead with her.

'Saira, it's all right, tell me what's happened,' she urged.

'Ammu, we need to lock all the doors – they will come after me,' I cried out in panic.

She pulled me close into her chest, clearly shocked at my plight, and reassured me. 'It's okay, you're safe here.'

I decided it was time to control my emotions and reveal the whole truth. So I took my beloved mother's hand in mine and told her that I loved her very much; she looked at me in anguish. I first told her the reason behind Sumayah's absence from me and that it was a result of the rumours that had been spreading amongst the villagers. I admitted that I only agreed to marry Hamid under duress, although my intention had been to make this marriage work. I then told her that fate had other plans for me, plans I had no control over. Feeling overwhelmed, I said, 'Please believe me, Ammu, all I wanted was to make you happy, and I tried to make things work, but they deceived me so badly.' I began crying hysterically, as Ammu held me close. Finally I divulged the bitter truth about Hamid, his family and the reasons behind this alliance, and how the family had behaved towards me. I watched the look of horror that spread across my mother's face, and then felt guilty as the horror turned into pain and utter devastation.

'You kept this all to yourself, my poor child – you did not think to share this with me once? Saira, I am so sorry, please forgive me, my child.'

'No, Ammu, none of this is your fault,' I cried back.

'I promise I will not let anything happen to you – you're safe now,' she said, holding me tightly. 'How dare he hurt you like this!' she cried out in anger, stroking my cold arms.

'Ammu, I hope Kamla is okay. If it weren't for her help then I would never have been able to escape,' I said, snuggling up into her chest.

'You're safe now,' she consoled me.

That night I lay next to my beloved mother, holding on tight in fear of Hamid or Amma turning up. She held me close.

The next morning I felt a great relief, an emotion I had not felt for a long while. The darkness of the night had begun to fade, making way for the light of a new day – almost a reflection of my current state of mind. Ammu brewed ginger tea for us both as I sat mute, overwhelmed by the many emotions I had endured the previous night and was still in battle with. My amazing mother seemed strong and determined; this was a side to her that I had never experienced. She was like a shield, ready to protect me should the need arise.

'I will speak with Hamid's family today. Don't you worry about a thing – you will never return to that house, no matter what the consequences,' she said sternly. She held my face gently and said, 'Saira, me and your Abbuji believed that one should always follow the heart and do the right thing, and today I'm immensely proud of you for doing that, but remember that the road ahead may be rocky and I need you to stay strong. Can you do that?'

'Of course, Ammu,' I replied.

'You're home now and you're safe here. I want you to gradually put all of this behind you,' she added with a look of determination in her eyes. 'Will you be all right for a short while? I need to pop out for something urgent,' she asked.

'Yes, Ammu,' I replied wearily.

'You're safe here and I won't be long,' she assured me, and left. I immediately locked the door and watched through the open window as Ammu disappeared into the winding valley leading out of our village. Just then I noticed the shawl I had been wearing the previous night. I picked it up and thought about the stranger who had so kindly helped me in my time of greatest need, and smiled, wishing I had been able to express my gratitude to him. I then carefully placed the shawl into my closet for safe keeping. It felt good to be home, although memories of Hamid and the time spent with his family continued to haunt me throughout the day.

When Ammu came home she seemed exhausted, but immediately began preparing dinner for me. After much persuasion I finally managed to convince her to sit and take a rest. I served dinner whilst she informed me she had made contact with Hamid's father through Mesabji Chacha and that she had ended the marriage alliance between our families. 'Did they take the news well, Ammu?' I enquired.

'Let's just say that they were more concerned about how to preserve their dignity and status,' she said, caressing my hair.

'You don't know them, Ammu, they will come looking for me and take me back,' I cried out.

She held me close and said, 'Saira, you're safe here. You have me and everybody else in the village to protect you – just let them try.' I nodded, comforted by the safety of her arms.

Chapter 6 – Devastation of Barsha

I spent the next few weeks with Ammu, anxiety-ridden at the thought of Hamid and his mother coming after me. Most days I would check the door and surrounding area a dozen times and startle at the slightest sound. I avoided the villagers as much as possible in fear of being asked that unavoidable question, although I knew that naturally they would want to enquire about Hamid; and putting everything behind me seemed impossible. The monsoon season was fast approaching, bringing with it hope. I looked forward to watching the villagers grow and cultivate jute as my father had done. I was enthralled by the heavy rainfall, the humidity of the heat, the shapla flowers that would be floating almost everywhere in the village. All the while Ammu was right beside me, constantly reassuring me of my safety.

It was a hot and sticky afternoon, so I decided to take a walk as I had spent all my time indoors since my return. My mother had advised me that I needed to stop living in constant fear, and I stepped out of the house for the first time. Warily I began to walk down the muddy path, taking the route that I used to take to school. I recalled how much I had enjoyed greeting everybody I saw on the way; being a close community, mutual understanding and friendship was a feature of village life. That evening I wondered why the group of ladies I had greeted had completely ignored me. I sat near the stream in our back courtyard and brushed it off, thinking I was paranoid. After all, these were people I had known all my life; what issue would they have developed with me so suddenly? I stared into the shallows of the stream, which reminded me of Sumayah; I had not met with her since my return and missed her terribly. I missed our daily banter, our chats, the laughter, and I longed for the next time I would see her and wished for it to be soon.

That evening Ammu reached home carrying a heavy load of carrier bags containing a variety of different fabrics. I enquired about them, expecting that she must have received a large order. To my astonishment she said she needed to put in extra hours of sewing in order to keep up with the orders, as the lady who had been her partner for many years had suddenly decided to quit. 'What, Ammu, did you ask her why? How will you do all this by yourself?' I asked, annoyed. Ammu avoided my question and ended the conversation there without allowing me to explore it any further. I knew she was tired, so I decided my long list of questions could wait for another time. The next few weeks I witnessed how hard she worked, until she was physically exhausted and her mood subdued. She would leave very early in the morning and return late, and after dinner would continue cutting out the designs she had brought home with her. She hardly ate and only slept minimally. I once asked why she could not employ another lady from the village and her response was that nobody expressed an interest in sewing anymore, which did not fit in with her behaviour.

Although thoughts of Hamid and his family were gradually becoming a distant memory, my internal battle remained of the same magnitude and the fear strong. Most nights I lay awake terrified at the thought of them bursting through the door to summon me, and I would end up hyperventilating.

Barsha had finally arrived and the heavy rain brought great apprehension and anticipation to the villagers; the low-lying, fertile land around our village would be immersed in water for days or even months without respite. At times the water level would rise to such an extent that our school would need to stay closed and boats would be the only form of transport around our village. Although Barsha brought mainly devastation, with some villagers losing parts of their homes, there were some things that I treasured about the season. I loved how the almost extinct plants and greenery had a new lease of life after immersion in water. Ammuji loved the hilsha fish that swam in the Barsha waters, waiting to be captured by the fishermen.

I relished the company of my mother; being around her kept my mind occupied. Whilst the fear of Hamid and his family made me tremble most days and nights, I managed to conceal this from her with difficulty. The water level was now so high that the stream in our back courtyard had become a river after the overnight rain, which only subsided in the morning. It left the ground muddy and wet, making the floors inside our house slippery. Ammu and I loved watching the rain, it was almost cathartic. We waited for the raindrops to subside completely before leaving the house. I had planned to visit one of the pupils that I used to teach, as Ammu had suggested they may require home tuition since the school was closed. That, in turn, would keep me busy. The mudslides in the ground were shiny and wet as the rays of the sun reflected on them. We arrived at the house, which was a short distance away. Ammu knew the mother as a friend and greeted her. But she frowned upon seeing us. I enquired about the tuition, and she walked back into her house, leaving us bewildered. A few minutes later she returned and all we saw were papers and books flying up into the air and then falling to the ground around us. I stared in confusion at this lady's passive-aggressive behaviour. The commotion attracted other villagers, mainly women, who stared.

'Khala, why are you throwing books at us?' I asked firmly.

'Saira, because of you, people are pointing fingers at all of our girls. What will you teach any of our children?' she shouted at the top of her voice. I was angry and wanted to challenge her and ask exactly what she meant, but Ammu held me back by the hand, urging me to remain quiet, and firmly gestured for us both to walk away. The gathered throng stood still and continued to stare at us and the lady. This incident baffled me and on the way home I rebuked Ammu for not allowing me to say anything in our defence.

Ammu then sat me down to explain. 'It would have been pointless to engage in an argument as it's the mentality of the villagers that needs educating, and that can only be done through staying calm.' She was correct.

I soon gathered that this cold, angry, passive-aggressive behaviour of the local villagers towards us had been a consequence of my broken alliance with Hamid. I figured that the gossip mongers had succeeded in spreading the latest update regarding my broken marriage. My decision did not at all fit into the cultural and societal norms of my village; neither was it acceptable in their eyes. Although this cnraged me, I decided to remain calm as Ammu had advised and began to seek opportunities to talk to my fellow villagers, to get them to understand my decision. Perhaps at the same time I could change their way of thinking.

Over the next week I assisted Ammuji with her work. I secretly hoped that one of the local women would see past the prejudice and show an interest in working with her again. That did not happen, which came as no surprise.

Nightfall was fast approaching so we packed away all the different fabrics into separate bags and prepared for dinner. I turned at the sound of a deep male voice saying, 'Assalamualaikum, Saira,' coming from our front courtyard.

'Assalamualaikum, Chachu, please come inside.' I invited him in. He was one of the wise elderly members of our village council, who rarely visited anybody's house as people often took their minor and major disputes to him. I had always admired him for being fair and just; he had known my Abbuji and praised him at every opportunity. He smiled and asked to speak to my mother in private. I was intrigued by this conversation and attempted to listen in, but was unable to hear anything. I swiftly moved away from the doorway as Chachu bid goodbye to us both and left. Immediately Ammu became occupied with serving dinner, almost as if she did not want to tell me about the conversation, intriguing me even more. She was withdrawn most of the evening and only spoke when necessary. Even though she spoke very little, I was able to read the worry and panic imprinted upon her creased forehead. I sat quietly, analysing her behaviour in silence, wishing that somehow I could magically wave away her worry.

'Ammu, what's wrong?' I blurted out.

'Saira, I'm a little tired, that is all,' she replied, expressionless.

I persevered. 'Why did Chachu come to talk you privately?'

'Saira, why do you question everything? Not everything can be explained. I'm just very tired right now,' she said, seeming more upset than annoyed. That night I lay in bed wondering if perhaps Ammu had been right, and I should really not over think everything that happened. Eventually I surrendered to an unsettled sleep.

The next day Ammu continued with her sewing at home, as the rain was still very heavy and seemed set to continue. I stood and watched it, thinking of Sumayah; we were both enchanted by the warmth of the monsoon rain and would often put our feet out on the soil in our courtyard just so we could feel the warm water on our toes, and would giggle for ages as if we were enjoying a much-needed spa session.

'Ouch!' I heard coming from inside, and I ran indoors. Ammu stood leaning over some fabric holding her bleeding finger. I knew this was a consequence of her needing to complete the workload of two individuals. I cleaned her hand and put a cotton bandage around her wounded finger.

'Please, that's enough for today, you need to rest,' I declared. She ignored my pleas and continued.

'Saira, I must finish these orders, just in case we have to go away,' she said. My forehead creased in confusion. I couldn't recall Ammuji speaking about us travelling anywhere. She knew very well what I was thinking and turned away, so I could no longer see her expression. I followed her and demanded she tell me the truth. Finally she surrendered to my perseverance.

She said the people of our village had begun to spread gossip about Ammuji and I and that they did not agree with my decision not to return to Hamid. They had now brought this matter to the attention of our village council who initially intended to resolve it in the most amicable way possible. However, due to ongoing and aggressive pressure from the villagers it had become a pressing matter, needing attention immediately. The locals believed that my decision had brought shame and dishonour to our village and that all the unmarried girls would be considered undignified, just like me. Ammu said that yesterday they had again taken the matter to the village council, stating that it would be impossible for them to marry off their daughters as no wealthy or respectable suitor would approach our village for an alliance of marriage as long as Ammu and I continued to reside here. This had been why Chachu had visited our house. We had been offered two solutions: either I must return to Hamid or Ammu and I would be exiled from our village and our home. I was dumbstruck at this awful heart-wrenching truth; my entire body turned cold and my hands trembled with fear like never before. My chastity and dignity was in question, all because I was not following the cultural norms and expectations of my village. I couldn't understand their attitude. They cared little about the deception I had suffered or the brutal consequences that would await my return.

'Exiled from our home – where is the justice in that?' I whispered in despair. I sat down and bent over, covering my mouth with my hands, struggling to digest the barbarity of what I had just heard. 'Ammu, that means when Hamid and his family come looking for me, they will hand me over,' I cried out in distress.

She stood up tall and strong, brushed away her tears and looked intently into my eyes. Fiercely she said, 'You will never ever return to Hamid. Come what may we will face it together because God is with us.' That night I lay wide awake in bed in contemplation, looking around our house; every corner reminded me of Abbuji. This house was the home of the love between my parents and between the three of us; every single item within the house had a sentimental value. How could I have known that the trust I had placed in the villagers was an illusion? They would happily hand me over to Hamid to live a life of brutality and torture. Either I sacrifice myself or my mother would lose her home; the thought of leaving our home was beyond comprehension.

The next morning I woke to the sound of muffled voices – three or four males and females – or maybe more. My heart fluttered, worried that the voices belonged to Hamid and Amma. The urgency in their tone compelled me to rise out of bed almost immediately in search of my mother and safety. I ran towards our front courtyard and the voices gradually became louder. To my relief a crowd of villagers had gathered in our courtyard along with members of the village council, including Chachu. Much to my astonishment Ammu stood facing them; she appeared to be pleading or attempting to placate them, while they were angry and aggressive. I looked at the faces of everyone in front of us; there was Khala who lived a few houses away, Sumayah's father who I had known my entire life. I recalled Sumayah and I holding his hand as young children as we walked to the local bazaar. Even the lady who had worked with Ammu was standing against us today, demanding that we be exiled.

'There she is. It's all because of her that our daughters are being dishonoured and tainted.'

'She's brought nothing but shame upon us all.'

'What will people say about us keeping her in this village? She has brought us nothing but disrepute.'

'This is why girls should not be allowed to leave home without a guardian.'

My eyes flicked from face to face amongst the fierce throng. The audacity of these people confused me and broke my heart. This was the village that my father had developed with much love and held in such high esteem yet today those very people were standing against us as if we had committed a treacherous crime.

Apparently, after much deliberation, the council had decided that in order to maintain the harmony of this village, Ammuji and I would need to leave imminently, which came as no surprise to me. I was unable to look Ammu in the eye as we were ruthlessly instructed to leave by dusk. Silently Ammu began collecting essential items. All I wanted was to be able to offer her a little comfort; however, I failed in that task too. 'Ammu, I will go back to Hamid today, right now, but please – we can't leave our home,' I said.

'Saira, you will do no such thing, do you hear me?' she protested, holding my hand.

'We can't lose our home,' I cried.

'Listen to me. This is for the best – we can go someplace new where Hamid will never be able to find you. Now, get your things together.'

I packed our belongings, while Ammu glanced around at all the places that Abbuji had touched and where he had sat; she was truly devastated although she did not admit to it. The memories of my childhood were being snatched away cruelly leaving us helpless. I picked up our bags. Ammuji refused to let me carry hers, saying it was delicate so she must keep it with her. She stood quietly staring into the stream that had now become a river in our back courtyard. I knew instinctively she was remembering all the joyful moments we had had here. This spot was important to me, too, because it reminded me particularly of Sumayah. I longed to see her one final time and bid her farewell; no matter what had happened she remained as dear to me as she had always been. As I sobbed silently, I wanted to tell her that I would continue to cherish the moments we had spent together forever in my heart.

Sunset was fast approaching. Consumed by my own heartache I observed Ammu concealing hers. She held my hand and whispered, 'We must leave now, Saira – this is for the best.' We walked through our front courtyard hand in hand, bidding farewell to our beloved home, our memories and our village: the place where even the smallest shapla flower told a story about my beloved father. We took the damp and muddy village pathway leading to the school, Ammuji's tailoring hut and our village mosque where

Mesabji Chacha resided. Our destination was unknown; we had nowhere to go. For the first time I witnessed a look of defeat upon Ammu's face; her warm smiling eyes now only portrayed sadness. We were stranded and had been made destitute within what seemed to be the blink of an eye. Ironically, the monsoon rain that I adored so much began to fall heavy and strong, washing almost everything along our path, including me and Ammu. We decided to take shelter under the closed mosque doorway until the rain subsided. I stood in my wet kurta clutching my mother's caring shoulder.

'I am so sorry, Ammu,' I cried.

'You have nothing to be sorry for, dear, this is for the best,' she replied, wiping away the tears. The darkness of the night now beckoned and I longed to be back in the comfort of my precious home. Ammu held me close to her almost like a small child in need of protection as we stood together enveloped by the dark canvas above. Some time later, my eyes illuminated with joy at the sight of Mesabji Chacha's face.

His initial reaction was shock, when Ammu told him what had happened, followed by disbelief and then disgust at the actions of the villagers, especially the village council. He referred to them as cruel, narrow-minded and heartless. Mesabji Chacha took us into the mosque immediately, offering us warm clothing and food, which he kept for the many travellers that he often accommodated. He advised us to take shelter there for the night and in the morning a solution would be sought. Ammu was visibly tired and needed very little persuasion to rest.

The next morning, after dawn prayer, Mesabji Chacha was nowhere to be found. He returned a short while later seeming dejected. He told us he had been to visit the village council to discuss the issues regarding Ammu and me. He explained that even after pleading with them they maintained their decision not to allow us residence in the village. Ammu thanked Chacha for all his efforts. He told us kindly that we would always have his support, without reservation, as it was due to Abbuji's efforts and kindness that today he had this wonderful place of worship.

We collected our belongings to begin our search for accommodation, but Mesabji Chacha said he had a temporary solution which would require our approval. He knew of a man that was visiting his house in a nearby village who was in search of trustworthy maids to employ whilst he was in the country. Chacha had met with him a number of times as this man had approached him for help to build water wells in the remote villages surrounding ours. Mesabji Chacha emphasised that he was a kind-hearted man. We would have somewhere to live and receive a monthly wage. After a thoughtful pause Ammu nodded in approval.

'I think you are doing the right thing. This is a remote village and you will be safe there, Saira, away from Hamid, and he will not know your whereabouts,' Chacha said, looking at us both. I smiled politely although deep down I knew Hamid and Amma would not accept defeat without a battle. Ultimately we had nowhere to go, no relatives to call upon for support. So it was decided that we were now going to be employed by somebody who lived abroad and required maids to enable him to enjoy his opulent lifestyle: like Rahim Khan, who I quite detested, back in our village. This was a common occurrence, whenever the wealthier people from our village visited their grand houses from places such as the United Kingdom and America. They employed drivers and many maids to carry out household chores and serve them as if they were royalty. There was once a girl in our village who was employed by Rahim Khan to wash and iron his clothes in a specific way, as he watched and instructed her; Sumayah and I advised this girl to leave many times. However, now I was able to comprehend that she must have been compelled to take this job, as I recalled her telling us that she was paid well.

Chapter 7 - Exiled

That very afternoon, the three of us boarded a very small wooden sampan-like boat that was rowed by a young boy who could not have been much older than fourteen. It was common for young boys to undertake a job such as this in the monsoon as they received a small fee for transporting people from one side of the river to the other. This in turn provided an income for the less wealthy families. We sat underneath the small shelter situated in the middle of the flat-bottomed boat ready for transportation from our village to another one across the river. The tide was high and strong, causing waves to sway us from side to side. Ammu sat in the corner holding on tightly, trying to conceal her emotions. I stared back at my beloved village: the mud houses, the tin roofs, the fields, the riverbed I used to walk along almost every day, my school, the many floating shapla flowers scattered across the water; each one told a different story. I continued staring until the vision of my village merged into the greenery surrounding the river as the waves took us further and further away. I wondered if I would ever see my village again. At that moment I took an oath that whether or not I did, I would treasure my memories forever, with every beat of my heart. Unimaginable sadness overwhelmed me, although I knew I needed to stay strong, undefeated and courageous. So I suppressed my internal pain, glancing at Ammuji who I felt responsible for – for causing her the heartache of separation. An internal strength ignited within me; no matter the consequence or how much I was required to suppress my pain, I would remain strong and continually search for ways to bring happiness back to my mother. I took a second oath to live in her servitude, hoping that this would provide me with the opportunity to repent for the unforgivable pain that I had inflicted upon her.

The boat came to a jolting halt after a journey lasting around forty minutes. Ammuji appeared preoccupied as we stepped onto the damp muddy pathway along the riverbed. I paused to look at her sad face, almost crying myself. In a strong supportive voice, I said, 'Ammu, don't be sad, God is with us.' She nodded in agreement, kissing my hand. It almost felt as if our roles had reversed, giving me new responsibilities that I was more than willing to undertake. Mesabji Chacha, who was a few steps ahead, gestured for us to continue walking as he carried our bags apart from the one Ammu refused to be parted from. The path was narrow and slippery, covering my feet completely in mud. It was about fifteen minutes before the locals of the village appeared. We saw a few mud houses close together and the residents had gathered along the pathway to stare at us suspiciously. I knew from my own village that this was a normal occurrence: whenever somebody unknown visited the village, curiosity and apprehension would result. Fearfully I wondered if they were staring because they knew we had been ousted from our own village and were now seeking shelter in theirs. Anxiety riddled me as the image of Hamid played through my mind and I wondered whether the villagers could read my fear. I vaguely heard the locals and Mesabji Chacha exchanging kind greetings, and attempted to maintain a neutral expression.

'Assalamualaikum,' I heard, and sighed with relief as we passed them. The path was becoming less muddy in the heat, enabling me to walk more easily. We walked past more mud houses and children who continued to stare in fascination. I refrained from making any eye contact as I had begun to panic.

The scenery was now beginning to change, becoming less barren and making way for more shrubs. I figured that we had now reached the more developed part of the village, because parts of the path were now concrete. I spotted henna trees that almost every household grew, with little flowery green leaves all over, giving off a fragrance that reminded me of Sumayah who adored decorating her hands and feet with henna. We were now approaching a few houses that appeared to be owned by the wealthier occupants of the village. They were very large, built of bricks and concrete, and the windows were carved in the shape of arches displaying intricate architecture. Each house appeared to have its own balcony and a large patio at the front and back, enhancing its beauty. Some were even two storeys high whilst another had a veranda on the roof, complete with furniture and even an enchanting flower garden; the petals of bright-coloured marigolds and roses could be seen swaying to the tune of the breeze. I stared mesmerised at the grandeur. Part of the house was painted in yellow and other parts in white. I then watched a lady dusting the high corners of the patio area and concluded that she must have been a maid, just as we were going to be.

Our new refuge was the village of Gobind Pur; it lay in the densely populated suburbs of my former home, Jahed Pur. It was around forty-five minutes' walk, and perhaps thirty minutes away by boat, the only other means to get there. Transportation by vehicle was not a possibility as the tracks were muddy and narrow. It was a much smaller village, consisting of only a few grocery shops, a mosque and a very small school. It had no bazaar or post office and the main sources of income for the occupants were agriculture and fishing. Mesabji Chacha had informed us that it was quite a remote village, and that most of the residents were wealthy and lived abroad and only visited once a year, perhaps less. I stood still in awe wondering which house we were to be employed in. Mesabji Chacha stood by a very large, enchanting house further away from the concrete path. This house was grand, full of character, and stood alone. The path meandered towards the house. We followed it and stood outside the white metal gates surrounding the front patio area that led into an open front veranda. It was a one-storey building, although quite high, complemented by an outdoor staircase leading up to a rooftop balcony. I looked up at the balcony; it had a white picket fence around the edge of the entire rooftop and was about three feet high. There was something about this house I found enchanting; something unidentifiable that instantly settled my unsettled mind. The walls were painted white and the door and window frames were coloured with a hint of green. An immaculately clean concrete pathway surrounded the entire house. The house had lovely cut-out windows on each side, and green steel doors. The curtains could be seen swaying in and out of the house with the light breeze. Ammu and I walked onto the patio. I secretly asked God to guide and bless me in this new trial in my life. The floor was tiled in green and white and the furniture was of jute, instantly reminding me of my Abbuji. The three of us were seated as the open gates let in rays of sun that glittered on the tiled floor. The veranda was wide and oval shaped, too big for one man, which made me ponder as to why he needed a house this grand.

Just then a middle-aged lady appeared through the hallway that ran through the middle of the house. She was short in appearance and dressed in a bright pink cotton sari that covered her face up to her nose. She was coy, giggling, and swiftly hid the rest of her face. This bewildering vision brought the hint of a smile to my lips. I glanced over to

Ammuji, who was resolutely immersed in her thoughts, and the harsh reality of our surroundings began to dawn on me again. Mesabji Chacha greeted the lady, as she presented us with water and dry sugary crackers, giggling again as she placed the glasses on the table. She then looked at the three of us individually with further giggles in between, while Ammu remained oblivious to everything. The lady informed us that she had been instructed by the owner to receive us and show us around the house. I figured she must have been a relative.

She started the tour with the hallway. It was quite long and had six rooms branching off; at the end was a very large kitchen with two indoor bathrooms attached to it. The kitchen was tidy with many different pots, pans and utensils, and a large dining table in the centre, which for me was a rarity in itself. She informed us the front two rooms were reception rooms for guests, and then presented one of the back rooms, which had been assigned to Ammu and me; it was close to the kitchen and comfortable. She then pointed towards a large room in the middle, which she said belonged to the owner; this was the only door that remained closed, intriguing me. Throughout the tour, the lady giggled each time she spoke a few words and would then cover her face momentarily, leading me to believe that perhaps this was a nervous trait to her personality. Either that or she found our faces to be amusing, but this seemed a little unlikely. The lady then led us back into the room that had been assigned to us and suggested we settle in, again giggling in between her words.

Nervously she looked at us and said, 'You all must be thinking that I am very happy.' Ammuji continued to be silent almost as if she had lost the will to live. Mesabji Chacha and I were puzzled more than anything. I asked her what she meant, to which she replied that ever since she had been a child she used to giggle nervously at everything, thus the villagers had named her 'Khushi'. Ever since that day her name and giggles had remained unchanged. She informed us that she had been working here as a maid for over a decade and due to her age was not able to complete all the tasks. She said her employer, being the kind man that he was, had agreed to keep her, assigning her lighter duties, thus enabling her to continue supporting her family, who resided in another village. Secretly I had already taken a liking to her, and her name befitted her colourfully vibrant persona. I respected her honesty as I knew all too well of the struggle to provide for one's family. Politely I introduced myself and Ammu, as Khushi giggled away. Khushi advised us to take rest, stating that 'Saheb' would return home very late today due to some important work he needed to complete. 'Saheb' was a word used to refer to royalty, and it baffled me somewhat that Khushi was referring to him in this way.

Ammu had been almost mute since our arrival. I silently observed as she sat on a bench near the window, consumed by sadness, which worried me immensely. Mesabji Chacha took his leave. 'Forgive me that I could not do more for you. I will always keep you both in my prayers and thoughts, and always remember that God is with you, and you will be safe here.' He touched my forehead as if he were blessing me.

Ammu looked towards him and whispered, 'Thank you for everything.' Mesabji Chacha nodded, smiled and left.

Our room was spacious, and furnished with a dresser with wooden drawers and two chairs in the corner. Its tiled floor provided coolness, just perfect for this intense heat. I sat on the double bed in the centre, which even had a thin mattress placed on it; only the wealthier people were able to afford luxuries such as a mattress. I stood peeping through the open window and closed my eyes, visualising my beloved village: the children chasing the roosters and baby goats, people milking the cow for their daily brew of tea. I missed my home, and most of all I missed the harmony of sitting near the stream, dipping my feet in and out to the tune of the croaking frogs.

My eyes opened and I sighed; the scenery here was almost like a parallel world – all I could see were some trees around the house. There were papaya, jack fruit, some pomelo and to my surprise a very tall and lean betel nut tree. Very few villagers could be seen or heard, apart from a few children I could hear laughing and splashing; I figured they were taking their daily bath in a pond somewhere in the distance, which I found comforting. Beside this house was another very large house. There were more houses at the side and back, all grand in appearance.

I looked over towards Ammu who was sitting anxiously on the bed. I hugged her tightly and helped her to lie down to rest. I had no words to comfort her, so I placed the few belongings that we had in the drawers and sat next to her. I still felt anxious, although I found comfort in the harmonious sound of the call to prayer as it reached my ears, immediately dispersing my worries. It provided me with internal strength as it reminded me of home. Silently I pleaded with God to help me care for my beloved mother through this unknown and precarious journey, and to keep me away from the clutches of Hamid.

A short while later Khushi entered our room inviting us to join her for dinner, which Ammu politely refused. I looked at Khushi and said, 'We will be right there, thank you,' to which Khushi giggled and walked away. I spent some time attempting to convince Ammu, and she only agreed when finally I resorted to emotional blackmail informing her that I refused to eat alone. Together we sat round the large table, where food had been served, but there was no sign of Khushi. Confused, I stood up to look around when I heard a giggle coming from behind me. Suddenly I saw the top of her head. She was sitting on the floor in a corner alone tucking into dinner. Khushi then informed me that Saheb liked everyone to eat their evening meals together, including maids, at the dinner table; however, she chose to sit separately as it made her more giggly to sit with others.

I reflected on the situation that had now become our reality. My poor mother, who had not uttered a single word since our arrival here, and the irony of Khushi, who giggled at almost everything, confused me making me just want to pour my heart out and cry. I noticed Ammu glance around the kitchen and could almost read the heartache imprinted all over her face. She was missing our home, missing the memories of my Abbuji. I quickly enticed her by inhaling in the garlic aroma of the piping hot dahl soup that we were both so fond of and then began eating in the hope that she would soon follow my lead.

That night I lay wide awake contemplating the future, which was full of uncertainty and which posed a thousand questions without providing a single answer. As the saying goes ‘You must hurt in order to grow and you must fall in order to stand’, and perhaps this was all predestined, a part of the plan that God had created for me. My faith kept me strong and the substantial concrete walls of this house provided me with security if nothing else, temporarily settling my mind.

The next morning I woke early, a feeling of dread in my heart. The memory of what I used to do at about this time of day was painful: Ammu and I would be busy preparing for work, drinking ginger tea; the village children would be outside causing a ruckus; the roosters; the cattle; the sound of clanging pots and pans being carried from here to there; the tune of the stream in our back courtyard where I had spent many cherished moments with Sumayah. Ammu was sleeping and she looked peaceful. As quietly as I could I wrapped my hijab loosely around my face and crept slowly out of the room. I figured Saheb would have a list of tasks for the day, so I wanted to begin while Ammu rested a little more. The sun shone right into the hallway, glittering across the kitchen tiles. The house seemed even larger in daylight.

'Khushi,' I called out, entering the kitchen. 'Khushi, are you there?' I figured she must have been asleep as I couldn't hear any giggling. I looked towards the open back patio; there was a light morning breeze sweeping across my face and I closed my eyes to savour it. I could hear the sound of birds, flapping cockerels, the chatter of women and children. The patio was almost the size of an entire room and very clean, with a water pump to the right side of the house – for easy access for cooking and cleaning I presumed. Further towards the back of the patio was a small pond; instinctively I searched for the shada shapla that I had become so accustomed to seeing every morning. I stepped outside, walking closer to the lake; it reminded me of my stream and the memories etched permanently into my mind. Perhaps I would find here what my heart yearned for.

This part of the house was beautifully decorated with many trees and plants, adding mystery and character. I soon discovered an entire avenue of what appeared to be palm trees. Taking a closer look, I noticed juicy papayas at the top of a tall tree trunk. Papaya leaves are huge and magnificent, although not very long lasting. In the past, Ammu and I had all but counted the number of days papaya leaves would last before withering away. Close to the papaya tree was another rather large tree almost enveloping the entire area with its magnificent high branches. Its root, which was similarly huge, covered the ground. I inhaled the distinctive sweet and fruity aroma of its fruit – called kathal – our national fruit. I was looking up at dozens of the largest tree-borne fruit in our country. Jackfruit was widely cultivated, mostly in hilly areas, and some of them could weigh as much as thirty-six kilos. The naturally distinctive sweet taste was loved and cherished by my father – he adored the taste of cooked kathal – whereas Ammu enjoyed devouring the soft and ripe ones in cakes and custard.

Ironically, this village had more similarities than differences to my beloved Jahed Pur. Hesitantly I retraced my steps and took the concrete path up to the mud houses we had passed the day before. I heard some children laughing and the sound of water being splashed. I then discovered another concrete path branching off from the one leading to the house, this one narrower. It felt strange not to walk on muddy soil. I walked to the very end of the path and to my astonishment there was a large pond with dozens of shada shapla flowers floating here, there and everywhere. Immediately my face lit up with joy – this was a vision I truly missed; I thought of Sumayah and smiled at the memory. Just then I felt an unexpected tug on the side of my kaftan which made me flinch with panic.

'Apa, would you like to play with us?' said a little angel – a boy who appeared to be around four or five years old. I sighed in relief, my heart stopped pounding and I stared at him in silence. 'Apa,' he called out again. Another reminder of my home: the children I had taught. I dearly missed their angelic faces and innocence. The boy tugged at my hand this time, bringing me back to reality. 'Are you new here, Apa?' he asked.

'Yes, my dear, I came to this Gao only yesterday, and will be staying here for some time,' I replied hesitantly.

'You will like it here, Apa. Would you like to play with us?' he asked again, smiling.

'I will definitely play with you all another day,' I assured him, stroking his angelic face gently. He was playing with a group of other children. They were each taking turns throwing stones and pebbles into the pond, their innocent faces laughing and joyful, and watching them gave me temporary peace of mind. A few ladies were standing knee deep in water washing and cleaning pots and pans; I assumed they were preparing to brew tea and begin cooking for the day. A young lady carrying pots in one hand and her young infant in the other walked past me, smiling as if to welcome me. I smiled back, as a chilling sensation of fear overcame me at the thought of them discovering my truth. I watched another lady who was beating out her dust-covered clothes on the steps of the pond, and the farmers as they began ushering cattle in preparation for the day ahead. I presumed they were headed to the fields before the onset of the scorching heat. This part of Gobind Pur was busier and people appeared happy, just like in my beloved home; ironically, it was also the less wealthy part of the village. Lost in my myriad thoughts, I began to walk back to the wealthier side along the concrete path leading to the larger houses. I stared at a lady sweeping a large courtyard as she smiled at me wandering past. I assumed her to be one of the maids looking after the house; the owners must be living abroad. My walking pace increased; I was anxious to return to Ammu as quickly as possible. Just then I heard a giggle and saw a fluorescent green sari. Khushi was standing there covering her mouth with the end of her pallu with one hand and carrying a large bowl of pots and utensils with the other hand.

'Khushi, I have been looking for you,' I said in astonishment.

She giggled and then replied, 'I went to collect some fresh vegetables from the field nearby. I'll be back shortly, just need to wash these.' She pointed at the pots and walked off without allowing me to say anything further. I struggled to fathom why she had decided to wash the pots in the pond when there was a water pump in the back patio. I concluded Khushi to be a mystery; perhaps Saheb could offer an explanation.

Chapter 8 – House Larger than Life

I almost sprinted back to the house, breathless, as the sound of my mother's voice startled me. I could hear her along with a male voice I didn't recognise. Immediately I scurried over to her as she sat beside the table in the kitchen. 'Ammu, are you okay? Why are you out of bed? You need to rest,' I blurted out hysterically. I ushered her back into our room without allowing her the opportunity to speak a single word. 'You should have waited for me to return,' I continued in a frenzied panic.

'Saira, I was only drinking tea,' she began.

'I would have made the tea for you, Ammu,' I said loudly.

'Saira, I didn't make the tea, Omar did. He wanted to introduce himself to us. We decided to wait for you to return so that he could meet you, and while we waited he brewed tea for the three of us,' she explained.

'I am sorry, Ammu, I just want you to rest,' I said in my defence. Feeling guilty and a little embarrassed about my behaviour now I stared at Ammu. She sent me straight back to the kitchen, firstly to apologise and then to meet our employer who was also the owner of this magnificent house. Feeling extremely annoyed with myself, with a lowered gaze I apologised for my untoward behaviour. I introduced myself asking what duties or chores he required me to complete that day. In the hope that he would understand and forgive my insolence I waited patiently for a response; however, there was silence. I asked a second time, 'What chores do I need to prioritise for today?' and again, silence. I decided either he must be extremely arrogant or he was refusing to forgive me. I looked up, confused, and to my surprise all I saw were an empty chair and three full teacups sitting on the table, which confirmed what Ammu had told me exactly. I wondered if he walked out whilst I had been speaking to him, which suggested two conclusions: number one – he was arrogant, and number two – he had taken offence at my behaviour. I hoped the latter to be untrue. The feeling of guilt refused to leave me. After all, I should have been ecstatic that Ammu had taken herself out of bed and had even spoken.

My attention suddenly diverted to the sound of a very loud 'clang' followed by a giggle. Khushi had returned with the washed pots and utensils and dropped them on the tiled kitchen floor; water sprinkled all over my bare feet. Immediately I rushed over to help her collect the shiny utensils and then stacked them on the low shelf across the man-made open stove used for cooking. Khushi continued to giggle some more as I stood in silence.

'Saira, Saheb asked me to inform you that he may be back very late today, and he sends his apology that he did not have time to meet with you,' she informed me in between giggles.

'Saheb has gone out?' I asked, surprised. Khushi then told me he had left approximately ten minutes before, which meant that he had been absent throughout my heartfelt apology. I decided I needed to wait for his return and then attempt it a second time. I peeped in to check on Ammu, who was resting, and returned to the kitchen to make a start on the chores. I was greeted by a variety of bags filled with bright-coloured clothing but just as I called out to Khushi she got up, saying that she had to leave now. Khushi was leaving, I thought; how would that even work? We had only just arrived. I had no idea what happened in this house. Not even an inkling about the menu, the tasks or the routine.

'What do you mean, Khushi? You can't leave, how will we cope?' I pleaded. Khushi explained her niece's wedding was taking place in a few weeks' time and that she had requested a month of annual leave to participate in the customary pre- and post-marriage functions. She giggled again and explained that Saheb had granted her this leave, and then miraculously he had been handed Ammu and me as substitutes.

'Khushi, I don't even know what chores Saheb needs doing,' I continued.

'Saira, you will be fine. Saheb is not fussy, he is a very kind man,' she replied. With that, Khushi collected her luggage, bade me farewell and left in a fit of further giggles. I began to feel annoyed, but I was unsure whether it was with Khushi's sudden departure or with myself. I stood feeling stranded and alone in this great big house; my body felt on high alert and my breathing was shallow. I had no idea what the expectations of a maid were. All I was sure of was that I missed teaching, my school, my amazing children and, most importantly, my home. A part of me wanted Khushi to return, although I knew I would have to go through this trial alone. I sat on the floor, tears streaming down my face, as this moment of weakness began to swallow me whole. Just then I heard the beautiful call to prayer for midday. I closed my eyes to dwell in its tranquillity and, as ever, the melody of it brought forth peace both in my mind and in my heart. Taking a few moments, I collected my thoughts and sat in prayer, pleading with God to provide me with the strength I desperately sought to continue with this unknown journey, regardless of the destination. I truly believed that life's most meaningful lessons were perhaps, learnt through pain.

The day was hot and sticky with beautiful rays of sunshine beating down on the patio and into the kitchen. I needed to make a start on lunch and dinner, sweep the house and clean the dishes. The last thing I wanted were questions regarding my integrity and commitment to my role as maid. I walked into my mother's room only to discover her empty bed. I found her sitting on the floor in the corner of the room in silence, and I knew she was thinking of the wonderful place that used to be our home.

'What's wrong, Saira?' she said, looking into my eyes.

'I was just wondering what you were doing... and if you needed anything,' I replied, and sat closer to her. I placed my arms gently around her as she cuddled me close. I knew very well the thoughts that were going through her mind, and felt her pain like an arrow through my heart.

'Don't worry, Saira, I am just being silly,' she said, turning towards me.

'No, Ammu, it's not silly to miss your home, to miss our village that has Abbuji embedded into every corner,' I reassured her, wiping away her precious tears.

'I am grateful that you're safe here. This is a new start where nobody knows you, and you need to put everything behind you,' Ammu whispered, holding my face gently. I held on to her as tightly as I could. I knew, ultimately, the bitter truth was that we could never return home. Neither the village council nor the villagers would allow that to happen. I thought of Hamid and his family and whether or not they had accepted I would never return; the very thought of him made me tremble like no other and it was a fear I was unable to suppress. I recalled Mesabji Chacha stating that Saheb was a kind man, although I wondered how he would feel if he discovered the truth behind Ammu and me ending up here in this village and in his house.

Ammu looked at me and said, 'Come on, let's make a start with the housework.'

I quickly composed myself and firmly said, 'No, you will not do anything, I can manage.' I was quite surprised when she sat herself down without protest. I felt fully responsible and accountable for her misery and sadness, and I was prepared to sacrifice everything to make her feel happy once again.

I dragged myself into the kitchen mentally making a list of chores I needed to complete that day. I was a little hesitant as this house was probably three times larger than what I had been accustomed to. Khushi had left without informing me where anything was kept, such as the sweeping broom, or even what Saheb's favourite food was. I began with the front courtyard and opened the great white gates to allow fresh air to circulate. I could hear the familiar sounds of water, people chattering, the laughter of children; these sounds brought me a sense of relief as they resonated happiness and joy. I peered into the houses near to ours, which mostly appeared empty apart from maids or lodgers who were safeguarding the properties, it seemed.

I was finally able to locate a broom in the corner of the large kitchen and began sweeping the courtyard; the dust billowed from side to side settling on my clothes. I pulled my hijab tighter around my face to save my hair from the dry dust that was now floating everywhere. The courtyard was large. I carefully swept the corners, and the sunshine felt extremely hot on my head; I searched for a little shade for a moment of relief and noticed that opposite this house stood a very small mud house, so small that in comparison it almost looked like a doll's house. I walked closer, taking comfort in its shade, and stood there for a moment against the coolness of the mud. My cheeks had turned bright pink as they used to when I returned from school and Ammu would rush to serve me water. I closed my eyes, sitting in the shade, and enjoyed the light breeze upon my face, as fatigue, to which I was not willing to surrender, enveloped my entire body.

I stood up to continue when suddenly I heard a soft meek voice coming from behind me. 'Would you like some water?' There stood a young lady holding a glass of water. I sat on the cool muddy ground and devoured the entire glass of cold water, quenching my thirst at once.

'Thank you so much,' I said to her, handing back the glass very carefully.

She smiled shyly and said, 'I saw you sweeping, so I thought you might be feeling hot and thirsty.' I smiled in appreciation of her kind gesture. She was coy; she had a small frame and a very pretty face, and was probably not much older than I was. She went back into the mud house in response to the sound of an urgent cry, a cry that belonged to an infant, to my surprise. Minutes later she returned with an adorable little baby girl cradled in her arms. I couldn't help but stare in awe.

'She is absolutely beautiful,' I said, enchanted by her baby gurgles. The lady smiled proudly. She introduced herself as Layla, and told me she was temporarily living in this mud house with her husband and brand new baby daughter. She informed me that they both looked after and lived in Saheb's house when he was in London, as they could not afford to live anywhere else. In return her husband maintained Saheb's land and looked after the crops. Layla placed her hand on my shoulder and said, 'He is a generous man, you're lucky to have found work here.' I nodded in approval. She welcomed me to the village offering her services should I need anything. I thanked her graciously and returned to my uncompleted task. I watched Layla from the courtyard cooing with her baby as she disappeared behind the mud wall. What a lovely encounter, I thought. This strengthened my belief that it was the smallest things in life that provided the most happiness, such as being with your loved ones.

Placing the broom back into its allocated space I thought about my next task of collecting water from the pump outside and taking it to the bathrooms for the day. I found the kholosh located on the kitchen floor and walked into the bathroom, to discover that Khushi had already completed this task. Ammu remained asleep so I decided to make a start with food preparation, only I had no idea what a maid should cook. Was there a menu I needed to refer to? And should I cook just one dish or many dishes? The questions continued to gather in my mind. After much internal deliberation, I decided to cook some of our favourite dishes hoping they would suit Saheb: dahl soup, chopped papaya cooked in herbs and spices with rice and a little fresh coriander salad. I began by collecting sticks that had been left in a pile at the far end of the back courtyard, by Layla's husband, I presumed. I then carefully placed the sticks deep into the stove, but the fire only increased the heat in the kitchen causing me to feel more fatigued. I walked out onto the patio and took comfort in splashing water all over my face, revelling in its coolness. I served some food on a plate and walked into Ammu's room; she was sitting up wide eyed. I forced a smile and said, 'Ammu, do you know there are so many papaya trees here. I will show you tomorrow, they are so juicy and fresh and smell wonderful. And look here – smell this!' Excitedly I placed the plate in front of her. 'Look, a little rice, papaya and dahl. I cooked it today, just like you.'

She smiled, inhaling the aroma. 'Dear, are you all right? You look tired, and what's happened to your clothes?' she asked, gesturing me to sit next to her.

'Nothing, Ammu. I went for a walk so they became a little dusty,' I replied, and then made an excuse to get her some water to escape any further questions. Ammu knew I was unable to handle the heat and would be devastated to learn I had been outside sweeping. I returned with water, urging her to eat, and then headed off to clean the kitchen and myself before my self-motivation completely disappeared.

It was dusk, and the harmonious sound of the call to prayer echoed through the entire house. Our first day here was now fading into the darkness of the night, as the sky slowly turned from blue to yellow, to red, to faded orange and then finally to black. There was silence throughout the house, in fact throughout the entire village. I listened for the return of Saheb. I found it difficult to comprehend that he had not returned yet, leaving two strangers in charge of this grand property. I noticed Ammu twitching her legs in pain, although she would never willingly admit to this. So I massaged them with the wonderful crushed stems of the shapla flower. The lady who I always saw as being inspirationally strong, was today fighting what seemed to be a losing battle against pain and sadness, and my relentless efforts to make her smile seemed to bear no fruit. The walls of this house were beginning to silently choke me, and I felt constricted by my new role of maid to an upper-class citizen who perhaps knew nothing of hardship. I felt like a bird with its wings clipped. How I longed to be that bird soaring high up in the sky, touching the clouds with not a burden in sight. How I desperately wanted to break free from the restrictions of life and this opulent house.

While my imagination travelled far and beyond, the sound of footsteps brought my mind back to the house. I figured Saheb was back and would need attending to because that was what maids did, and without further procrastination I intended to apologise. I heard a clattering sound from the kitchen and followed it.

'Assalamualaikum,' I greeted him as he stood in search of drinking water.

'Walaikumassalam,' he replied in a gentle voice. He was a tall man, medium built although quite lean, very smiley faced, and was dressed in casual jeans and a plain T-shirt with an expensive-looking watch around his wrist; this image did not fit with the picture I had created in my mind. I immediately poured some water and handed it to him. 'Thank you,' he replied. 'Have you guys settled in all right? I apologise for disappearing like that. I had something urgent to deal with,' he explained. He appeared somewhat tense.

'No, please don't apologise. I owe you an apology for my behaviour this morning. It's just that I'm...'

Before I was able to complete my sentence, 'You love your mother very much,' he concluded.

I stood in silence, and then said, 'I'm Saira.'

'I know,' he replied and walked out of the kitchen. I was puzzled by him to say the least. He made no demands, and, in fact, whether or not we had settled in was more of a concern for him. In comparison I thought of Hamid and his authoritarian mother whom Saheb appeared to be the complete opposite of. I realised that my expectation of Saheb's character was a little distorted and far from the truth. I had imagined him to be the duplicate of Rahim Khan back in my village, which was my own incorrect stereotypical misconception.

I laid the table for him and served dinner, and as he entered the kitchen, he asked, 'Are you guys not eating?'

'Maybe later...' I replied hesitantly.

'Did Khushi not explain that we eat together here?' he asked. I remained quiet, occupied with tidying pots and pans, and when I turned around to answer him he had disappeared. I recalled Khushi stating that Saheb liked everyone to eat together in the evenings as during the day he was busy, engrossed with one task or another. He returned a few minutes later, but this time Ammu was leaning against his arm. I stood staring as he pulled out a chair and supported her as she sat down, and then seated himself right beside her.

'Saira, this boy is strong headed, just like you. He said that he would only eat if I did,' Ammu said, looking at him. Pulling my hijab tighter around my face I smiled at her as I served the food.

'Shall we eat, Saira?' He pointed towards a chair for me to sit down.

'What will you have first, Ammu?' he said to her, to my surprise. The irony was surreal; we were his maids and yet here we were eating a meal together almost like a family. He and Ammu had developed a mutual liking, which fortunately appeared to have a positive impact on her. I watched her smile wholeheartedly as he explained how much he enjoyed papaya cooked in onion and turmeric gravy. I listened to the sound of their chatter as I relished my first meal of the day, and secretly thanked God for giving my mother a reason to smile even if it were only for this evening and through the aid of a complete stranger.

'Thank you, Saira, for a lovely meal,' he said in appreciation, to which I nodded and smiled. Ammu appeared tired and wanted to retire to her room. When she stood up she let out an unexpected pained shriek, almost freezing in an awkward standing position.

I scurried over to her immediately. 'What's wrong, is it hurting?' I cried.

'I'm all right, Saira, it's just a little twinge,' she said, reassuring me. I could sense she was in a great deal of pain so I began to rub her feet. Saheb walked over to her, placing one of her arms around his neck, shouldering half her body weight, and walked her to our room.

'Hold on to me,' he instructed as I followed behind. 'Are you okay?' he asked while supporting her onto the bed. He then carefully straightened out both her feet, placing them on top of two very soft pillows. It saddened me to see her in this plight and the little money that we had was not enough to fund her treatment. I only noticed Saheb had left the room when he returned holding a pain-relief ointment in his hand. He sat next to Ammu and to my surprise began massaging both her feet with this ointment. I immediately tried to intervene, but he paid no heed and continued.

I sat with her for a while afterwards until the pain began to gradually fade, and her eyes surrendered to sleep. My poor mother had spent her entire life working to provide me with a good life and happiness, and today she was living in a state of desperation and suffering, which I was to blame for.

My entire body ached with fatigue; as much as I wanted to retire for the day I knew that an uncompleted task still awaited me. I almost dragged my two feet into the kitchen. I was astonished to see that the plates, dishes, glasses and all other utensils had all been cleared away. The table had even been wiped down and the chairs were tucked under neatly. I stood in awe, unable to comprehend what my eyes were witnessing, and even questioned whether or not I had already cleaned up and had forgotten due to fatigue.

'Sorry, I'm not very good in the kitchen. I hope I've done this properly,' I heard Saheb say.

'You did all this?' I asked, bewildered.

'I figured Ammu needed you more right now,' he replied.

'You didn't have to, really,' I attempted to convince him as he began to walk away. 'Saheb,' I called out from behind, 'thank you.'

'Saira,' he said as I turned away. 'It's Omar,' he added politely and continued down the hallway. My mind and body were in a state of exhaustion: physically, emotionally and mentally. I anxiously reflected on my entire day here, contemplating what tomorrow would bring. All my ideas about Omar's character and personality appeared to be based on nothing but my own individual bias and prejudice, as he had only portrayed humility and kindness towards us. I felt grateful, more than anything, as it was due to this kindness and humility that I was able to bear the burden of this new journey.

The next morning I began by collecting water for the bathrooms. I knew this task would take a while and wanted to complete it while Ammu and Omar were sleeping. Firstly I collected the kholosh, which was larger and heavier than I was accustomed to. I struggled to lift the weight at first and I staggered, balancing it upon my hip. I managed to complete two rounds of the task, filling up the large empty water drums in the bathrooms. With a deep sigh I attempted to carry the water a third time, struggling to walk against the weight of it, and stumbled. I fell to the floor and the water spilled all through the courtyard and all over me. Omar immediately ran out to the sound of my shrieks and pulled me up swiftly. 'Saira, what happened? Are you okay?' he asked, glancing at the water all over the courtyard and me as I stood there, soaking wet. I began to dry myself with the towel that he now handed me. Feeling embarrassed, I explained I was collecting water for the day. 'I hope you haven't hurt yourself too badly,' he said, looking concerned.

I looked down at my grazed elbows and replied, 'I'm okay, thank you,' and walked inside, drenched.

Slightly hurt and with pain shooting through my lower back I entered the kitchen. I imagined the difficulty I would have trying to conceal this from Ammu today. I prepared breakfast quickly as I knew Omar left the house very early in the mornings. I then knocked on his door, and he followed me out into the kitchen. 'Your tea is ready,' I told him as he sat at the table.

'Where's Ammu, is she all right?' he asked, looking round the kitchen.

'Yes, she's much better, thank you,' I said, almost spilling the hot tea as I winced from the pain in my lower back.

'Saira, sit down, you must have injured yourself earlier,' he said pulling out a chair for me.

I inhaled a deep breath and politely replied, 'I'm fine, thank you,' and continued serving him breakfast. I felt literally useless; Ammu was unwell and here I was unable to complete one task successfully. I worried Omar may rethink his decision about employing us as maids, leaving us both stranded once again which would tear us apart, especially Ammu.

She appeared fast asleep so I crept back out of the room and began to collect the pots and utensils for washing and cleaning and headed to the pond. 'Saira, I will be out for most of the day,' Omar informed me. He was dressed smartly, sporting a light blue shirt with some casual jeans.

I nodded and then asked him, 'What chores should I complete today?'

'Saira, I trust you to take that responsibility,' he said and smiled. 'Before I forget, I have asked Abdullah to collect the water for the bathrooms every morning,' he added.

I was shocked. 'I can manage,' I protested.

'I have no doubt that you will manage, but I have asked him anyway and he has agreed,' he said firmly. 'By the way, if you need anything in my absence then Abdullah will look after you,' he said. I looked at him and nodded in submission. Omar's kind nature overwhelmed me, almost dispelling the panic and fear I harboured within. Abdullah was sweet Layla's husband who I had met only yesterday. He took care of maintaining Omar's land and harvested the crops as well as carrying out maintenance work around the house, and from the little I had observed he worked extremely hard and had immense respect for Omar.

Chapter 9 – Ray of Hope

I began to walk along the concrete path leading up to the big pond. Although it was hot, there was a distinct coolness in the morning air promoting a calm state of mindfulness. I indulged in the captivating sight of the birds and the ducks dawdling across the muddy ground pecking at seeds. I waved at Layla who was sitting out near our front courtyard with beautiful Khadijah. Passing the neighbouring houses I smiled and greeted the maid who again appeared to be dusting the metal gates near the entrance of the large property. I felt at ease, as if this walk to the pond had become cathartic, or was it that I was gradually discovering more similarities between this village and mine. Just then my eyes turned to the sound of splashing water. Children had gathered with a large branch of a banana tree, holding on to it with their arms whilst kicking their legs in a rhythmic beat. This was the technique used to teach young children to swim, and the monsoon rain provided ample opportunity. I smiled at this welcome sight, something I had almost forgotten how to do, and remembered my Abbuji teaching me to swim in this exact manner as Ammu stood by shouting out words of encouragement. Feeling joyful I felt a splash of water tickle my face over my hijab.

'Sorry, Apa,' said the little angel who was busy splashing water all over his baby sister, making her giggle.

'You guys are having fun,' I said, touching his cheerful face.

'Would you like to play?' he asked. I smiled and walked into the water up to my knees and began splashing the children as they laughed and splashed back, making me remember the children I used to teach. My eyes filled at the thought of Sumayah; I wondered how she was and if she had ever gone to sit beside our stream to think about me, even once. I thought about her for a while and how we used to be. I looked on as another lady smiled at me whilst she washed her pots and pans, which reminded me that I had placed mine on the side.

Upon my return I checked in on Ammu, who was sitting up, awake. 'How are you feeling?' I smiled at her.

'I'm fine. What time have you been up since?' she questioned as I began to tell her about the children I had just met. 'Are you comfortable here?' Ammu asked me, holding my hand. Unable to make eye contact with her I explained how lovely and serene this village was and how friendly its residents were. She continued to stare at me and I knew that she did not believe a single word I had uttered. I then applied some more of Omar's pain-relief ointment to Ammu's leg. My plan was to find treatment for Ammu's arthritis as soon as I was able to afford it. Lost in thought I didn't realise that Ammu had continued to stare at me as I began yawning and rubbing my exhausted eyes. She placed her hand on my shoulder and said, 'You look tired. You spend the whole day working in this house and you look after me. I'm sorry, dear.' She began to cry and this was one of the things that tore apart my heart.

'No! You have no reason to apologise, and I enjoy working in this house,' I said firmly, attempting to convince her. I sat her up and served her breakfast. 'Ammu, would you like to sit in the kitchen today? The sunshine is lovely this morning.' She agreed.

Omar had handed me the responsibility for this house and I wanted to fulfil his trust reverently. I began by sweeping the rooms at the front, followed by the patio and then the open veranda. I disliked the dust flying into my hair and hijab so tried to sweep as fast as I could. Just as I was placing the large broom back into its place, I heard a deep female voice.

'Is anyone home?' My heart began somersaulting at once and I trembled as I walked backwards into the hallway. 'Is anyone home?' I heard again and began to perspire at the mere thought that Hamid and Amma may have discovered my whereabouts. I stood, shell-shocked, and heard the voice calling out a third time. 'Omar, Omar, son, are you home?' Relieved, I peeped through the cracks in the door to take a closer look, and sighed at the sight of an elderly lady, who was very short and walking with the support of a stick. I wondered if perhaps she was a relative of Omar's, in which case I should attend to her.

Hesitantly I walked over and with chattering teeth said, 'Can I help you?' She carried a large sack beside her and was dressed in a beige-coloured tatty sari.

'Is Omar home?' she enquired, looking around and peering into the house.

'I'm afraid he's not. Can I help at all?' I replied politely.

'When will he be back?' she asked, dejected.

'Not till later. Are you a relative?' I enquired.

'No, I am not,' she replied sadly and began to walk away. I immediately thought about the people that used to come to our house back in Jahed Pur begging for food, shelter, clothes and even monetary support. Ammu and I used to donate large pots of rice, money and clothing to them on a regular basis. I knew that some people had no other option but to resort to begging from house to house just as a means of survival.

'Please, wait. Would you like to come inside?' I said. I invited her inside, assisting her to sit down.

She appeared very delicate and frail. I offered her some water to drink along with some papaya which she devoured very quickly. She then took my hand and kissed it saying, 'Thank you.' I smiled at her lovingly and embraced her frail shoulders.

'Dear, will you let Omar know I came by?' she asked.

'Of course I will,' I replied. She then told to me that she visited Omar on Wednesdays and that he gave her a large bag of rice and some money to take back with her; hence the sack she carried. She explained she had a physically disabled husband and two children, and no source of income. In order to survive she walked from her nearby village to the much wealthier residences to collect rice, money, clothing and whatever other donations people provided her with, and those donations were what she supported her family with. She explained that Omar knew of her hardship hence asked her to come by every Wednesday to collect rice and money. I fully empathised with this lady's heartbreaking circumstances and I continued to thank God for watching over and blessing me and my mother. I was thankful that at least we did not have to beg from village to village like this poor soul. I was grateful that at least we had a roof over our heads and basic amenities for survival such as food and water. I took the lady's sack and filled it as much as I could with rice before returning it to her, and watched as her face lit up with joy like a dark night filled with stars sparkling brightly up in the sky. Her joy and happiness were contagious, making me feel happy too.

She put the sack over her shoulder and looked at me with gratitude, saying, 'Thank you, and I will pray for you and Omar, may God bless you, dear.' I stood and watched her disappear along the path leading out of the village. I sat on the patio in reflection. Despite being wealthy, Omar really was a generous man – an unsung hero of good deeds it seemed.

Although he appeared honest and humble, there was a deep untold mystery about him, something that the eye was unable to see; a mystery yet to be uncovered. Many questions posed in my mind, such as why he lived alone in this great big house and where his family members were. Even though he gave away very little about himself, everyone he was acquainted with only spoke good of him. I brought my attention back to the chores and decided to dust the furniture as the cobwebs were becoming visible, making the house look untidy and unkempt. Even the furniture in the house was grand, which made little sense as Omar appeared to be a very simple man who lived a life that was far from luxurious.

The sun was shining intensely and my hijab stuck to the sweltering sweat beads across my forehead. I looked at my reflection in one of the mirrors in the large front room. My cheeks were bright red due to heat and fatigue; my rose-red cheeks and milky complexion had disappeared. My lips were dry and parched and I looked down at my dirty feet and dust-covered kaftan; what a sight I was. My forehead was creased, and my face showed tension and worry and sunken cheeks enveloped within a sweaty hijab. I sighed, wondering whether or not this was just the mundane life of a maid, and if this was now going to be my future. I walked into the kitchen feeling parched and sat down on the cool tiles for a moment.

'I wish I could help you with the work, Saira,' said Ammu with sadness in her voice. In my haste I had left Ammu sitting in the chair for goodness knew how long.

'Ammu, I am so sorry, I forgot I had left you sitting here,' I blurted out. Although she did not admit to it, I knew she was in pain, so I took her back to our room. Despite her resistance I served her lunch and encouraged her to rest, feeling angry at myself for neglecting her; how could I just leave her sitting in that heat? I reminded myself that Ammu was my first and foremost priority followed by the responsibility for this house. I knew that regret knew best those who had neglected their parents, and I did not want to be one of those, so I renewed my commitment to put my mother first and foremost above all.

It was nearly afternoon and I made a start on preparing dinner as Omar would soon be back. With a rag and some soapy water I scrubbed the entire kitchen floor, admiring the shine from the tiles. I then cleaned the stove before taking a much-needed rest spending some time on the front patio. I sat admiring the village scenery, and watched Layla collecting small branches and sticks. I presumed she wanted to use them as firewood while she cooked for her husband Abdullah and their daughter. I watched another lady chasing the cockerels into their bed for the night. The men were returning home from the fields along with their exhausted cattle that needed to be washed, fed and settled for the night into their mud sleep huts. This wonderful image refreshed my memories of my beloved home, allowing me to cherish them wholeheartedly. This was followed by the beautiful call to prayer which magnified the beauty of twilight a little more; it was melodious and peaceful, and at once replaced the anxiety that had been looming over me the entire day with an inner peace.

Just then I heard Omar entering the house. I greeted him and handed him a jug of warm water to wash himself with. I presumed he would be hungry so began to serve dinner.

Minutes later he walked back into the kitchen holding Ammu by her hand. 'Slowly, Ammu,' he instructed. I stared, astonished at how he seemed to have a way with her and somehow always managed to make her smile with his kindness and eloquently spoken words.

'I don't want to trouble you, dear, you have just returned, you must be tired,' Ammu said, looking at Omar.

He laughed and said, 'You are no trouble. Saira, we are ready for dinner.'

'Sure,' I replied and began serving them both. I watched as they ate and conversed over dinner; it brought me an unimaginable joy to witness Ammu smiling, and I was grateful to Omar for this. I listened attentively as he spoke, informing us that he had spent the entire day at a village close to this one where he had built a well for the less wealthy villagers, and from today it was in full working order. He spoke about the joy he had witnessed on their faces upon receiving clean water to drink. He talked about how thankful the women had been that they did not need to carry water for long distances just for the purpose of cooking and cleaning. I wondered if that had been the reason for his visit to Bangladesh; however, I was unable to muster the courage to ask him. Ammu praised him relentlessly for his wonderful act of charity as he smiled while his eyes twinkled coyly.

I cleared up after dinner, whilst Omar escorted Ammu back to her room. That night I lay wide awake in contemplation of how I desperately wanted to see her happy again and ironically she seemed to be happy around Omar. The next few days passed in the mundane tasks of completing chores around the house. Omar would leave early in the morning and return late in the evening. Every day he would return before dinner, and insist that Ammu join us and the three of us would dine together. Ammu and I both enjoyed listening to stories about his day. One incident in particular tugged at the strings of my heart. He talked about the time that he had visited a very remote village on the outskirts of the famous Sylhet tea gardens; the villagers there struggled with a lack of clean water and consequently the village children were made to walk two kilometres a day carrying water on their backs to the village and its people. He described the immeasurable joy on the faces of those children when he revisited the new well, and I sat conjuring this wonderful image in my mind. That evening I truly smiled and felt a sense of contentment after what had seemed to be an infinity filled with overwhelming sadness. Most importantly, I felt happy that there were still people like Omar who had not only taken us in, but chose to treat us with respect and integrity as opposed to maids at the disposal of his wealth and luxury.

I woke early the next morning to the gentle sound of Omar's footsteps and figured he would be heading out early as he always did, so I made a start on his breakfast. Abdullah would collect the water for the bathrooms, hence that was one chore less for me to contend with. It was a cool morning, although the sun was attempting to break through, making way for another bright sunny day. I liked the sun; it brought happiness, hope and a feeling of contentment as its infinite beauty nurtured much-loved memories I held close to my heart.

'Good morning, Saira.' I heard Omar's sincere voice as he walked into the kitchen.

'Morning,' I replied, placing my hijab neatly over my tangled hair. He was dressed casual smart as he did most days, and appeared ready to leave. I stumbled across the kitchen, almost falling as I hurriedly attempted to serve him breakfast.

'Careful, Saira,' he warned, standing up in case I needed rescuing from my own clumsiness. 'Is Ammu sleeping?' he asked.

'Yes, she is,' I replied.

'Did you sleep well?' he enquired.

'Yes, thanks,' I responded timidly. I looked down at my dust-covered kaftan; what a sight I must be. I decided to put cleaning myself and tidying my appearance right at the top of my priority list for the day. 'Is there anything that you need attending to today?' I asked while my elbow knocked over the bowl of tomatoes I had placed at the edge of the table, which I had planned to turn into a salad for later. Only now the tomatoes were rolling around in many directions across the kitchen tiles, most of them squashed. 'Oh my,' I gasped, on my knees as I began to collect them one by one.

'It's okay, Saira, I'll pick them up,' he said.

'They're all ruined,' I said, frustrated.

'We can get some more,' he replied as he collected them one by one, carefully placing them back into the bowl and then handing it to me.

'Thank you,' I replied, annoyed with my clumsiness. 'You didn't answer my question before I knocked over the tomatoes,' I repeated before he left for the day.

He appeared hesitant and then replied, 'I have some clothes that need washing if you wouldn't mind.'

'Of course I don't mind, that's what I am here for,' I reminded him. As Omar left for the day I began mine by sweeping the back courtyard before the arrival of the midday sunshine.

Chapter 10 – White Picket Fence

I gathered the laundry and headed towards the concrete path leading out of the house towards the big pond. I liked going there as it made me happy seeing the children play and interact and behave mischievously. As I approached the pond the sound of joyful laughter filled my ears. It was the same children and it appeared that today they had mastered the art of swimming, hence the absence of the banana tree.

'Apa, Apa,' shouted the little boy in excitement, running towards me. 'I have learnt how to swim – now look, watch me,' he said, diving into the water to demonstrate his swimming talent. I clapped my hands and laughed with him. I spent a short while watching and encouraging him as he swam around like an excited hilsha fish. I then began my primary task of the day. I fastened my hijab, tightening it around my burning head, and washed Omar's clothes as swiftly as possible. I waved goodbye to the little boy and set off to return to the house. I was becoming so used to walking on concrete that when I walked on the ground I realised how much I had missed the feel of the muddy soil under my bare feet.

I returned to the house with the wet laundry and looked for a place to dry it. It suddenly occurred to me that I had never been up on the rooftop. Curious, I unlocked the green gates leading to the outdoor staircase up to the rooftop. When I reached the top, I was immediately mesmerised by the sheer beauty. The rooftop was large with a white picket fence surrounding it. Three large benches were placed in the middle with flower beds scattered in the corners, planted with beautiful coloured flowers such as roses, lilies and marigolds. It was a beautiful, serene sight. I pondered how I had not discovered this place earlier. There was something peaceful about sitting here in the breeze amongst the aromatic fragrances of this enchanting flower garden. I closed my eyes, indulging fully in the moment, and remembered sitting near the stream with Sumayah, dipping our toes into the cool water. The serenity of this rooftop reminded me of all the happy moments spent in laughter with Sumayah and Ammu. I stood up and walked over to the front of the rooftop. I could see almost out to the big pond, past the concrete path and the neighbouring houses. I could even see the mud houses on the other side and watched as a lady played marbles with her children in the open mud courtyard. The trees lining the pond were visible, providing a perfect landscape for the eyes of the beholder. I watched Layla playing with her daughter. Seeing the village from this perspective increased its beauty, an image I otherwise could not have imagined had I not been standing here looking down at it from this point of view. My mind was truly captivated by this vision and I came to the realisation that the beauty of life does not decrease just because our viewpoint has altered. If anything, logically, a new point of view should only enhance the beauty of life. I wondered if perhaps this had been a subliminal message from God informing me that all would be well, and that this may be the next chapter in my life which I should throw myself into wholeheartedly, without a doubt or reservation. Perhaps this was the new beginning I needed, to be able to finally erase Hamid from my mind. I closed my eyes, taking an oath to remain positive no matter how difficult the struggle. With that thought in mind, I headed back downstairs, beginning my journey of a thousand miles with a single step.

I wondered whether physical exhaustion had overtaken me as I stared, puzzled, at the sight ahead, which initially I thought to be shadows. The papaya trees and the huge kathal tree I had walked by a few days earlier were splendid. But I was shocked to see Ammu standing near those trees today with someone who looked like Omar. She seemed to be leaning on him for support. I had presumed Omar would not return till late evening and I had left Ammu in bed. Immediately I began to walk across the back courtyard towards them. I wanted to run to Ammu to ensure she was all right, but I did not want to offend Omar, so I composed myself and walked over slowly. I enjoyed the sound of Ammu talking and laughing; she was telling Omar how much she and Abbuji enjoyed eating jackfruit and I smiled, listening to her serene voice. I heard Omar tell her that his late father had planted those trees, which was why he maintained them to ensure they stood strong. There was sadness in his voice that expressed an untold story.

Standing still, I wondered if I should approach them or turn back; I did not want to intrude on their conversation, especially as Ammu had ventured out of the house for the very first time since our arrival here. As silently as I possibly could I raised my foot to walk back, but stepped on a twig causing it to snap. Immediately they both turned around to find me standing behind them. I stood there, expressionless, feeling a little guilty for interrupting them. Ammu and Omar stared at each other smiling, only adding to my guilt.

Suddenly Omar raised his hands up in the air and said, 'I'm sorry, I should have let you know I was bringing Ammu here. It's very peaceful so I thought it would be refreshing for her, and she did warn me that you would worry. I promise I have been looking after her.'

I looked at him and smiled, feeling slightly embarrassed, and then looked over to Ammu. 'This is the place I was telling you about the other day, it's beautiful, isn't it?'

'Saira, why are your clothes wet?' she asked. I looked down to discover the bottom half of my kaftan soaked with water.

'Yes... I was just going to change. I will do that now,' I replied and swiftly walked back towards the house. Ammu appeared happy, which I was eternally grateful to Omar for; the kindness and hospitality he had bestowed upon us was immeasurable and something I could never reciprocate. I returned to the house and smiled as I saw them both pointing at a large jackfruit, and I hoped I had not offended him in any way. Now, after so long, I was beginning to feel a sense of positivity. It seemed that Omar's smile and love for life were contagious and he had infected both me and Ammu. I began dinner preparation as I could hear Ammu and Omar outside; he was holding Ammu with one hand and the large kathal with the other. He placed the not-so-ripe kathal on the courtyard floor as Ammu watched, and without explanation I understood that the menu for today was curried kathal – a dish relished by my father.

'Saira, I will ask Abdullah to cut it open and he can take half for him and Layla, and we will keep the rest,' Omar said.

It was twilight and I welcomed the moonlit night almost like an inviting beacon high up in the heavens. I intended to serve the cooked kathal with egg fried rice, and knocked on Omar's door to tell him dinner was ready.

That night I gathered a little courage. 'Thank you... thank you for taking such good care of my mother,' I stuttered.

He looked at me, smiled and then said, 'There is no need to thank me, I enjoy her company,' and walked towards her room.

The three of us sat at the table immersed in the sweet, distinct aroma. 'I have a confession to make,' Omar said, looking at Ammu with a stern look upon his face. 'I have never tasted curried kathal before.'

Ammu laughed in response, and her laughter made me giggle. She encouraged him to try the food, explaining that this was one of our favourite dishes and, to my surprise, just like my Abbuji, Omar decreed it had now become one of his favourites. It seemed today was a day of revelation. The many unanswered questions in my imagination received their answers. Omar divulged the mystery behind his grand house but simple lifestyle. He explained he had no immediate family and that he was raised by his paternal uncle and aunt, Chacha and Chachi, with whom he resided in London. His parents had passed away leaving him in the care of his uncle and the little memory he had of them was living in a tiny mud house with very little to call their own; this was the mud house that was now occupied by Layla and Abdullah. Omar told of how his parents always wanted a better life for him, so to fulfil their aspirations he worked hard, with little support from his uncle, and educated himself enough to start his own real estate business. He then built this very large house and bought acres of land where crops such as rice were cultivated and handed out to the needy villagers who, like his parents, had very little to survive on. He explained he visited once a year as it allowed him to feel close to his parents, and he spent that time building water wells for the less wealthy.

Ammu and I listened in awe and I could not help but notice the sadness in his eyes that told of the difficult life he must have led, but in which he had found the strength to become the exemplary character he was today. I wanted to applaud him; Ammu held his hand stating that his parents would have been proud of him. He smiled shyly and was deep in thought for a moment. I expected he must have been thinking about his parents, so attempted to redirect his thoughts to the dinner we had just eaten. I brought out the roasted oval-shaped jackfruit seeds. He seemed amused and said, 'I've never tried these before, either,' and began laughing.

I brewed ginger tea, which took me back to our happier times; now I was able to cherish those memories, after learning that Omar had not even had that, yet somehow he managed to live a life full of positivity, and perhaps I needed to take inspiration from that. We sat out on the front patio relishing the warm tea as the entire village slept. I listened as Ammu and Omar talked about his plans for the next day, for which he needed to leave early. I stared up at the scattered bright stars that gave light to the dark night and wondered where this journey would take me next, wondered where we would go when Omar returned to his home in London. Although we had only known him a short time our lives had become interconnected in more ways than one – whether it was through sadness or joy I was uncertain. I was sure about one thing: that this connection was one that ran deep and pulled at the delicate strings of my heart. I was thankful that he had entered our life at a point of much-needed hope, and he made Ammu happy in a way I was no longer able to. That night I lay in bed in contemplation and recalled a saying from my village: 'The darker the night the brighter the morning', and I secretly hoped this was true.

I rose early to the sound of birds and villagers preparing for the day ahead, under a perfect blue sky with clouds that were slowly moving from blue to white. I prepared Omar's breakfast, knowing he needed to leave early, and he sat at the table gulping down hot tea as quickly as possible. 'Saira, I will be back very late today, so please don't wait up for me,' he said in a tense voice. I nodded, wondering why he appeared tense and if there were anything I could do to help.

I checked on Ammu, only to discover her sitting up with her legs curled right up to her chest, grimacing in pain. I panicked and rushed to her side at once. 'Ammu, what's wrong? What's happened?' I asked her frantically.

'It's okay, Saira, I'm just having a little trouble moving my legs today,' she replied, clearly in excruciating pain. I squeezed out the remainder of her pain-relief ointment and began to massage her legs, but she complained of more pain.

'I'm so sorry, Ammu. I will go to the doctor right away to collect some medication for you,' I told her, almost crying. I grabbed my handbag securely placing the little money I had left inside it. I wrapped my headscarf tightly around my head covering all the bits of untidy hair flying around my face and wiped away my tears. I had no idea how to even get around this village or where I could take a rickshaw to get to the doctor's office. I went to Layla and asked that she look after Ammu. I was glad Omar was not around today; the last thing I wanted was for him to question my commitment to the responsibility for this house.

In confusion I ran to the big pond, oblivious to the women who were staring at me. Much to my relief the angelic-faced boy was splashing about in the water as usual. I asked him to show me where I could hail a rickshaw. 'Apa, come with me I will show you,' he said, taking my hand and leading me towards another path that led beyond the big pond – almost a secret path that no one knew about as it was covered by another tree canopy. I walked as quickly as I could, passing the route by which we had entered this village; suddenly I halted as the image of Hamid came into my mind. The thought of being discovered by him and his family sent shivers down the small of my back. But I had to cross the boundary of this village today out of duty to my mother. I sprinted back to the house and grabbed a thin, holey shawl and placed it around my head and shoulders.

'My Ammu wears one of those when she goes out,' said the little boy, taking hold of my hand again. I smiled at him. We came to a concrete bridge that passed over the river connecting this village to mine. I watched as people crossed the river in boats just as we had. The boy led me over the bridge and onto another, wider, mud path. I saw a gentleman sitting on the side of the path selling candy and various other household items such as bowls and fans from a rusty cart. The boy approached the gentleman and asked him to call the rickshaw boy. Just a few minutes later a rickshaw came round a bend and stood beside us. The little boy said, 'There you are, Apa, he will take you where you need to go and will bring you back here too.' I kissed him on his cheeks, forever grateful, and climbed up into the rickshaw, promising to buy him candy upon my return. The driver asked for my destination with a polite smile. 'The doctor's office in Jaggannathpur, please,' I replied anxiously, careful to conceal my face.

Jaggannathpur was another town that lay towards the eastern side of Sylhet, approximately an hour away. Dr Uddin had treated any ailments, be they minor or major, for me and Ammu for as long as I could remember, and I trusted that he would treat Ammu better than anybody else I knew. Jaggannathpur was a large town consisting of many shopping complexes, with a large bazaar and many official buildings providing ample opportunity for employment. Seeing vehicles here such as cars was common as the roads were made from concrete and much larger, accommodating the needs of the wealthy, whereas the less fortunate still relied upon motorcycles and rickshaws. I felt myself swaying from side to side in the rickshaw on the uneven road. The sun felt hot on my bare feet, and I anxiously waited to arrive at my destination; I knew that it would take a while, travelling in a rickshaw. The lightweight three-wheeled cart that was pedalled by a driver always fascinated me as a child. I loved sitting in the chair-like body mounted on springs and pulling the collapsible hood over my head. I closed my eyes as the wind blew over my face and recalled the time that Ammu, Sumayah and I had all squeezed into one rickshaw all the way to Jaggannathpur. We had laughed so much that Sumayah almost fell out. I looked around at the changing scenery; more rickshaws and cars were travelling alongside us now, as well as people walking, and animals strayed between the moving vehicles causing havoc on the road.

We finally arrived at the doctor's office. The heat of the sun was humid and sticky and I could feel a burning sensation on my head as I climbed down and out of the rickshaw. It was extremely busy and chaotic. The road was congested with people, cars and cattle. I could see a variety of stalls in the bazaar, vibrant with the colours of our native land. There were people gathering round a fish stall and a spice stall with colourful packages, containing cumin, turmeric, and fresh cloves of garlic to name a few. I hadn't been here for a very long time, hence the richness of its beauty fascinated me all the more. With a fearfully beating heart I walked into the doctor's office and asked the receptionist who already held a record of Ammu's treatment to prepare her medication. I waited anxiously as the lady handed me the bag, but when I went to pay I realised that I only had sixty takkas and the cost of the whole prescription was 130 Bangladeshi takkas. I trembled as I counted the money in my hand for a second and third time only to discover that I could not afford to purchase the medicines. I just about mumbled that I would return in a short while to the staring lady at the desk and walked out of the office as quickly as I could. I stood outside, unsure of what to do as the money I had would barely cover my travel costs. My distress gave way to panic. How could I return home without any medication for Ammuji? What could I say to her? I climbed back into the rickshaw and headed back to the village, quietly choking back tears of failure.

I stepped off the rickshaw, thanking the driver, and began to walk back to the house empty handed and dishevelled. My thoughts were jumbled and disordered as I thought about what I would say to Ammu. Exhaling a deep sigh I entered the house, where Layla stood with her daughter, giving me a warm smile. She informed me Ammu was feeling much better and was resting in her room; I nodded.

'Saira, Saira, are you okay?' I heard Layla call to me as I meandered past her.

'Yes, just a little tired,' I replied as I continued to walk into the house. I felt guilty that I was unable to care for Ammu the way she deserved, as if I had let her down. Swallowing intense feelings of anxiety deep into my stomach I entered Ammu's room. She was sitting up smiling, with both her ankles and all the way up to her knees covered in a thick green paste of crushed leaves.

'How are you feeling, Ammu?' I began. She smiled, handing me a much-needed glass of cold water which I drank almost instantly, splashing some of it onto my bright red cheeks and forehead.

I sat beside her as she held my hand and said, 'Saira, you look so tired, is everything okay?' I forced out a smile; a feeble attempt to conceal my distress and failure at the same time.

'I'm fine, Ammu. I have ordered your medication and it should be here soon.' I lied to her, feeling disgusted and ashamed of myself. I couldn't tell her the truth.

'I'm feeling much better now. Layla was kind enough to press neem leaves together. She has even massaged it onto my legs and it's helping,' she said, pointing at the paste. The neem plant was very popular in our village. The leaves were crushed and turned into a paste and used as a homeopathic remedy to cure and suppress ailments such as migraines, dermatitis, joint pain and arthritic pain. I spent a while sitting next to her staring at her angelic face while she slept, and felt physically sick knowing that today for the very first time I had resorted to lying to my mother.

It was nearly afternoon and I still had not completed any of the chores; the last thing I wanted was for Omar to return to an unkempt house and question what I had been doing the entire day. So I frantically began sweeping away the dust that had collected across the kitchen floor and tidied the stove so that I could start preparing dinner. My mind remained heavy and overwhelmed with worry while my body was paralysed with exhaustion. Today I missed my home and would have given anything to have my old life back: the life I lived before I fell prey to becoming a third wife and then a maid. I was holding on to hope for a miraculous solution to appear, although I knew the chance of that actually happening was minimal.

Chapter 11 – Memoirs of a Lost Village

I placed Omar's dinner on the table hoping that it would remain warm till he returned, and retired to bed. I lay down, stretching out my heat-swollen feet, allowing my entire body to sink into bed. I was physically exhausted but I felt alert. A thousand thoughts spiralled through my mind that refused to shut down, all coming back to my current dilemma. Staring up to the ceiling I thought about Sumayah, who always had a way to relieve my burden and managed to help me focus on the positive side of things; today I was in dire need of that support and direction.

The next morning I entered the kitchen to find that the table had been cleared and the chairs tucked away neatly. I couldn't remember whether or not I had heard Omar return.

'Morning, Saira.' I started at the voice that came from behind as I began to brew tea.

'Morning,' I replied, fastening my hijab securely around my face.

'How is Ammu?' he continued.

'She's not too great today,' I said. Before allowing me to finish my sentence he had begun walking in the direction of her room. I placed my hands on my hurting head and continued to prepare breakfast, then went into Ammu's room to find her sitting up beside Omar, chatting and smiling.

'Saira, can we have our breakfast in here today?' he suggested cheerfully. I nodded and served them breakfast, sitting close by. I don't know how he achieved it, but Omar had a way of optimising the little happiness Ammu had left; they appeared to enjoy each other's company in ways that were beyond my comprehension. I walked back to the kitchen, still anxious, and stood out on the patio staring at the meadow ahead. I was yet to find a means of purchasing the medication; the only resolution appeared to be resorting to Omar for support. How could I ask him for financial help? He was in no way related to us and we would soon leave this house, never to return. Why should he help us? He had already done so much by allowing us to be sheltered in his house when everybody else had deserted us. These questions filtered through my mind one by one, only increasing my anxiety.

'A penny for them,' I heard someone say. I turned around to find Omar standing beside me.

'Sorry, did you say something?' I asked, confused.

'You look a little distracted. Is everything all right?' he asked.

'Yes, I'm fine, just a little tired,' I replied.

'Why don't you take some rest with Ammu,' he advised.

'No, I am absolutely fine. I will clean your room today,' I said, returning to the kitchen. I needed to avoid Omar finding out the truth.

'Saira, if you're worried about anything, you know I'm always here to help,' he said, following me into the kitchen.

'Everything is fine. Can you please leave your laundry just outside the room,' I said and hurried out.

I then applied the remainder of the neem paste on Ammu's legs, massaging them thoroughly, and made a start on cleaning. I swept all the dusty rooms one by one, collected the dirty laundry and headed down to the big pond. It was nearly midday and the sun was out, bright and hot, with very little breeze, making the air humid and sticky. My feet were still swollen so I walked barefoot enjoying the warmth of the concrete path under my bare soles. I walked towards the inviting coolness of the water, greeting fellow village women who, just like me, had come to wash their laundry. Dipping my feet into the water I sat enjoying its coolness. The angelic-faced boy was far out into the pond today, swimming with a gentleman who I presumed to be his father. I waved at him and then began my mundane task of washing the clothes.

'Apa, did you find your doctor?' I felt a tug on my arm and then saw his sweet face looking directly at me.

I looked at him and replied, 'Thank you so much for your help, and I haven't forgotten your candy.' I looked over at his father who had followed him out of the pond to greet him out of courtesy. Much to my horror I turned around only to see Omar standing there, drenched, looking at me in confusion. I was shocked as I looked at him and then looked away swiftly.

'Shall we play cricket now?' I heard the little boy ask Omar, and they walked side by side towards the path I had taken yesterday. I was horrified to discover Omar here at the pond – what if he learnt the truth about where I had been yesterday? What answer would I give him when he questioned me about what he had just overheard? I didn't want to offend him, especially after the hospitality he had bestowed upon us. I returned to the house and climbed up to the white-picket-fenced rooftop with the load of wet clothes weighing me down physically, while panic weighed on me mentally. How many lies would I have to tell to conceal the cold reality of yesterday, I thought aloud. I stood on the rooftop staring out to the big pond. The serene sight gave me momentary relief from the magnitude of worries so painfully attached to this chapter of my life.

I scrubbed the bathroom floor, even though I had only completed this task a few days before, in the hope that this would be the best distraction from the thought of any questions Omar might have for me upon his return. Strangely enough I found this vigorous cleaning to be therapeutic, almost as if I was trying to scrub away my worries.

My much-loved time of day arrived quickly today; it was twilight and the sound of the melodious call to prayer brought me harmony, almost signifying a glimmer of hope. Omar had not returned, which left me imagining that perhaps he had discovered the truth, as he always informed either myself or Ammu of his plans for the day. Just as I had finished preparing dinner I heard the door open followed by Omar. I avoided making eye contact as he walked through the kitchen and down the hallway, and I began breathing so fast that I felt dizzy. I was still standing there when he returned to the kitchen with Ammu beside him. Smiling, I pulled out a chair for her and she sat down carefully.

'How are you, Ammu?' he asked her.

'I am perfectly fine,' she replied, looking at us both.

'Shall we eat, Saira?' he said, looking in my direction. I was taken aback to say the least. He was acting completely normally, which suggested that he had not discovered the truth, and if he had, why was he still acting normally? This debate continued in my mind all through dinner. In fact, I was so consumed by it that I sat obliviously scraping a spoon against my plate.

'Saira, what's wrong?' I jolted as Ammu asked, bringing my attention back to reality.

'Err… nothing. I was going to brew some ginger tea for us all,' I replied, rushing to the stove in an attempt to hide my face. I knew Ammu could read me like a book. I swiftly began to brew the tea as Omar began a conversation about cricket with Ammu, although she continued to look in my direction for a few more minutes and then immersed herself fully in conversation with him, much to my relief. The three of us sat out on the front patio drinking warm ginger tea – a perfect remedy to the hot and dusty weather, although there was a lovely breeze tonight. The stars were bright as I stared up at the beautiful moonlit canvas, momentarily resting my racing mind. Sitting here was perfect, as the darkness provided excellent cover allowing me to hide my emotions from them both.

I still had no solution to the problem of Ammu's medication, and now, on top of that, I needed to conceal it from Omar. Sitting quietly I listened to them talk about the village, which held a special place in his heart as it was the only connection he had with his beloved parents. He was truly praiseworthy in every way possible and I could only imagine how immensely proud his parents would have been had they been alive.

'You're very quiet, Saira,' said Ammu.

'Just a little tired,' I said.

'Thank you for another lovely dinner, Saira. I have an early start tomorrow and will be back very late,' Omar informed us. I tucked Ammu into bed and gladly surrendered my overworked mind for the night.

The next day I rose to the sound of the tweeting of birds and as usual rushed into the kitchen, fastening my scarf. I needed to prepare Omar's breakfast before he left so began to brew tea as fast as I could, then laid it on the table with his choice of snacks. The few days spent in this house had taught me about Omar's preferred cuisine – likes and dislikes. I waited some time for Omar to walk through to the kitchen as he usually did by this time. I knocked on his door only to find an empty room. The bed was neatly made up with his clothes tidy and the room was immaculate, as always. He had already left; which left me wondering why.

Ammu woke early so I served her breakfast and massaged her feet with the remainder of the home-made neem paste. 'Would you like to sit on the patio today?' I asked her. She agreed, as her pain appeared to have lessened. I figured the rays of sun would shine happiness onto her, too. I heard a voice.

'Is anybody home?' And then a second time. It sounded like a man's voice, which immediately sent my heart into a frenzy. Omar hadn't mentioned that anybody would come by today and I panicked in fear.

'I have a delivery,' I heard, and with sweaty hands approached the front patio. There was a young boy standing there in the white uniform of someone who worked in a doctor's office.

'Assalamualaikum,' I said, trembling, in the hope that this unexpected visitor was nothing to do with Hamid.

'Walaikumassalam,' he replied, holding up a carrier bag. 'I have a delivery for the name of Saira,' he said. I stood still, puzzled; I had nothing that needed delivering.

'What is it that you have?' I replied. He handed the carrier bag to me, said goodbye and left before I could enquire where he had come from and what the delivery was. The carrier bag was securely sealed so I took it inside and curiously opened it at once. To my disbelief the bag contained medication for Ammu matching the exact items I was unable to afford. The boxes were labelled individually with Ammu's name and the address of her doctor's office. I sat down, puzzled, unable to understand how and why this medication had been delivered here. Surely the pharmacy would not dispense it without any payment and if not, then who had paid and arranged for this to happen?

'Saira, what's in the bag?' Ammu called to me. I hurried out to her still holding the medication in my hand. Her face lit up with joy at once as if she had seen the light at the end of the tunnel; this made all my anxieties disappear right away.

I continued with the housework as Ammu appeared a little stronger today and was even enjoying slowly moving around the house, thanks to the effect of the painkillers. It made me sad to think that only a few weeks ago she had been a successful businesswoman and today she was almost bed bound, overcome with emotional distress that had affected her both psychologically and physically. I continued to ponder how the medication had arrived; this was a mystery I needed to unravel. My poor mother was under the impression that I had arranged this, all the while causing me to feel guilty and completely inadequate.

I planned to use the dozen fresh papayas that were literally hanging off the tree for dinner today as I figured it would be a lovely surprise for Omar. As I placed Ammu's medication safely into my cupboard I noticed that the telephone number of the doctor's office was written on the box. I wondered whether or not I should contact them. At least I would discover how the medication had arrived here and my mind would be at ease. Omar always left a spare cell phone in the house for me and Ammu to use in the event of emergencies. Hesitantly I took out the phone and dialled the number. Taking in a deep breath I informed the lady who answered of my name and situation, and then enquired about how and why the medication had been delivered here as I had not arranged for this. To say I was amazed and horrified at the same time would be an understatement when I heard the name of the person responsible. Shock turned into anger, and I struggled to understand the many emotions I was feeling. I contemplated whether or not I should confront this truth or bury it deep within me.

Dusk was beginning to approach and with it this long emotional day was coming to an end. I prepared dinner, wondering whether or not Omar would return in time or later than expected. Ammu had eaten and taken her medication, seeming a little tired due to the walking she had been doing today. I felt indescribably happy seeing her move about independently just the way she used to. I sat beside her, thinking over the events of the day, wondering if I should have been grateful for the outcome, although there was a part of me that just would not let go of anger. It was almost 11 p.m. and Omar still had not returned. I wondered if he was avoiding me. A short while later I heard the door open and then close, followed by his footsteps, and I waited in anticipation.

Chapter 12 – Misconceptions

Omar seemed shocked to find me standing here at this hour. He immediately made eye contact; I could see he was as anxious as I was. 'Saira, you're still awake,' he said, surprised. I did not respond and began to clear the table in a passive-aggressive manner. I had no intention of being cruel or unkind; however, for an unknown reason I had lost all control of my mental and emotional stability. 'Saira, is everything okay?' he asked.

'No it's not, nothing is okay,' I said, almost shouting and then bit my lip as I did not want Ammu to wake and learn about any of this. I held my head and began to walk away, frustrating him even more, it appeared.

'Tell me what's wrong,' he said firmly.

'What's wrong is that you have been spying on me,' I blurted out. I took out the medication and presented it to him as evidence; he stared at me, bemused. 'These arrived today and when I telephoned, they told me that you had arranged for them to be delivered for Ammu,' I told him.

'Yes, I did,' he admitted.

'But why? We are not your concern. I am very grateful that you are allowing us to stay here, but you have no responsibility for us. How did you even know I had gone there?' I continued in a fit of rage. I took a deep breath and for a few minutes we were both quiet.

'Saira...' he began timidly.

'I want to pay you back,' I demanded fiercely.

'You're being ridiculous, Saira,' he scoffed.

'I want to pay you back,' I repeated, anger echoing in my voice.

'Why are you being so stubborn?' he questioned.

I began to take off my thin gold bracelet that dangled around my wrist, which was a much-loved gift from Ammu, and for her I was willing to make any sacrifice. I took it off and handed it to him, saying, 'This should cover the expense.'

His face was now filled with rage as if it were a mirror reflecting mine. He took the bracelet and placed it back into my hands with a determination I had not witnessed before. 'I will not accept money or jewellery from you, do you understand that?' he said, in a firm, angry voice. I had clearly offended him although that had not been my intention at all. 'If you really want to hear the truth, then fine,' he said in a submissive tone. 'Jamal, the little boy that plays in the pond, told me over cricket that you had been worried and upset and you asked him to hail a rickshaw for you to travel to the doctor. That worried me so I telephoned the doctor's office and they verified that you had gone to collect medication for Ammu.

'My only intention was to help Ammu to feel better… Since you arrived I have grown fond of Ammu and I just wanted to help her. I don't want anything in return, I assure you,' he explained. 'Anyway, I'm extremely sorry for upsetting you – that was not my intention,' he said in a dejected tone and walked into his room.

I stood in silence, wondering whether the events of my life had turned me bitter to the extent that today I was questioning the only person who had displayed nothing but integrity, kindness and compassion towards us. That night I lay awake in bed ruminating and reflecting, totally absorbed by my shortcomings. I was thankful that Ammu had slept through my altercation with Omar as I knew all too well how fond of him she was. I decided that the next morning my first and foremost priority would be to apologise to him as sincerely as I was able. I realised that sometimes you cross paths with people who teach you to live life with a dose of humility. I began to accept that perhaps Omar was an exceptional human being and, like he said, he just wanted to help my mother. For this alone I was immensely grateful.

I woke to the much-needed melody of the call to prayer and fully immersed myself in it, submitting all my worries to the Almighty with an abundance of gratitude. I rushed into the kitchen and began to brew the morning tea, noticing the stack of pots and pans which needed attending to. I served Ammu breakfast along with her medication and decided to knock on Omar's door, only to find it wide open, which suggested that he had already left for the day. Ammu had already enquired about Omar twice this morning and both times I avoided her question, distracting her swiftly with something else altogether.

I took the stack of pots and pans to the big pond, where I saw Layla walking with baby Khadijah. I greeted her and said, 'Layla, thank you so much for looking after Ammu the other day. I really appreciate it and if you ever need anything please don't hesitate to ask.' I had forgotten to thank her the other day in my panic. She flashed her lovely smile as always and continued playing with her daughter. For a moment I watched them laughing together; the love expressed between a mother and child is so pure, innocent and unconditional, like the love I felt for my mother. I couldn't help but think about Omar, and how as a child or an adult he had not experienced this unconditional love and perhaps that was why he felt inclined to help Ammu. I felt incredibly guilty about my behaviour towards him the previous night; how could I stand in his house and shout at him? I was appalled with myself. I saw angelic-faced Jamal splashing his legs high as he swam around, but to my disappointment he was alone and Omar was nowhere in sight. When I returned to the house carrying the clean vessels, Ammu was sitting in the open back courtyard looking out onto the captivating green scenery past the papaya trees. There was a serene, calm breeze complementing the brightness of the sunshine today, calming my mind for a short while. I loved the sunshine; it made me feel happy in so many ways. I missed my time with Sumayah terribly: days spent lounging in the heat, devouring the spicy, juicy flavours of fresh hog plum and lime Chanachur chutney prepared by Ammu. This was a delicacy back in our village – everybody loved Chanachur chutney prepared by her.

'Would you like anything, Ammu?' I asked, bringing myself back to reality. Every so often I took a glance around, wondering if Omar had returned; my mind was heavy with the burden of my undeclared apology.

I returned to the kitchen to serve Ammu some soup, thinking she would require sustenance by now. When I reached the stove I heard the chatter of voices, sounding like Ammu and Omar. I peeped through the small window directly above the stove and saw them sitting side by side sucking on cherry-flavoured cooling ice popsicles, which were taken round on a cart almost every day and sold to villagers, mostly children, to combat the scorching heat. I served two portions of soup and walked over to join them. With part of me too guilty to even make eye contact with Omar, I placed the tray beside them and began to walk away.

'Saira, here's one for you,' he called out, handing me a popsicle whilst pulling out a chair for me to sit next to them. I accepted, sitting close by, although I felt slightly uncomfortable at first. I desperately needed a window of opportunity to apologise, and needed to do this in the absence of my mother. The three of us sat there a little while immersed in the signature heat of our native land. I listened to

Omar telling Ammu about his day, and how he had had an appointment with a lawyer. He was preoccupied and lines of worry and tension were clearly visible across his forehead. I had no experience of meeting with lawyers, although I knew they were consulted to unravel both minor and major disputes through a court of law. I hoped that it was nothing major and prayed for it to be resolved soon.

Ammu chose to rest for some time, so I took the opportunity to apologise. I walked back into the kitchen where Omar appeared to be searching for something. 'Saira, I need some hot water,' he said looking around. I handed it to him, unable to make eye contact.

'Omar,' I said. He stopped momentarily, allowing me to speak. 'I am extremely sorry about my behaviour yesterday. I had no right to shout and be rude and obnoxious like that. I want you to know that I deeply appreciate what you have done and the way you make Ammu happy just by being around her. I am so grateful for that, so thank you.'

'Saira, you're most welcome, and no apology is needed,' he replied as if nothing had happened, which baffled me.

'If there's anything I can do to make up for my horrid behaviour…' I asked hopefully.

'There is one thing. I am a great fan of flatbread – if one day you could prepare some with curried papaya then that would be lovely,' he replied with humour. This was the very first time he had asked anything of me, or Ammu for that matter.

I smiled, nodded, and said, 'Consider it done.' I began to feel a light relief and was glad I'd had the opportunity to apologise.

'Saira,' he said, 'please continue smiling,' and then walked towards his room. A part of me agreed with him; I had stopped laughing or smiling and surrendered to a life of sadness.

The afternoon was fast approaching so I took out the leftover papayas from the other day that I had kept in the vegetable storage area and began to peel them in preparation for dinner. I began by kneading the chapatti dough ensuring the consistency was soft and stringy just the way Ammu did. I cooked the papaya with turmeric and green chillies and rolled out the chapattis ensuring they were as round as I could roll them. Just like every other day, Omar and Ammu walked into the kitchen, chatting together. They sat at the table as I served them and walked over to the stove to collect water. All of a sudden I heard a ferocious roar of laughter and it seemed both Ammu and Omar were laughing hysterically, holding up a chapatti. I looked up in confusion, only to realise that the chapatti was almost octagonal shaped, hence the laughter. I inspected all of them to discover that not one was circular. How I had remained oblivious to this while I was rolling them, I could not fathom. Just then both Ammu and Omar became silent, staring at my serious face. In retaliation I stared back at them and burst into laughter, which they soon joined in.

'Saira, I wonder if Omar knows that you could never master the art of rolling flatbread,' Ammu said, smiling.

'He does now,' I said, holding one up. That night had been memorable; laughter echoed throughout dinner and onto the patio where we drank warm ginger tea. I felt a glimpse of happiness return after what had felt like being stuck in a dark space, without a ray of light, for an eternity. I stared out into the darkness of the night taking a moment to contemplate, reflect and evaluate. I contemplated the journey I had taken to be here today. Then I reflected on life since our arrival in this village and I suddenly came to a realisation. How long could we live on Omar's hospitality and humility? I went to bed that night with a new-found hope, and a new perseverance that had awakened within me, leading me to believe that I needed to find the strength and passion to pursue a life that was based on happiness of the heart. What is happiness? I questioned, although I knew that I had been happy back in my Jahed Pur home. However, meeting Omar had taught me that perhaps the definition of true happiness is being content and thankful for whatever you have, be it little or large in amount.

The next day I woke up with a feeling of great purpose, a determination that, no matter what, I would think positive. No matter how much the past continued to haunt me, I would not succumb to it. No matter how strong the fear, I would replace it with courage and strength. It seemed Omar's infectious smile and optimism were truly contagious. I served them both breakfast and to my surprise Omar had not left early this morning; they were both walking along the dusty courtyard of the front patio deep in conversation and banter. Together they devoured mid-morning snacks and drank warm tea. I collected all the laundry, took it down to the pond and washed it thoroughly, mentally ticking off each task as I completed it. I returned to the house carrying the heavy bucket of wet clean clothes and climbed up to the rooftop balcony almost out of breath. When I reached the top and stopped to catch my breath, I was surprised to find Omar standing directly opposite me engrossed in a conversation on his mobile phone. As I moved closer, there was evident tension in his tone of voice. He spoke in English and I could hear him saying that he would never agree to sell his ancestral land and that he was willing to take this dispute to a court of law to resolve it. Abruptly he ended the conversation, walking swiftly past me, completely oblivious to the fact that I was standing there. I heard his angry footsteps descending the staircase and wondered who he was having this dispute with. Bewildered, I looked out towards the front of the house and could see Jamal still splashing in the water. I was beginning to convince myself that perhaps he was secretly a mermaid, the amount of time he spent in water each day; his angelic face always brought a smile to my lips. Just then I saw a gentleman walking fast towards the path beyond the pond; when I looked a second time I realised it was Omar and he was carrying a folder. I wondered where he was going and if something sinister had occurred, especially after the conversation I had unintentionally overheard.

I returned downstairs to give Ammu her medication, which was doing wonders for her, and lately I had even noticed she seemed happier, which I knew deep down was because of Omar's benevolent influence. I swept all the back rooms while Ammu sat out in the courtyard picking through spinach leaves for me to prepare for dinner. I found myself preoccupied and unsettled almost the entire day, mostly out of concern for Omar. I decided that upon his return I would ensure that he was well, just the way that he ensured we were; I felt an inexplicable obligation towards him and responsibility for his well-being.

Dusk was approaching and still there was no sign of him. Ammu and I ate dinner together and I sat with her for a while until she fell asleep. In anticipation, I laid out dinner for Omar and decided to take a walk to the rooftop balcony as sleep was a rather distant notion for my unsettled mind. I stepped out quietly into the dark back courtyard; the night felt warm and humid with a little soft breeze. I climbed the stairs slowly up to the rooftop and walked all the way to the front, looking out on the sleeping village under a perfectly aligned heavenly beacon of a thousand stars or more. I could hear Layla's baby crying, the sound of the waves in the pond crashing into each other, and the breeze blowing leaves from side to side. I heard the hum of the mosquitoes as they whizzed back and forth. You rarely heard cattle at this time, or people for that matter, as the entire village lay still, serene and composed; the irony was that this was the exact opposite of the chaos in my mind. I closed my eyes, momentarily surrendering to peace and harmony, and indulged in the gentle breeze that blew across my face.

'It's beautiful at this time, isn't it?' A voice startled me to the point that I jerked in rapid response. 'I am so sorry, I didn't mean to startle you,' said Omar looking out onto the same view I had been admiring only a few seconds before.

I wrapped my hijab tightly around my face, composed myself and said, 'Oh, I just didn't expect to find you, or anyone, up here.' I was astounded to find him here and my initial thought was to ask him about his conversation earlier; however, something was holding me back. 'It is very beautiful here,' I agreed, and then said, 'We thought you were out.'

'Sorry, I should have let you guys know,' he replied with a deep intensity in his eyes. He appeared upset and I could not help but wonder why, although I felt unable to ask him.

'Do you come up here often?' I asked in an attempt to break down the barrier that was preventing me from asking him anything more.

'I come up here mostly when I need space and time to reflect and think,' he said.

'Good thinking spot,' I confirmed. He appeared detached and not his usual self, and the infectious smile was nowhere to be seen. We stood in awkward silence, lost deep in thought. 'Is everything all right, Omar?' I blurted out. 'It's just you have been gone for the entire day so me and Ammu were wondering if you were okay,' I continued.

'Sorry, I have actually been sitting up here for the last few hours just trying to resolve something,' he said. Every crevice within me was shocked to learn he had been sitting here in isolation and despair. I wondered why he hadn't just come to speak to me or Ammu about his difficulties, why was he choosing to face them alone when he had shouldered our troubles; surely today we had a responsibility towards him.

'Please don't do it,' I said to him with urgency in my voice. I felt relieved that the night was now dark enough to conceal the expression on his face, as I dreaded that he may warn me not to interfere in his personal matters.

'Don't do what, Saira,' he questioned. I was quiet, speechless, unsure of how to answer his question. 'Saira,' he said again.

Hesitantly I said, 'What I meant is please don't give up your ancestral land, it's your last and only connection to your parents. Don't part with it.' Silence ensued for a moment and then Omar sighed deeply. 'I am sorry, I never meant to interfere, it's your personal matter,' I said dejectedly.

'No, you're absolutely correct, I have no intention of parting with that land,' he said, much to my relief. He informed me that the paternal uncle who had raised him after the demise of his parents was now forcefully demanding that he hand over a piece of land that had been lovingly nurtured by his parents. The most unfathomable aspect was that this was a direct consequence of his uncle developing a personal vendetta against him, only Omar did not disclose the reasons behind the vendetta. His parents had planted many trees on that land which today held invaluable importance. I sensed the pain in his voice and was able to completely empathise with him; thinking of my father, this was a pain I knew, recognised and felt all too well. He walked right to the back of the balcony, looking out. 'Saira, do you know which piece of land it is?' he asked, as I followed behind. He pointed towards the meadow of greenery that surrounded the magnificent papaya and jackfruit trees. Now I understood why he held that particular place in such high esteem. I left him standing there absorbed in thoughts of his parents and wished him goodnight.

Just as I began to climb back down the stairs I heard him call out, 'Saira.' I stopped and he asked, 'How did you know about the land?' I stood still, trapped by his question as I feared he would think I was purposefully eavesdropping on him and his life. He repeated the question, only adding to my stress. I decided to live on the edge and confess the truth. Hesitantly I explained that earlier that day I had been on the rooftop with laundry and had accidently overheard his conversation whilst he had been talking on the phone. Immediately I apologised, attempting to convince him that it was truly accidental. However, he appeared dismayed by my confession. 'That doesn't make sense,' he said, 'I had that conversation in English, so how did you…' he continued and then paused. The conversation had now begun to unravel many untold mysteries. 'So you can understand English,' he said in disbelief. I was quiet as the question deepened the pain in my unhealed wounds.

'I can speak and understand English,' I revealed. To say he appeared shocked would be an understatement and I was able to predict his next question without him even having to vocalise it. I informed him that I used to teach basic English to pre-schoolers and that my long-term plan was to continue pursuing my teaching career.

'That's amazing,' he said in awe. I sensed that this truth had exceeded his expectations in more ways than one.

'Wait, so how come you're here as a maid?' he asked, mystified. I became silent at once, as the answer to his question was the bitter truth full of memories I wanted to conceal and forget. I took in a deep breath. I figured he must have felt he had crossed a line, a line that for me only caused pain that was suppressed deep within my heart. Without a pause Omar wished me goodnight and retired to bed. It was late and the village was enveloped in darkness. It had been a night filled with revelation after revelation on both sides. It was ironic, but the three of us had almost been made captive in a bond consisting of unresolved pain, a deep passion for life and concern for one another. It made me question how sometimes the bond of humanity was perhaps just as strong and resilient as the bond of blood. Every inch of my physical being ached with fatigue and exhaustion. Whilst Omar's question continued to echo around me, I could not bear to reveal the truth to him, and I felt guilty for this. It was an expectation of his I could not uphold; it was too painful and raw to resolve with spoken words, so I deemed it best to keep it locked away from him as an undiscovered treasure, deep amidst the depths of the ocean.

I turned towards the spiral staircase and headed back down to the house, where the aroma of a sweet mixture resembling amber and sandalwood tickled the tip of my nose. I took a deep breath, inhaling the familiar fragrance of lavender mixed with the scent of the ocean. This aroma captured me right away. I'd recognised that it was in fact Omar's scent which I had become accustomed to by now. I recalled cleaning his room and seeing the Cool Water perfumed aftershave sitting on his bedside cabinet. I had smelt this umpteen times before without taking much notice. I was unsure why, but the darkness of this night seemed to illuminate the fragrance, causing myriad memories to resurface. I climbed down the stairs, struggling to understand the messages being sent from my mind to my body. I suddenly felt an untold inclination towards this fragrance as if I knew and recognised it from somewhere, as if I held a deep connection to it somehow. I continued walking into the house, puzzled, as I attempted to decode this maze I found myself trapped in. What was it that my subconscious mind wanted to reveal to my conscious mind, and why? The internal debate continued as I lay next to Ammu, watching her sleep peacefully. That night I tried so hard to close my eyes only my mind refused to shut down. I got out of bed and began to pace the room, thinking back to my beloved village. Perhaps I had recognised it from someone else, I questioned, but my subconscious mind denied all recollection. In haste I opened my closet and began to randomly pick out items just to sniff and investigate this aroma further, but my frustration gave way to anger as nothing seemed to fit.

Chapter 13 – The Discovery

I picked up a carrier bag that I had purposefully brought along with me to this village. Today I felt a strong inclination to open this bag once again, as if an unknown force was connecting the pieces of my fragmented mind.

I took out the beige-coloured shawl I had packed away so neatly, pulling it close to my nose and inhaling the aroma ascending from it. With a deep breath I let out a gasp, dropping the shawl to the floor. I felt a mixture of emotions rush through my veins: shock, horror, disbelief, anxiety and then panic. In need of reassurance I picked up the shawl one more time and sniffed it again. There it was: the sweet mixture of lavender, sea salt, sandalwood and amber so heavily imprinted into this shawl. This was the very shawl given to me to wear by the gentleman I had met the night I had stood stranded on the bamboo bridge, emotionally scattered into a thousand pieces. The night I had decided to finally escape the barbarity inflicted upon me by Hamid and his despicable family. The night that Kamla had so assiduously executed her carefully laid plan, in turn sacrificing herself to give me freedom. The night I vowed to bring back the part of me that had been lost. This had been the shawl that had kept me warm as I was shaking in the night fog. The shawl I had kept with gratitude as I never had the opportunity to thank the gentleman who had saved me, from myself more than anything, on that wretched night. The fact that the gentleman who had enabled me to reach home safely was in fact none other than Omar was far beyond my comprehension. This was why I had found the familiarity of his scent so overwhelming, almost as if standing on the rooftop with him in the dark had re-enacted the events of that night all over again. I sat down on the bed holding the shawl, completely overwhelmed by this discovery. How strange that my head and heart had made this connection. Perhaps I was destined to thank Omar; I contemplated that perhaps this was why fate had caused the two of us crossing paths again.

I realised that Omar had seen my face that night, which meant that he knew I was the strange girl he had rescued. The very first time we met here in this village, in this house, he was sure to have recognised me right away. How had I remained oblivious to this fact up until now? How had I not made this connection before? Why had he not directly asked me about that night? I thought out loud and brought my knees up to my face, feeling ashamed. He had seen me in my most vulnerable state. I felt unable to look him in the eye, feeling guilty and shameful at the same time. I lay down my head, ruminating over the events and revelations of the day one by one, until my eyes finally surrendered to much-needed sleep.

The next morning I awoke feeling tired and achy. My mind was like a cloud filled with dark grey areas. I felt trapped within this intricate web that had now become my reality. Slowly, I crept out of bed and then rushed to prepare breakfast. I heard Omar walking into the kitchen and quickly scurried over to the stove, attempting to avoid making eye contact with him. 'Morning, Saira,' he called out. I fastened my hijab, pulling it forward covering the majority of my forehead.

'Morning,' I replied, looking away and attempting to appear busy.

'You look tired, Saira,' he said, 'did you not sleep well?' I stopped to reflect on my discovery, which had been the primary cause of my lack of sleep.

'I did, thanks,' I replied, with an undertone of submission to my voice. I served him breakfast as I did most mornings, only today felt different. Today I served him with a new-found realisation, which brought along a new compulsion. I wondered whether or not I should confront him and ask him why he had pretended not to recognise me. I very much doubted that he would forget meeting an insane girl almost hanging off a bridge in the middle of the night. Just as I was about to confront him, I noticed he was wearing a big smile on his face from one side of his cheek to the other.

'Saira, I just wanted to thank you,' he said, beaming with joy. I stood, confused, wondering what he had to thank me for. 'Your kind words yesterday have helped me immensely, and you're absolutely correct. I will do whatever it takes to protect my father's land,' he continued. He appeared elated, and, astonishingly, that infectious smile had returned, this time with a meaningful purpose, it seemed. I held back my emotions, contemplating the consequences of what I was about to do. What would it actually achieve if I confronted him? Would it change anything or would it only bring about more distress to us both. To cause him distress was not my intention at all, especially now he had so much to deal with, and would it not be extremely selfish of me to repay his selfless gratitude with yet another confrontation? These questions continued to chase through my mind, without abate. After some thought I decided there was no need for me to inform Omar of the truth, burying this revelation deep within my heart. I walked over to the stove, and stared at Omar's smiling face.

First and foremost I was grateful to God Almighty; secondly I was grateful to Omar, for saving me from myself that night, and then teaching me that life still goes on no matter how deep or severe the wounds may be. He had taught me many things, especially the importance of self-belief, perseverance, and a passion to live life to its full. How did I have the audacity to want to take away his peace of mind when he had managed to return the smile to my mother, which I was unable to accomplish? I truly felt disgusted with myself and my actions, and decided that, no matter what, this was one secret I would never again contemplate divulging to anyone.

Immersed in a world of my own I had neglected to check on Ammu today and when I walked into the room she was wide awake. 'You all right, Ammu?' I asked her softly.

'I'm okay, Saira,' she said, pulling herself up gradually and out of bed. I served her breakfast followed by her medication. Ammu seemed different today; there was something about her behaviour, something unidentifiable, almost as if she was keeping a low profile around the house. I thought perhaps she was contemplating her precious memories of Abbuji, so I allowed her to sit out on the patio and have her moment, as I scrubbed the kitchen and bathroom floors. Then, one by one, I put the clean utensils back into their places. I was kneeling down, reaching for a pot on the floor, when suddenly I heard a very loud bang coming from one of the rooms in the house. Immediately I ran, my heart beating wildly. I gasped for air upon entering Ammu's room and discovered her lying on the floor face down.

'Ammu, Ammu, what happened?' I asked her urgently. I touched her head and face frantically checking to ensure she had not hurt herself severely. 'It's okay, you're going to be fine,' I shouted, reassuring her whilst attempting to lift her off the floor. Just then Omar walked into the room to discover us both on the floor. At once he lifted her up and onto the bed. I had been so immensely preoccupied with things that had been utterly meaningless that I had been neglecting my mother, I thought, with tears now streaming down my face. I gave her water to drink while Omar sat beside her. She drank a little sip and took a minute to compose herself. She explained she had been feeling weak all morning and dizzy which had caused her to fall.

I pulled her into an embrace so tight that she began laughing. 'I'm fine, Saira.'

'Why didn't you tell me that you were not feeling well?' I demanded.

'Saira, I am sure Ammu must have just forgotten,' said Omar attempting to lighten the mood for us all. I thoroughly checked her arms and legs for bruising. 'Ammu, are you sure you're okay?' Omar asked her again, massaging her legs.

'You both need to stop worrying, it was a little fall,' she replied. placing her arms around both our shoulders.

'I will ask the doctor to come and check you over,' Omar added.

'No, you will do no such thing. I am absolutely fine,' she persisted, looking at us.

'You rest and I will brew some tea for the three of us,' I told her. I stumbled into the kitchen almost breaking down; I wanted to crawl into a corner and cry to my heart's content. I felt terribly guilty; I had become so self-absorbed that I had become neglectful. I rebuked myself for not being more attentive and alert; then, perhaps, I would have noticed she was feeling dizzy and would not have left her alone for long periods.

I poured the tea, brushing away my tears, and carried a tray filled with snacks for the three of us. Upon entering the room I heard them talking and laughing so I completely immersed myself in the sound of Ammu's laughter; it was a beautiful sight as I sat close and listened to their banter. Fortunately Omar had no plans to travel out today. Hence he offered to sit with Ammu as I prepared dinner.

Dusk arrived with the sweet sound of the call to prayer, once again taking my breath away. I prayed for Ammu today, asking God to protect her always. When I returned to the room I discovered Omar and Ammu kneeling down in prayer together, side by side; my eyes filled with this beautiful image of Omar close to her, ensuring she did not fall a second time. How thoughtful he was; despite having his own difficulties to contend with, he chose to look after my mother, a woman he shared no blood relation with. He was truly commendable.

I quickly composed myself, informing them, 'Dinner is ready. Ammu, are you feeling okay?'

'How can I not be? I have you both looking after me,' she replied, smiling. Omar walked beside her to the dinner table as she appeared unwell and extremely fatigued. This picture of her was the total opposite of the busy working lady she had once been back in our beloved home. My much-loved Jahed Pur seemed a million miles away and I longed for it and missed it dearly. I missed seeing Ammu happy; in my memories she had been happiest with Abbuji. It had been an extremely long day and my feet ached in agony as I began to clear the table and the dishes.

'Ammu is all tucked up in bed,' I heard Omar say to me as he walked back into the kitchen. He seemed tired and I felt guilty because allowing us to stay here had now become another responsibility for him to shoulder.

'Thank you so much,' I said to him.

'You're very welcome, Saira,' he said, and retired to bed. That night I lay down almost unable to keep my eyes open.

With great difficulty I awoke earlier than usual the next morning. I wanted to ensure that Ammu had all her medications at the correct times and would be extra attentive and vigilant towards her. Dawn was still breaking, and gradually the village was coming to life with the sound of birds, cockerel, cattle, ducks, and the early swarming of mosquitoes followed by the breathtakingly beautiful call to prayer, along with the familiar sounds and movement of the people.

The entire house was dust covered and desperately needed attention. I began by preparing breakfast for the three of us, while Ammu was still asleep.

'Morning, Saira,' said Omar. Without even allowing me to reply he left the kitchen, heading towards Ammu's room, I presumed. A short while later both of them walked back into the kitchen and she appeared smiley and well rested, to my relief. I served them both warm tea with fresh home-made yoghurt and a milky rice pudding dessert sweetened to Ammu's liking. The day was beautiful, the sky was an azure blue and the sun was bright. It was hot and humid and I felt happy; happy to see my mother feeling much better, secretly thanking God in abundance.

I then started the mundane task of dusting the back courtyard and kitchen, but my attention was quickly diverted by the painful shrieks of my mother, making me sprint back into her room. She lay in bed with one leg curled up and her face screwed up in pain. I asked her what was wrong, to which she was unable to reply. I began to massage her legs frantically, instructing her to sit up. After a short while she was able to explain that she'd had another dizzy spell. We were soon joined by Omar who sat beside her, worried. I managed to calm and settle her back into bed but she continued to complain of an acute headache with dizziness. I sat beside her, desperately helpless. Just then Omar returned to the room informing us both that he had contacted a doctor and arranged for him to come over to examine Ammu; admittedly this was a relief to my ears.

The three of us waited patiently for the arrival of the doctor and that half hour seemed to last forever, with Ammu still appearing to be in pain. It broke my heart that I was unable to do anything to make her feel better. I continually massaged her feet and her forehead, while Omar sat close by with a face full of worry and tension, duplicating mine. The doctor finally arrived. He seemed friendly and was known to Omar, and resided in a village nearby. I hoped he did not belong to the same village as Hamid, and led him into Ammu's room as a matter of urgency. The examination took around thirty minutes, although it seemed longer, while Omar and I stood close by, the entire time. He looked at me with benevolence as if telling me to stay strong without the use of words, so I acknowledged his support by nodding. I began to wring my hands; overwhelmed with fear of what the doctor may conclude. The doctor then asked for a glass of water, which I brought over right away, and then he instructed Ammu to take some medication which he had brought along with him.

The doctor sat Omar and me down, and said that Ammu's blood pressure was extremely high, causing dizziness, blurred vision and severe headaches. This was in addition to the acute arthritic pain she was already suffering. I sat beside Ammu, terrified, as this information engendered a new fear within me. The doctor then prescribed a new set of medications; Omar thanked him and left for the local bazaar, where there was a large pharmacy, to collect the new prescription.

I sat massaging Ammu's head as my subconscious mind began to accumulate a number of dark thoughts. Somewhere, somehow, I knew I had contributed to her slowly becoming this unwell; the amount of stress placed on her in the last few weeks was unimaginable. My head began to hurt as I thought about the many tragedies we had confronted, beginning with the end of my deception of a marriage, then being ousted from our village and leaving our beloved home, to arriving here, consequently losing everything that we had ever known and loved. Even now the fact was that we were in hiding from the clutches of Hamid; should he ever discover my whereabouts then I knew that the consequences would be dire. These events were mostly caused by me and now my beloved mother was suffering the consequences. I should have thought about her well-being more and sacrificed myself if needed, then maybe today she would have been all right, she would have been her old self: well, healthy and happy. I watched her sleep while I ruminated over a thousand possibilities and thoughts, brushing away the tears that were now flowing uncontrollably.

A short while later Omar returned with the new medication. He unsealed the bag, explaining the medications to me one by one as I listened attentively.

'Saira, are you okay?' he asked, no doubt noticing my red eyes and nose.

'Yes,' I muttered, trying to understand what he was explaining. 'I'll go and sort you out some lunch now,' I said to him, standing up.

'Saira, stop, I won't die of starvation. I think it's best you stay with Ammu, don't you?' he said with a stern face. If I were honest all I wanted was to sit next to my mother and care for her and ensure that she made a quick and full recovery.

Sometime later she opened her eyes as I remained beside her holding on to her hand, just as she used to nurse me when I was unwell. I asked her softly how she was feeling.

'I am much better, my darling,' she replied, slowly sitting herself up. I gave her some juice for sustenance and massaged her head with some balm.

'Ammu, I'm just going to get you something to eat,' I said to her. I figured a hot drink and bread would suffice until I managed to clean the stove, wash the pots and then eventually prepare dinner.

I ran into the kitchen; I was mesmerised by the sight of Omar standing over a hot stove stirring a pot. My initial reaction was to stand and stare until a feeling of guilt overcame me. The fact remained that I was a maid here, and I had been so caught up in my own emotional battle and instability that poor Omar had been left to prepare his own meals.

'Saira, does this look right? I am not sure if I have added all the right ingredients,' he asked, pointing down at the pot with that infectious smile he always wore. I looked into the pot to discover that he had prepared one of our native dishes, comprising a mixture of rice and lentils with added spices to enhance the flavour.

'It looks lovely,' I said. 'I will serve it now,' I told him as he walked towards Ammu's room. Secretly I added a little more turmeric, while I admired his initiative. Did his generosity never cease? I contemplated. I served up the khichri and walked into Ammu's room with three steaming plates.

'Looks delicious, Saira,' Ammu said.

'I can't take credit for this, Ammu, this is the handiwork of Omar,' I told her as he laughed.

'You have many talents, my dear,' she told him. I then encouraged her to eat, and I followed. To my surprise the khichri tasted exactly as I would have prepared it, and I wondered how he had managed to prepare this all by himself.

'Okay, so I have a confession to make,' Omar said, looking at Ammu, who was just as surprised as I was. 'I asked Layla to help me prepare the khichri,' he revealed. I smiled as Ammu began to laugh, with Omar now joining in.

'How are you feeling?' I asked, sitting close to her. I could tell she was having another severe headache. Swiftly I cleared away the plates and, when I returned to the room, the lights were turned down low as that appeared to ease the discomfort of her eyes. Omar then retired to bed; I knew he would be leaving early in the morning for a land-related meeting he needed to attend. Sitting beside her I prayed with conviction, asking God to make her better; even with the new medication I was beginning to see only a little improvement.

Chapter 14 – The Miracle that Never Came

The next morning I brewed tea and placed it on the table along with Omar's favourite snacks. My eyes were tired, and that weariness was accompanied by an aching body and a hurting head and heart.

'Morning, Saira,' Omar called, followed by, 'how is Ammu?'

'She struggled to sleep,' I said quietly. Prior to leaving he requested I contact him should we need anything, which I appreciated immensely. He had already helped me so much; how could I ever express my gratitude, so I did the only thing I had left. Along with Ammu I kept Omar in my prayers, hoping that his land dispute would be resolved, enabling him to hold on to his precious memories of his parents. I returned to Ammu who was now wide awake and perspiring. I rushed to her side immediately with a wet flannel to cool down her burning forehead. Worry and panic overtook me as I had never seen her this unwell before. It was almost as if she was physically, emotionally and mentally exhausted and had altogether given up on life itself. I deliberated about whether or not I should contact Omar, then realised I might jeopardise his important legal meeting.

Shortly after nightfall I heard the door open and secretly welcomed his return. Immediately he walked into our room smiling and greeted us.

'How is she?' he asked, looking in my direction. I informed him the medication was having little effect and that she had been perspiring with a fever for most of the day – all of which Ammu denied, stating that I was exaggerating. She continued to stubbornly insist that she was feeling well and did not require medical attention. Omar, exercising his own stubbornness, then firmly informed her that he would be contacting the doctor first thing in the morning whether she liked it or not, and I watched as she surrendered to his insistence.

I sat near the stove crying my heart out until I heard Omar's voice. 'I thought we could all have some tea,' he said, smiling.

'Yes, you're right,' I quickly replied, grabbing a pot and filling it with water to place upon the stove. We both sat next to Ammu drinking tea that night, while she was perched up on pillows. All the while I felt a deep anxiety in my stomach and throat that refused to leave, causing me to feel further unsettled and worried.

That night there was no laughter, only a few quiet polite exchanges and smiles, mainly from Ammu, almost as if she were vicariously living through us; I merely felt sombre with an underlying deep concern. I desperately wanted my old life back, where at least my beloved mother had been in the best of health; deep in my heart I knew that what had gone would never return. Omar retired to bed, advising Ammu to rest, and he directed a reassuring glance towards me. I remembered Hamid who was vile and did not possess an ounce of humanity, and was a depleted human being for that matter. In many ways he was accountable for our plight today. Then there was Omar who was kind, generous, and humble; words were not enough to praise him.

My attention diverted to the sound of Ammu's voice. 'Saira,' she called.

'Yes, Ammu,' I replied, expecting she might need something. Strangely enough she smiled, instructing me to open her closet, which I did. She then pointed towards a carrier bag that lay at the bottom of the cupboard. I recalled this being the same bag she would not allow me to carry while we were leaving our beloved home. This had been the bag she had held close to her through the journey here. She told me the bag held something precious that was meant only for me and that I should open the bag when the time was right. 'Ammu, how will I know when the time is right?' I asked with curiosity. 'Will you tell me when?'

'You will just know, dear,' she replied softly, with a beautiful angelic smile, and wished me goodnight. I stood still, captivated by what had just happened, and later lay in bed wondering what the bag held that was deemed so precious and meant for me. What had she meant by 'I will know'? What would I know? I figured perhaps Ammu was just extremely tired and delirious or perhaps the strong painkillers were causing some sort of hallucinations. I was tired and achy and very quickly surrendered to the call of my exhausted eyes.

Dawn was breaking through, and as usual my day began with the beautiful call to prayer; this time my prayer included both Ammu and Omar. I noticed Ammu was shivering in her sleep, so I wrapped her with a blanket and held her close to me. But when I touched her face she was burning hot with an extremely high fever. I immediately ran into the bathroom and got two wet flannels to place on her head. I was oblivious to the fact that Omar had followed me into the room after seeing me running across the house in a state of panic.

'What's wrong, Saira?' he asked with worry.

'I don't know, I don't know, she's hot, burning with fever, and not waking up. I don't know...' I replied hysterically. Omar immediately contacted the doctor for medical assistance. I felt a deep fear pierce through me, a fear so uncontrollable and fierce it was beginning to wither me away like melting wax on a burning candle. We must have sat with her for an hour before the doctor arrived to find Ammu almost unconscious. We both stood over him, anxiety ridden, frantically explaining what had happened overnight. She was still burning hot as the doctor examined her with a subdued look on his face that scared me witless. What had he discovered and what was wrong with my mother? The doctor then asked us both to be seated, and my heart began to pound at the thought of what he was about to divulge; I felt a lump in my throat finding it impossible to swallow. The doctor said it was vital for Ammu to be admitted to a hospital; I took shelter in the kitchen, standing against the wall, helpless.

I hadn't even realised that Omar was standing right behind me until he said, 'Saira, please, you have to stay strong for Ammu, she needs you right now. Come on, it's very important we listen to what the doctor has to say.' He stood strong and tall, towering over me as the resounding voice of logic. I took a deep breath, wishing away my tears, and walked behind Omar back into the room. I listened as the doctor reported Ammu's blood pressure to be uncontrollably high, accompanied with a high fever, as she lay semi-conscious, almost in a lifeless state. He informed us that she was physically so weak she would be prone to further complications, which was why she needed to be admitted right away for acute intensive treatment in hospital. His words felt like daggers piercing right through my heart. How could her health have deteriorated to this extent, this rapidly? Once again I felt the tears begin to flow and tried to suppress them to no avail. I sat next to Ammu, listening to Omar as he made arrangements for her to be admitted right away. He turned to me instructing me to pack a few of her things. The doctor then left, informing us that he would send an ambulance to collect Ammu and take her to Sylhet Town, which was the nearest hospital to us that had all the specialist facilities she needed.

I continued sitting next to Ammu, staring into her face, pleading with her to wake up.

'Saira, you heard what the doctor advised. Ammu needs treatment. You need to get a few of her things together, so that we can leave as soon as the ambulance arrives,' said Omar. Again he was right.

I silently kissed Ammu on her cheeks and whispered, 'It's okay, I will make you all better again.' This was something Ammu used to always say to me during my childhood whenever I was feeling unwell. Whenever I was sick as a child, Ammu would sit next to me rubbing balm on my forehead, my back and chest, and onto the soles of my feet. Today, here I was mirroring that same behaviour, only this time it was Ammu who was unwell and I would have given anything to trade places with her. I collected all her medication and packed some items of clothing to take along, and sat next to her waiting patiently for the arrival of the ambulance. I heard Omar's footsteps pacing along the front patio, and clearly sensed the stress and tension in his demeanour; he was worried just as much as I was as he stood against the grill gates, his eyes in search of the ambulance. I felt sick to the stomach as the fear of anything happening to my mother shook the foundation of my existence.

A short while later I heard a sweet angelic voice calling out. 'Saira...'

'Ammu, you're awake. How are you feeling?' I asked her.

'I'm feeling all right, just a little tired,' she said. I touched her forehead, which seemed a little cooler now. Then

I fetched her some water and painkillers and sat her up, enabling her to take small sips.

'Ammu, will you please eat something,' I said, elated to see her awake. Just then I heard Omar rush into the room, his face illuminated, almost like a starry night, upon seeing Ammu awake. He sat close to her, asking how she felt, and Ammu smiled back at him, saying she was feeling just fine. Omar informed us that the ambulance had been dispatched.

'Is everything okay, Saira? Why is there an ambulance arriving?' Ammu questioned, staring at us both. She was behaving strangely, completely oblivious to the fact that she was extremely unwell and could barely lift herself out of bed; she began coughing and spluttering.

'Ammu, you have been very unwell since last night,' I told her, softly touching her warm forehead.

'I am fine – you two worry too much about me,' she complained.

'No, Ammu, please listen to me.' I sat next to her and explained how her health had deteriorated, and that the doctor had advised that she be admitted.

She thought this was a travesty. 'Admitted to hospital?' She laughed. I was shocked that she was unable to comprehend the implications if she did not receive specialist treatment.

'Ammu, please, we will come with you. I promise I will stay with you, you have nothing to worry about,' I reassured her.

'Dear, I'm not worried at all, I am absolutely fine and I don't need to be in hospital. You and Omar are doing a wonderful job of looking after me here,' she said, looking at us both.

I pleaded with her. 'You don't understand, your blood pressure is high, anything could happen. You need to be stronger, that's why you need to be in hospital.'

'Saira, I will not go anywhere,' she said.

'Please, Ammu, I'm really scared and I just want you to get better.' I tried to reason with her.

'Saira, I will not go to a hospital and that is final. I like staying here, in this house, it's peaceful and I will be fine,' she said adamantly.

'Ammu, please,' I cried out.

'Saira, my dear, it's going to be okay.' She smiled, placing her arms around me while Omar stood and watched, speechless. I ran out into the courtyard unable to hold on to my many emotions: tears, pain, anger, confusion, all at the same time. I stood staring out onto the courtyard desperate for a way to convince Ammu to go to hospital. I was scared, scared of what consequences may lie ahead. I hoped Omar would be able to persuade her somehow, although I knew this would be nothing short of a miracle. I wiped away the beads of sweat from my forehead and turned to return to Ammu's room. Omar walked onto the patio looking subdued.

'What is it, what's wrong? Is she okay?' I panicked.

'It's okay, she's fine,' he quickly reassured me. 'Sit down a minute, Saira,' he instructed, which I did. 'Look, I have just been speaking to Ammu,' he continued.

'Did you convince her?' I asked hopefully.

He looked at me, stating that he had tried his best, even suggesting that she only attend for a check-up and return to sleep here for the night. Even then she remained adamant and determined that she would not leave this house, Omar said. I knew that Ammu, like myself, was headstrong, and once she had reached her decision, she would remain loyal to it come what may. 'Saira, I am confused about one thing. Why is

Ammu adamant about not wanting to leave this house? I will never ask her to leave,' he said. I knew all too well the pain Ammu felt and that inevitably it had a part to play in the state she was in today. I continued to stare at the floor, while the silence drowned out Omar's question entirely. 'Saira, what's wrong?' he repeated.

'I just want her to be in hospital, I don't want to risk anything happening to her, ever,' I replied.

'I completely understand what you're saying, but she has made her mind up and I think we have to respect that and start to think about how we can best look after her here,' he advised kindly. I nodded, trying to quell my emotions, but no matter how much I tried I was unable to eradicate them. I knew it would not be beneficial for Ammu to see me in this state, so I placed my hands together in supplication and conversed with my Lord, praying for strength to withstand this storm, and pleaded for the return of my mother's health. I walked back into her room only to discover her sitting there smiling. She pulled me closer to her, telling me not to worry and that everything would be okay. I smiled back in return at her, wondering where she was able to find this innate strength to pretend that all was well.

Gradually I made a start on dinner; nobody had eaten and I especially wanted Ammu to eat and regain some of that lost strength. The three of us sat side by side for dinner after what had been a trying day, while I gently encouraged Ammu to eat. She appeared weak and frail and complained of dizziness throughout the evening. I forced her to eat as much as she could tolerate and then tucked her into bed just as the shivers returned. I held on to her soft hands for reassurance, although all I wanted was to cry out in despair as nothing I did eradicated her pain or mine.

It was now late into the night, humid and sticky, and Ammu's fever had returned, this time with a vengeance it seemed; her entire body was burning hot as she drifted in and out of consciousness. I sat next to her for hours holding her hand, rubbing her feet, massaging her head, placing cool flannels on her forehead, and continuously prayed for her to make a full and complete recovery. I was petrified of what this dark night may bring. Omar opened the small windows of the room allowing cool air to circulate. I stared into Ammu's beautiful face and kissed her burning cheeks, while he sat beside her feet, mirroring my distress. I assumed seeing Ammu unwell like this was perhaps reminding him of unhealed wounds.

'Omar, get some rest,' I said to him.

'No, I am fine,' he said, fanning Ammu with a small handheld fan. I attempted to wake her many times, but she was unresponsive as if she were asleep. How ironic that the strongest person I had ever known was today lying here so physically weak and bed bound. Her bones felt brittle to the touch, her skin papery and translucent.

After a long and trying night, dawn finally arrived bringing with it the beautiful call to prayer. Little did I know that these were Ammu's last moments; like sand in an hourglass my beautiful, beloved, most precious person, my mother, had departed from us, falling forever into a deep sleep. While I sat holding her hand and Omar her feet, her body began to feel colder and colder as I continued grasping on to her life as tightly as possible. She had made the inevitable crossing from this realm into the next: the hereafter, departing from everything in this world, including me.

I struggled to breathe; I struggled for air and was just about able to sit next to her staring into her beautiful face. I heard Omar whispering to me that she had gone; he must have been unsure of whether or not I had accepted her sudden departure. I continued sitting close to her for the next few hours. We were now surrounded by daylight, but I felt captive in a darkness that encompassed my entire being.

Suddenly I noticed the entire room was full of people. I wanted to shout and demand that everyone leave and let her rest, only I was unable to speak. It was as if I had become paralysed. The room was filled with familiar faces, people I had been in contact with and seen around the village. Some were hugging me, while others touched my head and shoulders at which I flinched, and offered me words of condolence along with their prayers and blessings. A lady then attempted to remove my hand from Ammu's, but in retaliation I held on tighter. People had surrounded Ammu, leaving only her hand in sight. I began to feel disorientated, unable to comprehend the activity around me. I heard chatter about shrouding her body and arranging her burial. These words continued to ring in my ears as I sat frozen and shell-shocked. I wanted to tell everyone to leave her alone. I wanted Omar to tell everyone to leave, but he appeared to be delegating tasks to various different people.

A short while later I felt the warmth of somebody's hand on my arm. When I looked over I saw Layla standing there, reflecting my grief-stricken face in hers. She placed her arm around me, gently unlocking my hand from Ammu's, which I tried to prevent but was unable to muster the physical strength. I brought my hand up to my nose so I could continue to smell the sweet aroma of my beloved mother, as Layla walked beside me to another room away from everybody and away from Ammu. Layla sat me down on the bed, seating herself next to me. I wanted to shout and scream and cry, but nothing came out of my mouth. I wanted to demand that she take me back so I could stay near my mother, so that I could feel the touch of her skin upon mine once again. I wanted to ask everybody why they were determined to separate me from her. I sat on the bed fixated on one spot on the floor, while Layla sat close to me, only allowing a few people in at a time who wanted to personally pay their respects.

Chapter 15 - Departing with an Angel

Layla offered me some water, which I refused, shaking my head vigorously as I battled with my inability to speak. Just as twilight struck, between light and dark, Omar entered the room to find me sitting in the exact same position staring at exactly the same place. He asked Layla whether or not I had eaten, to which Layla answered, 'She hasn't eaten or drunk anything, neither has she spoken a single word.'

Omar stood in front of me while I continued to look down. 'Saira, I have just returned from Ammu's burial. Everything went smoothly and… the place where she is resting is close by. It's very peaceful there,' he said. 'I'm very sorry for your loss,' he continued. The word 'burial' replayed in my mind, ripping through the walls of my heart like a dagger, and all I could think about was my beloved mother all alone in the ground, beckoned by the will of the Almighty. I wanted to ask Omar why he had just left her there all by herself, as I thought about how lonely and scared she must be feeling. 'Saira!' I heard Omar shout my name and I flinched, looking up at him and then looked away.

'Omar, getting frustrated is not going to help,' Layla shouted back at him.

'Why will she not talk, Layla? She's shut down and not processing any of this.' I heard Omar and Layla continue talking about me as if I wasn't even in the room with them. It almost felt surreal, as my conscious mind debated whether or not all this was reality.

The night was dark, reflecting my myriad thoughts. No matter how much I tried I was unable to stop thinking about her face, her smell, her touch, and how within the space of one day and one night she had taken her last breath and was now in her humble abode along with my beloved Abbuji. All the local well-wishers and villagers had left now and a grotesque silence echoed throughout the entire house, giving substance to my cold reality.

'Saira, I need to leave now. I will be back in the morning,' Layla said, placing her arm around me as I clutched onto her warmth and nodded. She laid me down, leaving some water by my side, and left. I felt the ghastly silent roar of the house surround me like waves crashing into one another deep in the ocean, and sat up, immediately out of breath. I ran to take shelter in Ammu's room. Her bed appeared the same as I had left it that morning and the very few belongings she had lay scattered around the room. I picked up her shawl, bringing it up to my nose to inhale her fragrance some more. The entire room held precious memories of her: the place she used to sit, where she used to sleep, where she had prayed. Even the things she had touched today in the exact same place, only she was somewhere else, some place far away, and completely out of my reach. I stood in the centre of the room burying my head in her shawl, trying to preserve as much of her as I physically could.

'Saira, what are you doing in there?' I heard Omar's voice echo as he walked into the room. I put my hand up, gesturing for him to leave. 'If you need anything I'm here,' he said softly, and then unwillingly left the room. I lay down on Ammu's bed, recalling her voice around me as if it were melody to my ears, only to discover that it was the imagination of my subconscious mind. I lay thinking about her almost that entire night until my eyes closed and I surrendered my grief-stricken exhausted body to sleep.

The next morning I opened my eyes to find myself covered with a thin blanket; in my hand was Ammu's shawl and Layla was sitting next to me. I could hear the chatter of people and the devastating reality pierced right through my body, reminding me that my mother was no longer amongst us. I sat up to see that it was bright outside and figured that I must have been sleeping a while. I looked towards Layla, who smiled at me lovingly, informing me that almost everybody in the village had come by to enquire about me. Most of them had brought food and other items which they felt we may need. Omar walked into the room immediately, enquiring about me; Layla replied that I still had not spoken.

'Saira, please will you say something, you can't continue like this… it's not good for you,' he said to me. I continued to stare out through the window, mute, as some women entered the room. They hugged me, offering their heartfelt condolences, only this was not enough; nothing was and nothing would ever take away this ache in my heart. I desperately wanted her to return, I wanted to feel her touch and hear the sound of her melodic voice that I missed so much. The women left the room, discussing how I needed to process my loss. Was she just a loss? Because to me she was my everything: my heart, my world, my lifeline, my guardian angel, and without her I was unable to breathe or speak, so how could they expect me to process my loss. I wanted to scream out at the top of my lungs from the rooftop that to me she was so much more than just a loss. I spent most of the day in her room holding her shawl closely against the warmth of my chest, detesting myself for not doing more for her. Feeling responsible for her death; if only I had taken better care of her, if only I could have persuaded her to be admitted to hospital then today she would have been right here beside me. A thousand questions came into my mind one by one, causing internal chaos. I fell to the floor, weighed down with sorrow, and Layla rushed to my side calling Omar hysterically, telling him that I had fallen. Together they lifted me up off the floor and Omar instructed Layla to take me into another room. She sat me down in one of the front rooms.

Omar turned to me, saying, 'Saira, we are all so worried about you, you haven't eaten or spoken for almost two days now, and I don't know how to help you.'

'Saira, please, you need to speak or cry, please, just say something. We are both here for you,' Layla said, holding my hand.

'I can only imagine what you are going through, but please, you can't give up, not like this, you need to stay strong. Please just say something,' Omar continued. I remained quiet, unable to find the courage to speak, and brushed away the glass of water they offered me. I lay down, turning away from them both.

'Layla, do you think we need to call a doctor?' Omar asked with a deep concern in his voice.

'I think we just need to give her some time,' Layla replied. They continued to converse about how traumatised I must be feeling, so I closed my eyes in an attempt to drown out their voices, to no avail. Omar left the room and, just like the day before, Layla continued to sit beside me as he had instructed. She placed a blanket over my tortured body; perhaps she thought I was sleeping. Just then there was a gentle knock on the door so I kept my eyes closed in pretence. I heard the voices of more women who had come by to pay their respects. They crept over to look at my face, talking amongst themselves about how important it was for me to rest and eat. They had brought along enough food to last a few days and asked Layla to serve it to me when I woke.

As soon as they left the room I opened my eyes and recalled the time my beloved Abbuji had departed from us in a similar manner. Back then, just like today, almost everybody visited me and Ammu offering their condolences; many brought along gifts while others brought food and household items they thought we may require. Only today was more painful as I had nobody to shield me from the storm and, as the saying goes, 'When it rains it pours'. The person who protected me the most and who had been my shield and teacher and everything I had ever known was no longer in this world; she had departed for the next. My head began to feel extremely heavy and my throat became lumpy; I was filled with anxiety. I jumped out of bed and stood in front of the open window, gasping for air as the breeze brushed over my face.

'Saira, Saira, what happened?' I heard Layla shouting as she came towards me, with Omar following her.

'Layla, what's wrong?' he asked.

'I don't know, it was like she was struggling to breathe,' Layla informed him.

'Saira…' Omar said, looking at me. I closed my eyes, inhaling air deep into my stomach. 'Will you drink some water?' he continued, at which I shook my head. He turned to Layla saying he felt helpless.

'She really needs to drink something,' Layla continued. They were so preoccupied with my well-being, when all I wanted was to curl up into a ball and go someplace far away and never return.

It was almost afternoon and the day was hot. I pulled Ammu's shawl closer to my nose, taking in her fragrance with every breath I inhaled, while Layla watched me constantly saying that I should not upset myself like this. I heard the door again, followed by Omar's voice along with some others I assumed to be fellow villagers who had come again to enquire about me. I listened as they entered the room and closed my eyes in pretence of sleep, expecting a repeat of the previous mantra.

I felt a gentle touch on my hand that surprised me, a touch that I recognised almost instinctively, followed by a softly spoken meek voice saying, 'Saira.' Immediately I placed my hand in hers, standing up to look at her smiling face. I embraced her at once, crying my eyes and heart out into her chest as she lifted my head up, wiping away my tears one by one. I looked up at her unchanged face, just as it was when I had parted with her.

Sumayah was standing right in front of me along with Mesabji Chacha, who placed his gentle hand on my head, stating, 'Dear, you don't cry for the departed, you pray for them.' I began to sob inconsolably, holding on to both Sumayah and Mesabji Chacha.

'She's gone, Sumayah, she has left me all alone. She has gone, I couldn't make her better.' I continued sobbing. They sat me down, wiping away the tears. Sumayah brought me some water, forcing me to take sips, and I did find some relief from the surge of sadness in my heart.

Mesabji Chacha looked at me and said, 'Saira, dear, you have to stay strong. Just like your father, your mother was a wonderful person and she would dislike seeing you in this state. Have faith that she is dwelling peacefully within the beautiful gardens of Jannah. Now you must continue to live your life, if not for you then for your wonderful mother. Let her live through you.' He placed his hand over my forehead as if to bless me then left the room. I looked at Sumayah who smiled at me and then embraced me again.

'I still can't believe that she's gone. It feels surreal – how will I live without her, Sumayah?'

'You will find a way, I promise. God will guide you,' she explained. Slowly the darkness of the night was beginning to loom over us. Sumayah and I sat out on the patio sharing stories about Ammu for a while. I wondered how she had reached me here in this village. Sumayah told me how Omar had gone to visit Mesabji Chacha that afternoon, distressed by Ammu's sudden demise, and explained that I had become mute and had stopped eating and drinking altogether. Mesabji Chacha was extremely concerned upon hearing this news and went to Sumayah's parents to ask their permission for her to visit me here.

'How's the village?' I asked her with deep sadness. 'You remember the stream, Sumayah, and how we would sit there every evening with Ammu and our ginger tea. I can't stop thinking about her beautiful face,' I continued.

'I wish I could have seen her one last time,' Sumayah whispered, and I began crying uncontrollably again.

'Saira, please don't cry anymore,' she said, pleading with me.

'It's my fault, Sumayah. After we left our home she became so weak and unwell. I gave her so much tension and stress with everything that happened with Hamid – and her blood pressure had… I couldn't even look after her, what will I do now?'

'No, Saira, none of this is your fault, or even anything that happened before, nothing is your fault, do you understand that? You know they say God takes the people he loves the most and I bet she is now in Jannah with your Abbuji talking about how much they love you and want you to continue living and being happy,' she said.

I expected she was right; Ammu always had a soft spot for Sumayah. I recalled how she always put aside for her a portion of every meal we had. 'You know I longed to meet you again, I just didn't expect it to be in these circumstances,' I told her. The night was dark and warm with a soft breeze;

how ironic that Sumayah was sitting here with me and Ammu was sitting somewhere up in the heavens, where I guess we would meet again someday. With that thought in mind I stared up into the dark starry night.

'Saira,' Sumayah said, holding my hand as I turned to look towards her. 'Do you remember that saying of Ammu's?' she asked.

'Which one?'

Sumayah closed her eyes and said, 'The world is three days. Yesterday has perished along with all that was in it. As for tomorrow you may never see it. Today is yours and you must live it.' She opened her eyes and smiled.

I inhaled a deep breath, deep into my abdomen, understanding all too well the message she was giving me. 'Sumayah, I feel scared – I don't know how to live without her,' I said.

'Saira, you will be absolutely fine,' she replied, and we sat there together for a moment in reflection. 'Saira, will you do something for me?' she asked.

'Of course I will,' I replied.

'Do you promise?' she asked hesitantly.

'Without a doubt, I promise,' I reassured her.

'Will you eat something with me?' she asked innocently. I looked at her, now bound by my promise, and nodded as she smiled in approval. She walked to the kitchen and returned with two plates. I suspected that this was most likely part of Omar's master plan. Nevertheless I sat with Sumayah to eat my first meal in almost three days, and admittedly felt physically better for it. Sumayah and I laughed over how Ammu had always overfed us, serving us before herself. Everything about life reminded me of my mother, as though she were all around and immersed in me.

'Saira, I have to leave now,' Sumayah said.

'Of course, it is very late,' I replied. Mesabji Chacha, Layla and Omar joined us out on the front patio.

Chacha placed his hand on my head and said, 'My dearest Saira, your parents would be so proud of you today. Stay strong.' I nodded, thanking him for his support and kind words. Sumayah hugged me one more time as I clutched on to her tightly; tears had now made a comeback for a third time.

'No, Saira, don't. Promise me that you will look after yourself, promise me,' she said firmly.

'I promise,' I told her, thanking her for visiting.

'God willing I will see you again,' she whispered as I gradually slipped my hand out of hers.

I stood in the patio, watching as Sumayah and Mesabji Chacha disappeared into the darkness of the night, and closed my eyes, secretly thanking God for this sweet endeavour. I pondered the glimpse of hope they had resurrected – hope to continue living for my mother, as I was now also accountable to the promise that Sumayah had bound me to.

I sat out in the dark patio for some time, retreating into a state of mindfulness.

'Saira, I will need to go now. Do you need anything else? I will be back in the morning,' Layla said.

I turned towards her and said, 'Thank you Layla, I'm fine.' I sat watching Layla walk home into her cosy little abode sculpted out of mud; she had been so kind and affectionate towards me over the last few days, leaving her daughter with her husband for long periods just so she could look after me. I must remember to thank her, I thought. I looked at Ammu's shawl which I was still clinging on to and drew it tightly around me, indulging in her aroma as the cool breeze blew over my face. Just then I heard gentle footsteps approaching the patio.

'Can I get you anything, Saira?' Omar asked in a soft voice.

'Omar,' I said, turning to look at him, 'thank you for bringing them both here today. I appreciate it immensely,' I said, choking back tears.

'As long as you're okay, that's the most important thing,' he answered. I wished him goodnight and retired to bed. This was the hardest part: sleeping in Ammu's bed in her absence. I touched her clothes; everything lay intact, only she was missing, never to return. I lay in bed right where she used to sleep, taking in her sweet fragrance, sobbing into her empty pillow. Darkness and silence pervaded the entire house, leaving an irreparable hole in my heart and soul. I missed her with every bone in my aching body and with every breath that I took; I knew that nothing would bring her back. But I remembered my promise to Sumayah and placed my hands together in submission to the Almighty, and prayed with conviction that wherever my beloved mother may be, she may be surrounded with peace and tranquillity in her new abode.

The next morning I opened my eyes and turned to where Ammu used to sleep, and my subconscious mind attempted to enact what used to be that was no more. Then, memory by memory, the last few days flashed right before my eyes in various images and conversations. Seeing Sumayah yesterday had given me perspective and I knew she was right, I knew that deep down Ammu would want me to continue living. I prayed that one day we would meet again... in Jannah. I asked God to give me strength: to live, to breathe and to continue. I wanted to continue living and make my parents proud of me, although I found myself struggling with that notion on more levels than one. Ammu had been my guide, my direction, my shining light when all was dark, the one I turned to in times of joy and distress; she was the one who taught me to speak, to walk, to live. She taught me courage in defeat, strength when I felt weak, and told me to be brave when I was afraid. Everything I had become was due to her love and nurture – how could I continue without all these things? Paralysed, I stood near the open window; I hadn't been outside in the open air for what seemed like an eternity.

I walked into the kitchen – everything appeared different as if something was lacking or amiss. I felt suffocated, so I decided to take a walk out in the morning air, in search of a change of scene. I walked along the concrete path leading to the pond; although I had no reason to walk there at this time my feet took me there and my body followed. The pond appeared the same and I was greeted by familiar women who were preparing for their day ahead, who appeared bemused to find me there. I stood and stared into the water.

'Apa.' I felt a tug on my arm. I looked down to see the angel-faced boy standing next to me, smiling. Even though I had discovered that his name was Jamal, I much preferred to call him Angel Face. 'Apa, please don't be sad. God will look after your Ammu,' he said to me and I felt my eyes swimming in tears.

'Yes, you are right,' I told him as he hugged me tightly wiping away the visible tears on my cheeks. I stood and watched him playing in the water, laughing with the other children, full of life and joy as I once had been. The sun was now shining brightly over the pond and the entire village, making everything sparkle. I pondered how the village had remained the same; only my perspective and outlook were different. I turned to walk towards the concrete path leading back to the house. Many people were out and about now; some were transporting cattle, some were washing pots, and some women were washing their laundry. This picture made me realise that life still continued for everyone, apart from me. I felt trapped between yesterday and today and was unable to muster the courage to go on to tomorrow, just as Sumayah had said I should.

I spent the next few weeks in an almost lifeless state, deeply introverted, as if I was being taught how to live all over again. But this time my teachers were Omar and Layla as opposed to my beloved mother.

Chapter 16 – Untold Revelation

A few weeks later

The morning was filled with a cool breeze as I enjoyed my walk, taking shade near the big pond to watch the children play, engrossed in laughter and happiness. I smiled as splashes of water fell onto my face and arms and I took in the rays of sunshine beating down. Just as I was about to walk back to the house, a group of local women approached me to enquire about how I was coping. They clearly had a set of pre-planned questions, to which I said nothing. I stared at them vacantly. It was as if their words were daggers that did nothing but refresh my unsung pain. The women then walked towards the pond and I began to walk away. Their words as they continued to talk amongst themselves reached my ears almost immediately, halting my steps right where I was standing. I heard them talking about me, saying that I was now a vulnerable, young, unmarried woman living under the same roof as an unmarried man. I heard another lady join in to add that this was not ideal for my reputation, especially now I no longer had a guardian to protect my chastity from disrepute. Their cruel gossip hit the epicentre of my already emotional mind, sending me to the edge of despair. My hands trembled and my legs wobbled beneath me, while my vision became blurred. Little did these women know that I was already a product of disrepute – a woman scorned – and in the eyes of society I was no longer a woman of integrity. I gasped for air, almost running into the kitchen, bumping into Omar with a loud thud.

'Saira, Saira, what happened?' I heard him shouting. He sat me down and told me to breathe slowly. After a few minutes my vision gradually cleared and my breathing returned to normal. My palpitating heart began to slow down as I found myself sitting in the kitchen next to Omar, who had now summoned Layla to my assistance. Omar brought me over a glass of water while Layla placed her hand on my shoulder, asking what had happened. Confused about the entire incident, I explained that I had gone for fresh air; then suddenly I began to recall the incident and stopped talking – I did not want to tell them about the scandalous gossip I had been subjected to.

'Why did you go alone, Saira?' Omar said. 'Layla, please take Saira inside to rest while I call the doctor,' he instructed.

'I'm all right now, there is no need for a doctor,' I said adamantly.

'I will not negotiate about this, Saira,' he said with an intense look in his eyes. Layla held my arm and led me out of the kitchen. She encouraged me to lie down while she enquired about whether or not I had eaten anything. When I told her I hadn't she looked at me with disapproval, reminiscent of the exact look that Ammu would have given me. She brought me some juice and dhal soup. I could not stop thinking about the gossip that was slowly spreading, echoing through my system and evoking further questions.

I began to eat the soup to avoid any more questions from either of them. In my mind I continued to debate whether or not those women had been correct; the fact of the matter was that I was a young woman living with an unmarried man who was no relation to me except through the unfortunate circumstances that had led me and Ammu to this house. My heart skipped a beat at the thought of Hamid;

technically we were separated although I knew that he and his family would never give up their search until they found me and summoned me back to the abhorrence I had escaped from. I glanced around the grand house complete with its grand furniture and pondered how much longer I could continue to live here like this. People would begin to gossip and slander me, raising questions about my chastity and dignity. I knew all too well about the mentality of people in our villages, especially regarding the reputation of a young woman. The harsh reality was that I no longer had anybody to call my own and I needed to accept this. I asked God not to attach my heart to something that was not mine, especially this house and my life here. The short time I had spent here with Ammuji had created a bond to this house and to this village. I knew I had to rid my mind of this short-term arrangement, just as I knew that to continue living here like this was an illusion and my reality was someplace far away. How long would it be before Hamid connected the dots and traced me to this house? I questioned. The fear of Omar becoming entangled in this horrific maze sent shivers down my spine.

Just then I heard the doctor arrive. He entered my room accompanied by Omar and Layla and I quickly gathered my scattered thoughts. 'Assalamualaikum,' I greeted him politely. Omar paraphrased the events that had taken place over the last few weeks, finishing by informing him about this morning. The doctor was friendly, smiling at me, and then performed a full examination. He asked me a few questions regarding my health and then turned to Omar and Layla. He concluded I had been traumatised by the loss of my mother, and that it was essential for me to avoid any further stress and tension. I sat quietly whilst Omar walked the doctor out, thanking him repeatedly.

Omar returned to the room and looked at me. 'Please, Saira, you really need to start looking after yourself, if not for you then for Ammu's sake.' I looked at him and then looked away.

'Saira, you rest for a while,' Layla told me, and they both walked out of the room.

For the next few days I was under strict orders to only rest and eat. At times I wandered aimlessly around the house, lost in deep thought. Whenever I offered to help Layla with anything, I had them both to contend with. One evening after dinner I sat in my room unable to sleep. Layla had gone home for the day and Omar had retired to bed. I suddenly felt a rush of anxiety and began to walk around the room, wrapping Ammu's shawl around me, immersing myself in her fragrance; I missed her so much, beyond any reason or explanation.

Some days I wanted my heart to stop beating just so I could gain control over my thoughts. I recalled the nasty words of those women at the pond and began to contemplate to what extent they may have been correct. That night I lay in bed for a few hours, ruminating over everything that had happened, and wondered where my life would take me next. I knew that the change I needed to implement was to depart this house, to which I had no real connection. I figured that if today a few ladies were gossiping, perhaps tomorrow the entire village would imply something similar if not far more sinister. I cared very little about my own reputation but felt a huge amount of respect for, and gratitude towards Omar; he was well respected and was a role model in this village and community. The last thing I wanted was for anyone to raise questions about his integrity and reputation, especially because of me. Most of all I needed to protect him from Hamid.

Early next morning the sound of something pelting towards the front of the house woke me so suddenly that I immediately climbed out of bed as the noise became louder and more repetitive. This was an unfamiliar sound at this time of the morning so I began to walk down the corridor as fast as I could, only to find that objects were being thrown into the house through the gates of the front patio. At first I figured it was children playing, but when I stepped onto the patio it was almost as if I had walked onto a battlefield; there was an angry crowd of villagers I had not seen before who were hurling abuse as they threw stones at me. I raised my hands up to my face in defence. I stood, confused, and a stone struck my hand and my cheek. I cried out in pain and fell to the floor.

A woman shouted, 'There she is, she needs to be punished, it's a good job the fisherman informed us about her real identity.'

'She has defamed her own village and has now come to do the same to ours,' shouted another villager, and the rest of them cheered on in agreement: 'Hear, hear.'

I was terrified. I knew all too well that word had finally reached this village and they had discovered the reason I had been exiled. Many times I had heard that the punishment for women who had brought about shame and defamation was to be stoned to death or set alight, which had happened to a young girl who lived in a nearby village who had decided to marry against her elders' wishes. I had not thought this would be my fate until I stood with blood dripping from my injured hand. I closed my eyes in surrender to my fate of being returned to Hamid and his horrific family, while the evil cursing continued. I had no one left to protect me, and so I prepared myself to face this wrath.

'Stop, stop this madness right away!' I startled at the sound of an angry voice. Omar grabbed me by the hand and quickly placed me behind his body, acting as a human shield as the shouting of the angry crowd continued. 'Stop this or I will have you all removed from my property,' he shouted back in retaliation, as he protected me with one arm and addressed the crowd with the other.

'She has brought shame to our village and needs punishment. You should not be harbouring her in your house,' shouted a villager.

'Leave my property or I will have you escorted off if need be – and stay away from her,' Omar said aggressively, but they continued. I stood embarrassed and ashamed at the state I had been reduced to.

'Who are you to be harbouring this wretched woman in your home?' came a high-pitched voice that made me tremble in fear. My instincts had been correct and, when I looked up, Amma was standing right in front of me, leading the villagers. 'How are you related to this wretch, may I ask?' she demanded of Omar, moving closer to me, screwing her face up all the more. I began to hyperventilate and my hands shook with fear at the mere thought of Hamid and Amma and being escorted back to that place again.

'Whoever I may be, I don't feel I need to justify that to you,' he shouted back at her, now standing between Amma and me as a shield.

'She hasn't informed you that she is married to my son, which means I have every right to take her back and that's what I am here to do.' Amma laughed in his face.

'Well, if you want to take her back you will have to go through me,' Omar replied in fury, holding me behind him now, much to the roars of disapproval from the watching crowd.

'What relation do you have with her that you're going to stop me? She is my daughter-in-law, and little did I know that she has been living here with another man,' Amma screamed at the top of her voice, defaming me all the more.

Omar then turned around to address the crowd of villagers. 'Did you know that it is illegal to demand dowry, and this lady has been demanding unreasonable amounts of dowry from Saira, consequently making her life miserable? I have heard that the police are treating such cases with special care and handing out punishments to people who demand monetary items in the form of dowry. In my opinion I think this lady should be handed over to the police. What do you all think?'

The entire crowd went quiet until one lady spoke very timidly. 'We all have daughters and demanding dowry is wrong and she needs to be punished.' This was then repeated by many other villagers.

'Omar, we trust you to hand her over to the police,' shouted an elderly wise man, much to Amma's protests. Omar then suggested the crowd disperse, which they gradually did. I stood on the patio barely breathing beside Omar; Amma was furiously staring at us both.

'How dare you lie?' she said scornfully to him.

'How dare you come to my village and my home and threaten Saira like this? You heard what the villagers said – they want me to hand you over to the police, and I am sure you have heard the punishment for people who demand dowry these days,' he told her.

'You wretch of a woman,' Amma spat at me as I held my hands up to cover my face.

'That's enough.' He intervened, guarding me with his body. 'Leave this village right now, and if I ever see you here again or anywhere near Saira, I will personally hand you over to the authorities,' he warned. At once Amma frowned and walked away, much to my relief. Omar closed the grill gates and guided me into the kitchen, where he washed my bloodstained wrist. He then handed me some ice to place on my swollen cheek that was slowly turning from blue to purple. I stood shaking in disbelief and shock.

'It's okay, Saira, you're safe now. I won't let anything happen to you,' he assured me. I was unable to make eye contact with him; what was I to tell him? I was embarrassed more than anything. How could I possibly explain what had just happened? I took some deep breaths as he handed me some water with a couple of painkillers. 'These will help, Saira,' he said softly.

I looked at him and said, 'I'm terribly sorry for all this, it is entirely my fault.'

'You have nothing to feel sorry about,' he said steadily.

'Will you not ask…' I began to say, hesitantly.

'I need no explanation or justification from you, Saira. You stay here, while I go and speak with those unreasonable people,' he said, and left.

I was terrified, thinking of what may have occurred had Omar not intervened. The audacity of these villagers devastated me and I cried out in pain and despair. If only Ammu was here. 'She would know just what to do,' I cried out.

Omar returned a short while later to find me sitting in the same spot he had left me in. 'Are you okay?' he asked. 'Does it hurt?'

'I'm okay, thank you,' I replied.

'They won't bother you anymore, Saira. I assure you, they are just a minority. I promise to keep you safe here,' he said with assurance, and retired to his room.

This ordeal had only strengthened my belief that leaving this house was what I needed to do. With that thought in mind I began to pack the very few belongings I had. I planned to talk with Omar and explain my concerns to him prior to leaving the next morning. I began by collecting a few of Ammuji's items that were still scattered around the room and placed them carefully into a bag; these items held myriad precious memories that I wanted to preserve until my last breath. I then opened her cupboard carefully and her aroma hit me like a gust of fresh air. I closed my eyes, momentarily wishing away the horrific memories of today.

I noticed the carrier bag still lying on the bottom shelf and picked it up curiously. As soon as I touched it I recalled her exact words the night before her sudden demise. I remembered how she had told me that she had left a bag which contained something of mine in it. I recalled how she had told me that I would know when to open it. I held the bag in my hand, perplexed by the secrecy of it. It began to feel as if she knew she would not be around, hence she had left behind a precious keepsake. I wondered whether or not I should open the bag, as she had specifically mentioned that I would know when the time was right. I wondered what she had meant and what may have been going through her mind at the time.

After an internal deliberation, the option of opening the bag won. My initial reaction was a gasp of awe, followed by sobs. As I held up the ivory gown, the scattered shiny golden stones and beads sparkled across the ceiling and walls of the entire room. I held it up in admiration. Its beauty was still intact, just as it had been when Ammu presented it to me the very first time, just before my Nikkah to Hamid. It was the very same dress that my Abbuji had gifted to her for her Nikkah, which they then gifted to me for mine. At the bottom of the bag lay the antique gold coloured necklace, with its many sparkly stones lighting up the room with their beauty, which Ammu had purchased herself. I sat and sobbed at the evidence of my mother's love for me. I recalled how she had carried this bag close to her chest when we had left our beloved home, Jahed Pur; little did I then know the depths of her maternal love. Her love was so unconditional that even when she became bed bound, she had not forgotten this bag and managed to tell me about it. A few weeks into my marriage to Hamid I had sent the gown to Ammu for safe keeping, as the extended relatives had begun to take a liking to it. I knew that Ammu would be the best person to preserve this dress for me just the way she had been doing all these years. I wondered if perhaps she had known that God was calling her. I did not know what use I would have for this gown now, though, apart from as another memory for me to cherish.

The house was unclean, with fluttering cobwebs in almost every corner as I hadn't dusted for a long time, so I planned to clean and dust prior to leaving the next morning. I woke early to find all my bags still intact in the corner of the room. I began with prayer, submitting all the worries I held deep within me to God Almighty, and in return asked for courage, strength, patience and peace. The new path I was about to embark on today, I knew, would involve great difficulties and tribulations. I would bid farewell to this house and be alone once again, with no abode and no destination, just courage, strength, patience and an immensely strong faith in God to make everything well once again.

Dawn had passed now, giving way to daylight; another beautiful day as the sun shone upon the entire village. I listened for one final time as the sleeping village gradually came to life; sounds of people, cattle, birds, children singing and the fresh smell of soil under the open blue skies of my native land. Today I had woken with a great purpose. I recalled my goal for the day and began to dust all the rooms one by one, beating out all the cobwebs. I then scrubbed the floors with soap and water until they were immaculate and shiny. Just then Omar walked into the kitchen to find me vigorously scrubbing the stove.

'Morning, Saira,' he said softly.

'Morning,' I replied, full of self-motivation.

'How's your hand?' he asked, looking at my bandaged wrist.

'It's fine,' I replied. He walked away with the look of disapproval on his face. I prepared breakfast for him, a task that I had not undertaken for some time, and recalled how he used to sit with Ammu at this time of the morning immersed in conversation, and how much I used to enjoy listening to their chatter filled with laughter and happiness. I continued to tidy the rest of the house while Omar wandered around aimlessly, and neither of us broached the subject of the previous day's ordeal. It was as if we were both attempting to erase it from our minds altogether.

It was nearly midday and the sun was shining brightly into the kitchen, gleaming all over the tiled floor, pots and utensils. I thought now would be the best time to leave, as I would need to find somewhere to sleep for the night. I felt a deep surge of sadness overtake me. I was sad to leave – devastated to part with the memories of my mother that were embedded deeply into the concrete walls of this house. One by one I recalled all that had happened here, the things she had said, the places where she had walked. I thought of the dinner table and how the three of us would congregate here every evening telling stories about our lives. I locked away the memories deep within my heart, which was now almost like a deep ocean filled with secrets waiting to be discovered. I took a walk to the front patio and glanced around. I saw Layla collecting water in a kholosh with sticks in the other hand, as Khadijah walked beside her, amused by the splashes of water on the ground. I intended to say goodbye to her and wanted to thank her for all she had done for me over the last few days; after all, I was a complete stranger to whom she had shown loyal support when I had needed it the most.

I walked into the room that was mine and Ammu's and touched the place she used to sit, almost as if I could still smell her. I exhaled, feeling lost and abandoned, I knew that my life needed to continue, but in which direction? I felt I was in an emotional spiral, slowly losing control. I carried my packed bags into the kitchen, carefully placing them near the back courtyard door and taking a final look around while I searched for Omar. I sat on a chair, staring down at the shiny tiles, oblivious to the fact that he had walked in.

'You've sorted through Ammu's clothes – you should have asked me to help,' he said in a soft voice.

I looked at him, bewildered, and said, 'It's not just Ammu's clothes.' He looked perplexed. 'I have been meaning to speak to you all day,' I began and he sat down immediately, giving me his undivided attention.

'Of course you can talk to me, Saira.' I began to feel guilty: a guilt that was beyond any level of comprehension. 'These bags are my belongings, Omar. I can't thank you enough. Even if I was to thank you a million times it would not express how grateful I am to you. Everything you have done for Ammu and me since we have been here… I deeply appreciate it and will never be able to repay you for any of those things. Especially what you did yesterday – I will never forget that and will remain forever indebted to you, but I have decided to leave this house, this village, today,’ I said, choking back tears.

I saw an array of emotions displayed across his innocent face, beginning with confusion, then fear, some anger, and then pain. ‘Leaving, why? Where to and why so suddenly?’ He stood up.

I collected my bags and turned away from him, while I fastened my hijab tightly around my face. ‘It’s time for me to leave. What happened yesterday was not fair on you, and I don’t want to defame you anymore.’

He was now standing in front of me, looking angry, and I avoided eye contact with him. ‘Where will you go?’ he asked in a stern voice.

‘I don’t know yet,’ I answered. I knew that he was hurt by my ungrateful behaviour although that had never been my intention.

‘Saira, do you really think I would let you just walk out of here? How would I ever face Ammu?’ he continued.

‘I am sorry. I know I should have given you more notice to find another maid, but I really think this is for the best,’ I said, almost sobbing.

‘A maid,’ he scoffed to my surprise, ‘you think this is about finding a maid?’ I stood in submission allowing him to have his moment. ‘I’m sorry, I’m being rude. I just… I just can’t understand why you want to leave like this, where will you go? Have I done something to upset you?’ he asked in a gentle voice.

‘Omar, no, please – you have done no such thing. But this isn’t right. How long can I continue living here like this? We share no relation and the entire village is against me and is spreading malicious gossip, and I don't want to cause any further harm to your reputation.'

He was angry; standing up immediately he placed his hands up to his head in distress.

'Omar, you live abroad, you don't know the culture of the village and the mentality of the people here. I don't care what they say about me, honestly, it makes no difference, but I don't want anyone to raise questions about your integrity and reputation, which is why the best solution is for me to leave,' I explained to him.

'Saira, you're wrong, no one has the right to question your integrity and reputation either,' he said calmly.

'Omar, unfortunately this is part of the culture and traditions of us villagers,' I told him and began to walk out.

'Saira, wait,' he called from behind. 'So they are gossiping because we don't share any relation, right? That does not bother me whatsoever, but I can see that it is affecting you. So what if you were to continue living here in this house as co-owner of this house, as my wife?' I turned to look at him, aghast. I didn't know if this was some sort of a joke, although the expression on his face was serious.

'Omar please, I don't expect a gesture that grand from you, this is absurd,' I told him.

'Saira, look at me. I am serious. I want you to become my life partner, my wife, my best friend, I want us to build a life together,' he continued. I stood still as if held captive as his prisoner. My mind travelled back to how Ammu and I had been ousted from our beloved home by the villagers who had raised questions about my chastity. Ironically, history was now repeating itself, and who knew what the consequences would be this time? I recalled my short-lived marriage to Hamid and what had followed from there. Omar knew nothing about me or my history and all the skeletons I came with, and I wondered how he would react should he discover the whole truth. I questioned whether he would still feel the same and still be determined to commit his life to me. 'Saira,' he said, bringing my attention back to reality.

'Omar, I thank you from the very bottom of my heart for this wonderful, kind gesture, but there are so many things that you don't know about me, about what's happened with Hamid and his family,' I told him.

'I don't care about the past, and nothing you tell me will make a difference.'

'It will, Omar, it will, I have done so many things that…' I continued, now distressed.

'What did you do? You didn't return to Hamid and his evil-minded family because you wanted to protect yourself. None of that was your fault and the fact that you were both made to leave your home just because of small-minded villagers is disgusting,' he blurted out. I turned my face away from him, feeling ashamed that he had discovered my innermost secrets, feeling bare and vulnerable. 'Saira, please believe me, none of that matters to me,' he said softly, attempting to convince me further.

'Please, Omar, I am not the person that you think I am. I'm tainted and ill fated,' I reiterated.

'Shush,' he said holding his hand up. 'No, you're not, you're pure and more than enough for me.'

I wiped the tears from my face and asked him firmly, 'How do you know everything?'

'The day I asked Sumayah and Mesabji Chacha to come and visit he appeared hesitant about bringing Sumayah here. When I asked why, he told me everything.' I stood in silent awe, unable to find any words. 'Saira, please believe me, none of that makes a difference to me. I want to marry you for the person that you are,' he said, looking at me. We sat down and an awkward silence encompassed the entire room. 'Can I suggest something?'

'Yes,' I replied. He said he realised I must be in shock and that decisions such as these should not be made lightly. He suggested I sleep there that night and take some time to think, and give him my decision the next day.

'Look, Saira, I don't want to force you into anything, and if your answer is no, then I am willing to accept that, too, and I will happily escort you wherever you want to go,' he said. He took my bags back into the room and then went to his. I sat in contemplation for a while, trying to comprehend what had just unfolded. Times such as these I needed my mother, who would have known just what to do; this was one of the most important decisions of my life and I craved support and her much-needed guidance. I had been prepared to leave this house, and instead had received a proposal of marriage. My emotions were in turmoil.

Omar spent a while in his room. I procrastinated about whether or not I should check to ensure he was all right, then turned away from his door silently. I made a start on dinner, setting out two places, and the cold reality once again ripped through my heart. My mind was heavy with many conflicting thoughts running wild, only increasing my emotional burden. I knocked on Omar's door to let him know that dinner was ready and sat at the table as he joined me shortly after. He appeared subdued and preoccupied with his own internal battle.

'Saira, you're not eating,' he said. I was holding a spoon and staring at it. I looked at him and took some sips of water to allow my blood to circulate oxygen around my body. 'Look, Saira, I'm sorry if I said anything out of line before. If I have upset or offended you then please forgive me,' he said in a soft, apologetic tone of voice.

‘No, you haven’t,’ I replied firmly and began to eat. He had known the innermost secrets of my life and still continued to only want the best for me, without a doubt, without pausing to think about what the consequences would perhaps be for him and his reputation. He was truly the definition of inspirational. We sat mostly in silence throughout dinner, both of us slightly uncomfortable amidst the awkward silences and pauses in the little conversation we engaged in. In my grief I had completely forgotten to enquire about what had transpired regarding the dispute over his father’s land. ‘Omar, I’m sorry, I completely forgot to ask about your land issues, are they sorted?’ I asked him.

‘No, they are not, the official papers are still being processed,’ he replied, quite obviously worried about it all. I cleared away the dishes and left Omar in the kitchen drinking tea. I wished him goodnight and retired to bed. It had been a long, tiring and eventful day and the soles of my feet were aching. I was exhausted but sleep was probably the furthest thing from my mind, which chose to remain alert. I sat near where Ammu used to sit, battling with the internal dilemma I now had to contend with.

Chapter 17 - Crossing the Distance

I sat in thought, reminiscing about how we would wrap up in thick woollen blankets to escape the chill of the Grishmo nights and drink warm ginger tea to warm our cold bodies. I opened my cupboard and took out my most prized possession: my beloved Abbuji's prayer mat. I had preserved it all these years, only bringing it out when I missed him terribly and wanted to feel his presence close to me. I placed it on the floor, inhaling the musky aroma of the perfume I recalled him rubbing onto his wrists and cheeks almost every morning, perfume which he would then rub onto mine. Both of us would then laugh for ages, and Ammu would wonder what the joke had been. In response, Abbuji would tell her that it was a special joke between father and daughter. I sat on the mat in submission, relieving myself of the burden within. I asked for guidance and entrusted my utmost faith in God to show me the path that was best suited for me. My faith remained immensely strong and I knew that whichever path I was destined to walk, that would be the one deemed best for me. Sitting here like this brought me hope, happiness and a feeling of contentment, and I liked the notion of my parents dwelling together peacefully in the gardens of Jannah, holding hands side by side in eternal bliss.

I then thought of Omar; in many ways he resembled my father. He was kind, loyal, humble, liberal minded, successful, extremely handsome and always wanting to do good for others; he had a heart of gold. He had strong faith in himself and somehow managed to elevate the people around him, especially me. Everybody in the village had immense respect for him and the majority had even asked for his hand in marriage for their daughters at some point; it seemed he was the most eligible bachelor in this village as well as the surrounding ones. I lay down my heavy head as my imagination continued to flit between my deserted home and the one I was lying in right now. I desperately sought clarity, but it wouldn't come. I needed to reach a decision, a solution. I knew Omar was a good person – how could he not be? He had arranged my mother's funeral so assiduously, allowing me to do nothing but grieve and, even when I had become mute, he summoned Sumayah, bringing hope back into my life to enable me to continue living. The way he protected me through the unexpected appearance of Hamid's mother was incomparable. Inexplicably, he brought happiness, hope, growth, guidance and strength into my life, be it through words or actions. It was like the morning sun rising out of darkness bringing with it a new day, a new experience, a new moment and a new ray of hope.

One by one I began to collate and recall the many tragedies I had battled with. The first one being the dreaded night I had escaped via the bamboo bridge, which it later transpired was my very first encounter with Omar. The second was being ousted from our home before Omar had employed us as his maids. I reflected on the way he showed us hospitality throughout our stay here, treating us more like family members than employees, and the unprecedented way he had cared for Ammu, paying for her treatment, ensuring she had eaten, taking her for walks and making her smile with his presence alone. Throughout her last moments it was Omar who had sat beside her taking care of her as if she was his own mother. All through my grief, he had stood strong beside me, wishing me well and supporting me in the best way he knew. We had shared many moments of both joy and sadness, through which we had stood side by side as one another's strength and courage. In my moments of darkness he had been the one to show me the light. In many ways we had formed a bond: a bond that was based on concern for one another, a bond based on humanity. Only today this bond was in question; my existence in his house and in his life was in question. Today societal expectations required a name, a definition of this bond, and perhaps marriage was the most appropriate course of action for us both. Perhaps this had been the reason that fate allowed Omar and me to join our paths at a time of calamity, intertwined so unimaginably that departing from one another would be a challenge in itself. I wondered if perhaps this was all part of my destiny, and if this was God's subliminal way of telling me that Omar was meant only for me.

I thought about the way Ammu had interacted with him; he seemed to elevate her with his presence alone. She was always so happy and comfortable around him, and even missed him in his absence. She cared for him as she had cared for me. My mind then halted – and I questioned why she had told me about the gown the very night that she had passed away and what significance this held. Did it mean that perhaps she had known that she would be gone, and I wondered if this was another coincidence, or again was it fate unfolding my destiny? I wondered if Ammu had known all along and she had already granted her blessings to this alliance; perhaps that was why she and Omar had a connection almost from their first meeting. I contemplated how my beloved Abbuji longed for me to be able to live a life away from the cultural and societal expectations that were imposed upon women in our village. He was a strong, courageous man and if he were with me I knew his very words would have been, 'My dear Saira, follow your heart and be happy.' He always taught me and Sumayah that when choosing a life partner, you should always look at two characteristics: a person's character and their manners. In this case, those words were befitting for Omar, as he possessed qualities and mannerisms that were both praiseworthy and impeccable. The deeper I thought the more my mind and heart surrendered to the idea of binding my life to Omar. I had never contemplated becoming betrothed to him, hence the mere thought overwhelmed me.

Dawn was almost here so I decided to go to the place that had given me the clarity and perspective I was in dire need of today. I quietly climbed out of bed and went out through the kitchen door, carefully unlocked the green gates and went up to the rooftop balcony and stared over the white picket fence and everything beyond it. I looked over the front of the house onto the pond, the line of trees and the greenery beyond. The sunrise was beautiful and I watched the black sky give way to yellow, orange, red, white, and then blue. It was so full of light, renewing my belief in the saying 'The darker the night the lighter the day'. A new day had begun, ironically reflecting the start of something new and perhaps extremely beautiful. I closed my eyes, immersing myself in the dewy, morning-fresh air. Just then the beautiful early morning call to prayer made its mark, harmoniously resounding through the entire village. It took my breath away as ever, only this time it was further confirmation that I had reached a clear and correct decision. With that thought in mind I opened my eyes to embark on the journey of a lifetime with one single step. I climbed back down and went into the house. Splendid is the sun that never ceases to rise, out of its dedication and commitment to the Earth. Similarly I should perhaps dedicate and commit myself to Omar.

I stepped into the kitchen knowing that this decision would now shape and contour my existing life and what was yet to come. I also knew that whether or not this decision would bring me joy was a gigantic question in itself, one that I was unable to articulate at this point.

I must have been standing lost in thought for a short while, when I heard a softly spoken, 'Morning, Saira.'

'Morning,' I replied, pushing away the strands of hair that were covering my face.

'You look tired, did you sleep well?' he asked, evidently concerned. 'Are you feeling unwell again?' he continued.

'No, I am feeling fine, thank you,' I replied, turning away so that I could conceal my tired-looking appearance from him. I began to occupy myself with cooking breakfast. My entire body felt tense at the thought of Omar approaching me about my decision before allowing me to conjure up the courage to speak to him about it independently. To my surprise he spoke no more and chose to stand outside on the back patio looking ahead into the intricate maze of trees. I looked at him, observing his subdued expression. The sun shone brightly onto the contours of his face, illuminating the twinkle in his eyes as I continued to stare, mesmerised, until I noticed his forehead crease with apparent lines of worry. I disliked seeing him distressed or upset as we shared a mutual concern and respect for each other, and perhaps in many ways this was the solid foundation that was required in order for us to continue forward on this journey together as one.

'Breakfast is ready, Omar,' I said to him, stepping out onto the hot patio floor. He sat himself at the table, clearly immersed in a world of his own. I took a deep breath, right into my gut, and attempted to conquer my fear of the conversation that was the deciding factor in our combined fate. 'Omar,' I said, and then paused.

'Saira, take a seat.' He pointed to a chair opposite him. I sat down, almost unable to breathe. 'I spent most of last night thinking about everything: what you said, the time I have spent here, and the… I think you're right about what you suggested.' I was speaking in a jumbled and confused manner. He appeared a little unsettled and fidgety, as perhaps I wasn't articulating exactly what I had planned to say. 'I only have one request, if you're agreeable,' I continued.

'Of course, Saira, anything you want,' he said with a determination in his voice.

'I, erm… would like a very small ceremony and would like for Mesabji Chacha to conduct our Nikkah, and Omar I don't want anything from you, if you're happy with those things,' I asked.

'That is absolutely fine, whatever you need.' He smiled reassuringly. There was an awkwardness between us following the dreaded conversation, which continued throughout breakfast.

I began to clear the dishes when suddenly I heard, 'Saira,' and I turned to find Omar standing in front of me with a fearful expression upon his face. 'Are you positive about this?' he asked.

'Absolutely,' I assured him, and smiled.

Chapter 18 - Nikkah

I swept the front patio, which appeared to be in great need of a deep clean as the dust flew up into the air, sticking to my sweaty face. I heard laughter through the grill gates of the courtyard and could just about see Layla throwing a ball into the air, playing with her daughter. This made me smile and I immediately thought of Ammuji and Abbuji; how much I missed and longed for them.

'Saira, Saira,' I heard Omar call out to me. 'What's wrong?' he enquired. I was completely oblivious to the fact that I was sitting down on the patio, dust covered, holding a broom. 'What's happened, did they come back?' he asked as he stood me up and guided me to a chair. I sat down and Omar brought me a glass of water and offered me his handkerchief. 'Take a sip, it's okay,' he said gently as I wiped away my tears. We sat in silence for a few minutes and he handed me the glass of water again, offering me relief from the humidity, although the emotional turbulence remained the same. 'I guess asking if you're okay would be an irrelevant question,' he said softly.

'No, it wouldn't be. I'm really sorry. I'm just being silly,' I replied, rubbing my eyes.

'It's not silly to miss your loved ones,' he said. He knew me better than anyone else so it came as no surprise that he was able to analyse and hear the thoughts in my head well before I had expressed them. I briefly looked into his concerned eyes and then looked away.

'I saw Layla playing with her daughter and I guess it made me a little emotional, sorry,' I explained to him.

'It's absolutely fine,' he replied. 'Look, Saira, I can only imagine how heartbreaking this must be for you – you're still grieving and then dealing with all this stuff. I wish that I could make it all better.'

'I want you to feel assured that I will take care of you to the very best of my ability,' he said as I nodded in submission. 'I need to pop out for a short while – will you be all right? Abdullah and Layla are around if you need anything,' he said.

'Yes, thank you,' I assured him. I watched him walk down the concrete pathway until he finally disappeared behind the big pond. I sat in contemplation for a short while, uncertain about many things in my life, and pondered about where this journey would take me. The one thing I was absolutely sure about was that Omar was a man of outstanding character both internally and externally, who led life with the guidance of immaculate principles and morals. My heart longed for Sumayah, to see her and to tell her about my decision to bind my life to Omar through marriage. I wondered whether or not she would approve, and I even contemplated visiting her. I quickly abandoned this idea, though, because I knew as much joy as it would bring to me, she would most probably receive nothing but taunts from her father and the villagers.

It was nearly midday as I continued dusting and sweeping the front and back rooms. I then sat on the bed in Ammu's room, in the place she used to lie, and took out her shawl from under my pillow, embracing her fragrance. I figured she would be happy with my alliance with Omar as in a way she had already given her blessing. With that thought in mind I spent the rest of the day cleaning the windows and washing pots that had been left in various places around the house, and prepared our evening meal.

The day had gone by so quickly and before I knew it, it was twilight. I sat down on the bench on the front patio looking out onto the village; it was peaceful and serene at this time. I enjoyed looking at the beauty of the sun setting for the night and watched how the colours in the heavens above gradually meshed into each other. They changed from orange to yellow with bits of red, then grey, and then finally darkness loomed with the glitter and sparkle of the beaming moon decorated with an array of silver stars. I smiled as I watched Layla collect her daughter's toys to take them in for the night. I relished the sound of cattle being ushered into their huts and women hurrying their children inside and then washing tiny dust-covered hands and feet, just as Ammu used to usher Sumayah and me indoors as soon as the sun had set. Suddenly the village was quiet in the darkness of the night, the only visible light coming from inside the houses accompanied by the indistinct voices of people talking indoors. I wondered where Omar was, and anxiously anticipated his return home.

Just then I heard the door open and close, followed by Omar's reassuring footsteps. I waited a few minutes to compose myself and then walked into the kitchen and began to serve dinner for us both. 'I'm sorry, I should have told you I would be returning late,' he said.

'It's okay,' I replied.

'Shall we eat?' He gestured at the table and I nodded in agreement. I stared at the chair that Ammu used to sit in and then calmly looked away. 'Saira,' I heard Omar say, bringing my attention back to dinner. 'I went to visit Mesabji Chacha today to ask him about whether he would be able to conduct our Nikkah. He has agreed to come over tomorrow morning – is that all right with you?' he asked. I nodded in agreement, only my mind was someplace far away. We ate together in an awkward silence. Omar assisted me to clear the table and then retired to bed. I lay down in the spot Ammuji used to sleep in, feeling strange; it was a feeling I was unable to explain or express. How could I do this without her? How could I start such a significant chapter as this in my life without her advice, support and guidance? The questions continued in my mind almost like an erupting volcano that refused to subside.

The next day I opened my eyes to the sunlight gradually breaking into the house through the window. Almost immediately I felt the panic return, but today it seemed deeper and stronger with a profound purpose. Today was the day my Nikkah to Omar would be solemnised. I lay in bed listening to the many sounds that surrounded me: the chirping of birds, the herding of animals, the clatter of pots and pans, the splashing of water in the big pond as the children laughed. There was a gentle knock on my door, which surprised me. I sat up and wrapped my scarf around my face, expecting it to be Omar, and called out, 'Come in.'

'Good morning,' said Layla with excitement in her voice. She was standing in front of me wearing a big smile that went right across her face.

'Hi, Layla,' I said to her.

'Don't look so shocked to see me…' she began.

'Sorry, I didn't expect to see you here this early, that's all,' I explained.

'Omar has given me the great news and requested I assist you with getting ready this morning, if that's all right with you?' Layla said.

'Sure, I would really like that,' I said with a knot right in the middle of my gut which I struggled to undo. Layla smiled and walked out of the room, saying she would return shortly. She was lovely, always smiling, and in many ways she reminded me of Sumayah. She returned carrying soup and ginger tea. 'Somebody told me that you like ginger tea, so I have prepared you a little breakfast. It's going to be an adventurous day and we need you to stay fit and healthy.' She handed me the bowl of lentil soup and pointed at the cup of tea. How ironic that Layla was attempting to do the job that Ammu would have done. She opened the windows to a hot and humid day with very little breeze. I heard Omar talking to another man who sounded like Mesabji Chacha.

'Is that…?' I asked Layla.

'Yes, he's already here, so as soon as you finish we need to get you all ready for Omar who is waiting eagerly,' she continued. I looked at her and looked away, as I began to feel the intensity of my palpitating heart. I sat quietly, deep in thought, as Layla braided my hair and tied it up into a high bridal bun, attaching silver diamanté clips all through the braid. I was painfully reminded of Hamid by the repetition of this process.

'Does that feel okay?' she asked, and I nodded in silence and compelled my mind to detach itself from the ordeal of those horrific memories. 'What are you going to wear, Saira?' she asked. I walked over to the cupboard and handed her the bag. Layla took out the dress and placed it against my body; her jaw dropped in awe of its beauty. 'This is absolutely beautiful, Saira,' she gasped.

'Yes, you're right,' I said, choking back tears. 'This is the dress that my father gifted to my mother to wear for her Nikkah, and before she… died, she gave it back to me,' I said, fighting back the tears.

'Oh, Saira, sit down.' Layla comforted me, placing her arm around my shoulder. I took deep breaths to compose myself. 'Saira, I know how hard this must be for you, but I also remember how fond of Omar Ammu was, and I think if she were here today she would have been the first person to choose him as your life partner,' she said, to which I nodded in agreement. 'Now come on, let's sort your face out.' She laughed.

I sat as Layla applied make-up to my face, helped me to get into the dress and then placed the glittering necklace around my bare neck. She then instructed me to stand up while she gently placed the matching off-white scarf over my braided bun, clipping it in gently as the delicate net swayed downwards over my hair. It felt as if I was covered in an array of scattered diamonds and made a significant change to my normal attire of dust-filled cotton dresses. 'Oh my, Saira, you look absolutely mind blowing, so beautiful,' Layla screeched. 'Close your eyes,' she instructed and walked me over to the other side of the room. 'Now open them,' she said softly. I opened my eyes to find myself standing in front of the long mirror right in the back of my room. The flattering layered white chiffon gown took my breath away; it was still a perfect fit and the layers of fabric swayed from side to side as I walked. The netted sleeves felt soft and smooth against my skin. The diamanté stones shone in the mirror like a moonlit night. My hair was neat and tidy and my make-up immaculate – it had a finish of pink lipstick and glittery silver eyeshadow, and there were no marigolds, much to my relief. The net scarf over my head was soft and sparkly, and I could almost smell Ammuji within this dress; I indulged in the realisation that she too had worn this very same dress for the very same occasion. Although I had worn it before, this time felt surreal and special and much more meaningful, marking the significance of the day ahead.

Layla took my hand in hers and said, 'Are you ready?' I nodded, looking down at the layers of fabric touching the floor as I walked. 'If she were to see you today she would have been extremely happy,' said Layla. I nodded again, blinking away the tears that were welling in my eyes. 'Shall we go, Saira? They will be waiting.' I took a deep breath and placed one foot in front of the other, as Layla walked beside me holding on to my arm in support.

A rush of anxiety went through me and I began to gasp for air; then I watched the layers of fabric swaying with each step, letting out my Ammuji's fragrance for me to immerse myself in. We walked along the corridor and into Omar's room, which today seemed to take an awfully long time. I held on to Layla tightly, unsure of whether or not it was to stop myself from falling or to reassure myself that I was doing the right thing. As usual, Layla remained calm, instructing me to take deep breaths. We entered Omar's room and my vision became a little blurry, and then returned to normal as I balanced my breathing.

Omar was sitting in a chair wearing a traditional white, subtly decorated kaftan. I saw him look at me, captivated, and then look away as my eyes met his. Abdullah sat close with his daughter and raised his hand up to greet me, while Khadijah babbled away.

'My dearest Saira, you have made a very wise decision, and if your parents were here today they would have been extremely proud,' said Mesabji Chacha, placing his hand on my head. I couldn't help but cry. 'No, my dear, don't upset yourself. Your father would be very proud that you have chosen Omar,' he said, wiping away my tears. Layla guided me to sit as Omar pulled forward a chair, placing it next to him. A part of me still couldn't believe I was marrying Omar. Mesabji Chacha began the ceremony by taking consent from us both and then recited the blessed prayer. He then spoke a little about the values and principles that needed to be instilled into a marriage such as mutual respect, trust, taking care of one another, communication, supporting and guiding one another. He explained that these attributes would support us in building a solid unbreakable foundation based on love and trust. I listened to his words carefully, as they reflected the relationship of my parents.

'You're married – yippee!' Layla shouted in an attempt to make everyone laugh.

'Yes, they most certainly are,' said Mesabji Chacha, smiling. Omar looked at me and smiled. I smiled back and noticed the elation in his eyes that lit up his entire face.

'It's time for lunch – everyone in the kitchen,' Layla instructed, and we all followed her. I offered to help her serve the food, but she declined, insisting I stay seated next to Omar, so I sat down beside him. I watched as everybody chatted and laughed with joy as Layla excitedly served lunch. Although I was surrounded by happiness, I couldn't feel the same, no matter how much I tried. We ate lunch together and then congregated outside for warm tea. I watched all three men play with Layla's baby as I sat in the shade, shielding myself from the heat, which only seemed to heighten in my gown. I saw Omar cuddling the baby and she laughed; it seemed he enjoyed the company of children.

'How is our bride doing?' I heard Layla ask as she sat down beside me.

'Thank you, Layla, for everything,' I told her.

'Don't be silly, I am so glad that Omar has you as his wife. You two are truly made for each other,' she stated. 'Saira, the concern he has for you, I see that in your eyes, too. Allow yourself to be happy with him and entrust everything else to the Almighty,' she said kindly and I smiled in appreciation. We spent the entire afternoon out in the courtyard immersed in conversation and laughter, in my case listening to everyone as Layla served us all snacks and cold drinks every so often. Layla was nothing short of inspirational; they had very little wealth but they appeared to be extremely happy and blessed in so many ways; the three of them shared an immense amount of love, almost a solace from this cruel world.

Before I knew it, dusk had approached announcing the end of what had been a memorable day, with some moments of sadness. Layla and Abdullah left with their exhausted little bundle of joy, followed by Mesabji Chacha, who placed his hand on my head, smiled sweetly and said, 'My dear Saira, always stay happy and smiling. I know that Omar will take good care of you.' He bade farewell to us both and disappeared into the wilderness of the night, another reminder that my life was now moving rapidly away from my beloved Jahed Pur and all the memories that were attached to it, especially my Abbuji and Ammuji.

'Saira,' I heard Omar call from the hallway. 'I can make a start on clearing up in the kitchen, if you want to rest a while. It's been an eventful day,' he said. I smiled and nodded and walked into my room feeling lonely and isolated. I went to the mirror and stared at my reflection. I could hardly believe that we were now married; this thought invoked a new anxiety within me, a new fear, one that I was unable to explain. A part of me felt as if I was in a parallel world, where I would suddenly wake up and find Ammuji right beside me, but deep down I knew that this house and Omar were my new reality – perhaps in many ways a new-found absolution. Choking back unwanted tears I slid out of the dress and neatly placed it back into the cupboard, just the way Ammu had kept it all these years; this was one memory of her that I would never let go of. When I returned to the kitchen Omar was attempting to wash up the remaining utensils.

'Omar, I can finish up now, thank you,' I said.

'We can finish it together, Saira,' he replied. I secretly wished he wouldn't treat me this well; I felt undeserving and unworthy of him. A sudden awkwardness seemed to overtake us both, and I wondered if this was perhaps normal considering the unusual circumstances. 'Saira,' he said, and I turned to look at him. 'Can we talk for a few minutes?' he asked.

'Of course,' I replied; he gestured towards the table, and I followed and sat down beside him.

'I noticed that you seem a little uncomfortable and I don't want you to feel like that. Just because we are now married does not mean that our relationship has to change. What I mean is, I don't expect anything different from you or expect you to behave in a certain way or do certain things. I would much rather we stay as we are. This bond that we have is special and I don't want our friendship to change. I don't want you to feel that you have to change. We don't even have to share a room – you can stay in yours – so please don't look so overwhelmed. I want you to feel safe.' Again he had exceeded all my expectations; he never ceased to amaze me. The way he had been able to comprehend my thoughts only lured me closer to him a little more each time. This was another confirmation that perhaps the Almighty had moulded us to dwell together as one soul.

'Thank you,' I whispered, teary-eyed.

'No, please don't cry,' he said.

'I'm not,' I said and smiled again.

'Okay. I'm a little tired so I'm going to bed. I will see you in the morning – and by the way, you looked absolutely beautiful today,' he added, prior to retiring to his room. Admittedly I felt relieved and the internal burden began to feel a little lighter. I walked out onto the front veranda; the dark night was warm with a humid breeze. My mind and body were exhausted as I contemplated where I should lay my head to rest tonight. I headed to my room and then realised that

Omar may think I was regretting my decision, and that was something I wanted to avoid. So I took a deep strong breath and made my way towards Omar's room, and with an inner strength I never knew I possessed I pushed open the door. Every one of my senses was elevated. Much to my relief Omar appeared to be deep in sleep, his angelic face calm and peaceful. Carefully I crept into the space next to him, almost holding in my breath in fear of waking him. I reflected on the entire day, analysing my past and contemplated what my future would bring. I stared at Omar's sleeping face; he was beautiful. He was truly the definition of loyalty; he chose to stand by me through my most difficult times. In a way a part of me was relieved that we had missed the honeymoon phase of marriage. Most people had told me that this phase was the most difficult, because expectations were extremely high on both sides, which often led to conflict and the desire to change each other rather than embrace the differences along with the similarities. Fortunately Omar and I did not have any differing expectations of one another and neither did we want to change each other; it appeared that imperfect had become perfect. Most of all he made me feel safe – something I had not experienced in a very long time. With that thought in mind I drifted into a deep sleep.

The next morning I opened my sleepy eyes expecting it to still be dark outside. I listened out carefully, unsure of whether I had missed the call to prayer. I rose to peep through the window, only to discover that it must have been mid-morning as everybody was already out and about in the village. I could even hear the children splashing out in the big pond. I gasped at the realisation I was standing in Omar's bedroom as I recalled the events of the previous day. I sat down on the bed in my own world of turbulent emotions. I wondered where Omar was, and if he had purposefully left the room to enable me to feel comfortable. In a hurry I placed my scarf around my head loosely and walked down the hallway; the tiled floor felt warm underneath my bare feet. I walked into the kitchen to find Omar sitting at the table sipping tea. 'Morning,' he said.

'You should have woken me,' I said to him sternly.

'I thought you could do with the rest,' he replied. 'Let's sit outside,' he suggested, handing me a warm cup of tea. We sat in the shaded area and just as I had expected he chose not to highlight or comment on the fact that I had chosen to share his room. We sat in silence for a short while as I gazed at his olive skin, shining in the sunlight.

'I was thinking of giving out some Mitai to some of our neighbours, if you would like to accompany me, Saira,' he asked. Mitai were a delicacy in our villages, shared between family, friends and neighbours during celebrations such as engagements and weddings. It seemed fitting for this occasion. I must have been deep in thought when I heard 'Saira,' again.

'Yes, I would like that, but I don't think our neighbours would be very accepting, you know, given what's happened,' I replied hesitantly.

'Don't you worry about that, Saira. I am a part of this village just as much as they are, and you are now my wife and this is your home and village,' he said with assurance. I looked at him, nodding, knowing all too well that the villagers would never accept me here as I was a woman scorned, with a tarnished reputation, who served no purpose in their traditional society. I also knew that Omar, being the man he was, would go to any extreme to make me feel accepted here, even it meant distributing Mitai to people whose views and opinions he did not accept.

I attended to my appearance, trying to imitate what Layla had done yesterday. Omar carried bags full of Mitai that were pre-packed in delicately decorated boxes. Our first stop was Layla and Abdullah and their adorable daughter. Layla welcomed us with open arms, smiling wholeheartedly. They both appeared to be overjoyed by our visit as well as the sweets. Our next stop was the big pond where Omar handed out a box each to the children who were playing. Little Jamal made his way towards me, embracing me with open arms at once. 'Apa, don't you like playing with me anymore?' he asked with an angelic expression on his face.

'Oh, sweetie, I will come soon to play with you again,' I said and he smiled before diving into the water, splashing Omar. I watched as he laughed and then playfully splashed water right back at him. He appeared elated in mood, happier in himself, and his eyes sparkled just a little more when he smiled – or perhaps I now had a different perspective. Together we continued our journey and visited a few other houses close to ours, handing out a box of Mitai to each; mostly, people welcomed and congratulated us. I watched Omar smile coyly as one of the older ladies of the village told me that my face was now glowing as a newlywed, at which I looked away politely without responding. We walked back towards the concrete path with the heat of the midday sun now beating down. While most of the villagers had been welcoming and accepting, there was a small minority that remained quite clearly intolerant of our alliance, which was clearly expressed through grunts and whispers as we walked past. However, Omar ignored them and engaged me in conversation; secretly I was grateful that we hadn't been verbally abused or pelted with stones.

'Saira, I need to go out for some urgent work. I will be back shortly,' Omar said as we entered the kitchen.

‘Sure, that’s fine,’ I replied, relieved that the ordeal of going round the village had now ended.

Chapter 19 – So Long, Gobind Pur

I climbed up to the rooftop to collect the drying laundry. I enjoyed spending time there as it was peaceful and provided me with space to free my mind of any thoughts, if only for a short while. I walked to the front and looked out onto the village, and saw local men preparing their nets for a day of fishing. They often brought their catch back to the village and would go round from house to house to find anyone who wanted to purchase the fish at the end of the day. I recalled the time a local man had come here carrying a large jute basket on his head. As he placed the basket on the floor of the front patio and opened the lid, a dozen eels jumped out onto the floor, slithering as if they were in search of water. I began screaming as the man explained that they were fresh fish literally just out of his net. Ammu and Omar had sent him away and Omar politely asked him never to return. The thought of Ammu filled my eyes with tears once again, leaving me paralysed with grief.

The sun had set. I welcomed in the light of the moon, and waited for Omar's return. I wondered what the urgent task had been that was taking him the entire day to complete. On his return, we spoke a little about his day, but over dinner he informed me that his uncle no longer wanted to continue with the fight for his ancestral land as the legal fees were increasing for him. 'That's great news, Omar, I am so pleased for you,' I said cheerfully. He became silent for a few minutes, appearing worried.

'It is good, although it has ruined my relationship with the only family I had left,' he said, sounding dejected.

'Yes, I'm sorry about that.'

'Life goes on,' he said slowly. We went to sit on the front patio, taking comfort in the warmth of our tea. 'Anyway, how was your day?' he asked. 'You have spent the entire day thinking about Ammu, haven't you?' he said when I didn't reply. There was a short silence between us before he said, 'Tomorrow I will have to plan another tour of the village to keep your mind busy. Perhaps we can visit the remainder of the elder ladies so they can tell you how you are glowing again.' I laughed and he joined in, teasing me some more. 'You finish your tea, I'm going to bed,' he said, walking down the hallway.

I sat in contemplation for a short while, mostly in disbelief that he had been aware of my innermost secrets and not once had he become judgemental. Even today when he was evidently distressed he continued his utmost to try to make me smile. He would much rather suppress his sadness to bring me happiness. We were two people who ultimately came together through sadness and grief, like sleepers in passing dreams. I desperately desired to free him of his burden and wanted to see him happy, only I was unsure how I could make that happen. I pondered whether our friendship would prove to be the unbreakable foundation that was required for a harmonious marriage. I recalled my parents and the way that they had spoken to each other, the time they spent together laughing, talking. They had been so happy and comfortable in one another's company. That was the kind of relationship, the kind of bond and the kind of marriage I wanted to emulate and aspire to. They were truly the role models I needed in my life; their upbringing made me the person I was and for that I was eternally grateful. That night I carried Ammu's shawl into bed with me, wrapping it tightly around me, and fell asleep staring into Omar's angelic face.

The next morning I woke to find Omar sitting in the kitchen appearing subdued. He told me he needed to talk to me urgently and I sat next to him. 'Saira, I am terribly sorry that I have to even have this conversation with you, but I will have to… to leave,' he said, sounding devastated. I was confused for a moment and then understood that he must be referring to his return to the UK. 'I initially visited to resolve the dispute over my land. However, fate had other plans for me, which I'm not complaining about,' he continued. I stared down to the floor, lost in thought. 'Saira, are you listening?'

'Yes, I am,' I assured him.

'I had planned to stay longer as I don't want to leave you all alone here, but your visa for the UK will take a while to arrive, so I want to apply for that as a matter of urgency,' he explained. The word 'visa' replayed in my mind over and over again; I should have realised this would be the next course of action.

'A visa…' I said out loud, and he looked at me, perplexed.

'Yes, Saira, I have to submit an application for you to join me in the UK,' he said. I continued to listen as my mind and heart refused to process the information. 'I'm trying to arrange for a ticket for me to fly back in the next few days, and I have already consulted a solicitor who has started the application process, so I will just need to approve it,' he explained. I looked at him and nodded as he informed me about visiting the travel agent, and then sat in devastation and disbelief.

Omar was arranging for me to relocate and settle in the UK with him. I was expected to leave my native land, this village I was just beginning to call home, the muddy soil, the streams, the open blue skies, the sound of the birds, the open fields, and most importantly all the memories of my beloved mother that were etched into this land. How could I leave all that behind and travel to the UK in search of a new life? I walked out onto the hot patio, cooling my feet in the water from the pump outside, appreciating the greenery that surrounded me as I listened to the many wonders of my land. I listened to the sound of birds, the chatter of people. I could hear a lady shouting, 'Who wants bangles, green, yellow, pink, blue? I have every colour!' repeatedly. She would go round from house to house every morning carrying a large jute basket on her head that held an assortment of different coloured bangles for people to purchase, and she never seemed to take a day off. I inhaled the open, fresh village air feeling free almost like a bird about to fly over the high skies. This land was my home – how could I depart from it? It was embedded into my subconscious mind and soul.

Omar returned just before dusk, hot and bothered as a consequence of the levels of humidity in the air today. I offered him cool water to drink and then watched as he splashed it all over his face, prior to serving him late afternoon snacks. 'Saira, I have managed to book my ticket to the UK in three days' time. I hope you understand that I wouldn't leave in such a hurry if it wasn't for the fact that I want you to join me as soon as possible,' he said, and smiled.

'Omar, it's fine, I can continue living here,' I suggested to him.

'Saira, I promised to take care of you and I want to fulfil that promise,' he continued. He always chose to prioritise me and my needs before his; how could I not want to travel to the UK to live my life with him? 'Don't look so despondent, Saira,' Omar said, 'I won't leave you here all alone. I will ask Layla and Abdullah to stay here with you and take good care of you, I promise,' he assured me.

'I'm not worried about that, Omar, I trust you completely,' I told him. That night, after dinner, I lay in bed sobbing silently. Omar lay asleep next to me as I stared at his immaculately perfect face. How could I disclose to him that I did not want to relocate to the UK, and most of all depart from my beloved mother? How could I explain that the thought of this was ripping through the cords of my heart? I wanted to stay here where my Ammuji's memory was very much alive and I could cherish it all day, every day. I knew that if I revealed this truth to him, it would probably break his heart, and seeing him upset hurt me. If anything, I wanted to shield him from pain and sadness. He had become my guiding light through the darkest nights, so surely I could make a sacrifice for him and his happiness – which ultimately meant our happiness. No matter how much I deliberated I was unable to convince my mind and my heart that this was the path meant for me; *this* was where I was meant to be.

A few days later

It was mid-morning and Omar was busy preparing to leave for his flight to London. Just as he had suggested, Layla and Abdullah with their daughter had moved into our house, ensuring I had some company and security. I assisted him with the last of his packing and then walked into the kitchen to bring him an early lunch prior to his departure. 'Do you have everything?' I asked him.

'Yes, thank you,' he replied, checking over everything one final time. I began to feel strange suddenly, a feeling I was unable to comprehend. Watching Omar pack confirmed the reality of actually being apart from him, and secretly I longed for him to stay. I had become so used to his company that the thought of being without him was inconceivable.

'Saira,' he said, and gestured for me to sit next to him. He looked into my eyes, smiled, and softly said, 'A lot has happened in the last few weeks. We have experienced lots of happy moments and some sad ones too. I know you think about Ammu every second of every day, and I wish that I could take some of your pain along with me. What I want to say is – while I am gone please take care of yourself. I care for you more than I can express. So whenever you need me, night or day, please don't hesitate to make contact. I just don't want you to feel lonely or that you have no one to turn to because I will always be here for you. Besides, I have given Layla and Abdullah strict instructions to take care of you, and should Hamid or his family turn up again then don't you worry – Abdullah will take care of that too, I promise.'

I was overcome with emotion by the sheer sincerity of his words. 'Omar, don't worry about me. I will be just fine here – thank you for everything,' I said, choking back the tears.

'No tears,' he whispered, and took my hands in his, brought them up to his face and gently kissed them. Just then there was a knock on the door.

'We will need to leave now,' Abdullah stated.

'Yes, just coming now,' Omar informed him, as he picked up his luggage. Together we walked through the hallway and into the kitchen and I noticed Layla look in my direction to give me a cheeky smile, which I reciprocated. 'I have everything, Abdullah,' Omar told him, as he bade goodbye to Layla and their daughter.

'Omar, I want you to be completely free of worry. Be reassured that we will take care of Saira,' Layla told him with determination, and then laughed with him, looking at his tense face. 'Don't look so worried,' Layla continued to tease him.

‘Saira, are you sure you won’t accompany us to the airport?’ Abdullah asked me. I shook my head. I felt as if I couldn’t speak. Was Omar’s departure affecting me more than I had expected, or was it that I had just become so used to being around him that the thought of separation was now unbearable.

‘I will call you on the other side,’ he said softly, and left with Abdullah. I watched from inside the grill gates of the front patio as he walked down the concrete pathway leading to the big pond, until he disappeared beyond the path leading to the road out of the village. I waited until I could no longer see him and began to feel uneasy and restless. I walked up to the rooftop and stood close to the immaculately clean white picket fence. One by one I began to recall the myriad events that had taken place here, which had miraculously transformed into a marriage. My mind flitted to thoughts of my mother; I missed her so much that words were unable to express the pain inside. Although Omar was a great man and I knew he had all the qualities I needed in a life partner, there was still a part of me that did not want to let go; I wanted to hold on to this part of my life, this village, and all the memories of my mother. I did not want to part with a place that was vividly alive with her existence, and wanted to preserve her memory for as long as I could. I took comfort in the image of Omar’s angelic sleeping face and the warmth of his hand upon mine; we had developed a bond, a connection that I was beginning to hold very close to my heart. That moment, as I stood looking out onto the village, sobbing silently, with thoughts of my parents, Sumayah, and then Omar, I decided I would never allow him to know of my reluctance to leave this land.

A short while later I felt a gentle touch on my shoulder which took me by surprise, as this had been a place that was only known to and shared between Omar and me. I looked over my shoulder to find Layla standing there, staring at me with concern. 'Layla, is everything all right?' I asked her, quickly wiping my face.

She sat next to me and said, 'You missed a spot,' pointing to tears left on my chin.

'How did you know I was up here?' I asked her.

She just laughed and said, 'Your dear husband warned me that you may be up here reliving memories and upsetting yourself. I guess he was right.'

'He's worked me out.' I laughed.

'He cares for you deeply,' Layla stated. I should have expected this; I knew that he paid attention to the smallest of my needs and indulged them. 'Saira, believe me when I say that time is a great healer,' Layla assured me, and I nodded and walked back down the stairs into the house.

The next morning Omar telephoned as promised, assuring me that he had reached the UK safely. It felt good to hear his gentle voice once again, as he repeatedly instructed I take care of myself. Omar called me every day and sometimes even twice a day, when he would tell me about his day at work, what he had eaten, what the weather had been like, the humorous jokes shared between him and his work colleagues, almost as if subconsciously he was educating me about the UK prior to my arrival.

Back in the village Layla and Abdullah were taking great care to keep me occupied, whether it be engaged in conversation, taking me for walks around the village, or allocating me tasks. Most of all I enjoyed spending time and playing with their daughter, which I immersed myself in. Those three months went by very quickly, although a day did not go by when I did not think about my mother. Then one day I received a telephone call from Omar informing me that my visa had been granted and that he was in the process of arranging a plane ticket for me to travel to the UK to join him imminently. A large part of me was in denial, which soon became a feeling of dread, when a few days later Abdullah was arranging for a taxi to transport us to the airport. Before my mind was able to process any of this Layla was busy packing for me in excitement and joy. All I had wanted was for everything around me to slow down – I wasn't yet ready to leave this house and certainly not my memories. I felt unable to discuss any of this with Layla, so I guess she took my subdued state as nerves about my journey to my new home and the change of environment. My ticket had been booked and confirmed for the following day and everything had been set in place for me, except I was unable to convince my mind and my heart that in this lay my best interests. I now needed to accomplish one final task, so I went to Abdullah and requested his help.

It was nearly midday and the sky was a perfect blue with the sun beating down. I absorbed this vision fully and completely as if it were the last, as I waited in thoughtful anticipation. It had been a few hours since Abdullah had left so he should have returned by now. I stood up, loosening my hijab as it was hot and humid and the air was dry, increasing my anxiety a little more. I began to slowly pace the front courtyard, pausing at times to look towards the concrete path in desperate search for Abdullah and Sumayah.

'Saira, sit down, they'll be here soon,' said Layla, who sat near me appearing as anxious as I was. I smiled and nodded, although my heart was telling me something else altogether. Just then we heard baby Khadijah crying. 'I'll just check on her,' Layla said.

'Yes, of course, you carry on,' I told her. I sat down with sweaty palms and waited. An hour or so later I was still there when Abdullah returned and I looked for Sumayah, thinking that maybe she would be behind him. However, to my disappointment, Sumayah was not there. I stood up and looked at him.

'I'm ever so sorry, Saira, but she was unable to come,' he told me in an apologetic voice. Abdullah explained how he had informed Sumayah that I would be departing for London the next day and that I had wished to see her one final time. Abdullah even repeated this information to Sumayah's father and offered to escort her here and back, but her father declined unapologetically. My eyes filled with tears and I made a failed attempt to disguise it. 'Sumayah asked me to tell you that she is sorry,' Abdullah told me.

'I am terribly sorry, Saira. I tried my best,' said a defeated Abdullah.

'No, please don't be sorry. I appreciate your kind efforts,' I said to him and then walked into my room. I lay on the bed, sobbing uncontrollably. All I had wanted was to meet with Sumayah one final time to hug her and bid her farewell forever. I had known her and her father since we were young children and today he had denied me this simple request. I could not help but feel betrayed and dejected; surely Sumayah could have reasoned with him just a little more on this one occasion, I thought. I wondered what would have happened if she had come here without notifying her father, just this once. Perhaps I was being selfish expecting Sumayah to defy her father just so I could have met with her one final time. I soon surrendered to the idea that I would never meet Sumayah again, but I would hold on protectively to my cherished memories of her. I thought of Omar; times such as these I needed him and longed to feel his presence and the sweetness and comfort of his aroma. Layla walked into the room and I quickly composed myself, wiping away the evidence from my face.

'Oh, Saira, I'm so sorry,' she said, placing her comforting arm around me.

I smiled half-heartedly and whispered, 'I guess I was never meant to see her again.'

'Just think, this time tomorrow you will be beside Omar, and all this will be a distant memory,' said Layla, only I did not want any of this to become a distant memory. 'We have prepared you a special farewell dinner, so please come and join us,' she instructed. I took a few minutes and a few deep breaths and then walked into the kitchen to find a smiling Abdullah, Layla and Khadijah sitting next to the table where a feast was set out.

The dreaded morning arrived, the morning I was due to bid farewell to this house that I now called home. I held this village in high esteem as it had accommodated and nurtured a despised disdained woman such as myself – one who had been disowned and ill-fated in many ways. Remarkably my time spent here had developed me as a person and as a woman and if anything had saved me from my worst enemy: myself. The turmoil of events here had enabled me to grow and to learn about life and relationships; and I had also met some wonderful people here who had taught me that life goes on no matter what the situation or consequence and that no matter how much tragedy there was, one must soldier on and conquer the darker spaces within. Most importantly this house had played a large part in my finally being able to rid myself of the horrific memories of Hamid. I sat in my room staring into my already packed suitcase; this was the item I would be beginning my journey with, the irony being that I had come to this house with only a single carrier bag holding just a few pieces of clothing. Now, here I was leaving with this gigantic bag containing clothing and items that Omar had asked Layla to purchase on my behalf.

Layla entered the room after a gentle knock. She sat beside me and softly said, 'You will have to leave soon, Saira.' I looked at her and nodded. I entered the room I had shared with Ammuji for one final time and wrapped her shawl tightly around me, embracing her fragrance and wishing that I could drown in it. 'Saira,' Layla called from behind, 'I knew you would come here,' she said.

'I wish she was here, Layla,' I said, sobbing.

She placed her arm around me. 'Saira, she would never want to see you upset. I am positive she would want you to go and live your life to the fullest with Omar and she would want you to always be smiling.' I nodded in agreement. 'Go, Saira, go and be happy and let go of all this sadness. Ammu is at peace now, and Omar is right there waiting for you so go to him,' she told me. My instincts confirmed that Layla was absolutely correct and I cleaned up my face, tidied my hijab and walked round to the front of the house and onto the patio where Abdullah stood smiling, holding on to my rather large suitcase. I bade farewell to Layla and the baby, hugging them so tight I could almost feel the beat of my heart.

'Layla, you have done so much for me – words aren't enough to express my appreciation. Thank you so much, I will never forget it,' I told her.

'Don't be silly: be happy and tell Omar that we are here and will look after the house like it's our own.' She smiled. I took one final glance at the house and thought of our little house back in Jahed Pur; I thought of the stream that ran through the back of our house, the stream that I had spent hours sitting near with my feet dipped into the coolness of the water. As I walked down the concrete path I recalled my journey here, breathing deeply in an attempt to combat the well of anxiety. I walked past the big pond where the water shone in the scorching sunshine. Nearly everybody I walked past I bade farewell to and most of them blessed me with good wishes and congratulated me, as having the chance to travel abroad – and in my case to London – was perceived as a high achievement throughout the village.

Just as I was about to take the road beyond the big pond, with reluctant feet, I heard a sweet voice. 'Apa, you're leaving.' It was the angelic-looking boy, Jamal. I looked at his sweet face and embraced him.

'I am, but I will come back to visit very soon, and when I do I promise I will bring you back a very big bag of sweets from London,' I told him.

'Do you promise?' he asked. I nodded, smiled, and kissed his wet forehead as he ran back off again to play. I continued walking behind Abdullah towards the waiting taxi that was going to transport us to the airport, where I would begin my journey of a thousand miles or more.

With an ache in my heart I bade farewell to the feel of the mud, the sound of the waves, the open blue skies, the heat of the sunshine and the floating shada shapla. I bade farewell to the enchanting sunset, the chirping birds at dawn, the laughter of my childhood, the fresh smell of jute, the open air and, most importantly, my precious memories captive in my beloved native land: Bangladesh. I silently prepared my mind, my heart and my soul for the new journey that lay ahead.

Chapter 20 – Solace in his Arms

I opened my eyes to another cold, foggy, frosty, grey morning in London, surprised to find myself tucked up all neat and warm in bed, shielded from the early morning cold and feeling somewhat confused as my thoughts were no longer in my native land with my beloved mother. I looked over to Omar's empty pillow; it appeared cold and unslept in, which left me wondering if perhaps he had spent the entire night at Kareem's house. Exhaling a deep sigh, I recalled the events of the previous night's function and began to feel extremely guilty, firstly for doubting Omar and then for shutting him out and asking him to leave. Placing my hands over my head in shame I wondered how I had got into bed, as the last thing I was able to recall was curling up on the sofa and sobbing to my heart's content. I had been unable to comprehend my erratic emotional state lately; one moment I was perfectly all right and the next I was consumed with guilt, grief, anger, and pain, and poor Omar was dealing with this turbulent flight of emotions without even letting out a sigh. I got out of bed and looked through the window at the grey and cloudy sky; rain covered the streets and everything in sight – typical British weather. I needed to see Omar at once, firstly to apologise and then to ensure that he was okay and to set things right. As I reached out for the door handle I noticed a small envelope lying on the floor. Curiously I picked it up and opened it, to discover that it was a letter addressed to me.

My Dearest Saira,

I am positive that the horrible events of last night have left their imprint upon you and are perhaps haunting you as much as they are me. However, I have come to the conclusion that I should shower you with love more often and tell you the significance that you hold in my life. I want you to know that I'm overtaken with joy that you and I are bound together in marriage and I cannot contemplate anybody else ever taking your place in this life or the hereafter. I want to take this opportunity to tell you that for me you are the air that I breathe, the orange sun in the sky and the light of a thousand stars. You are my silver lining amongst the dark clouds. You have my heart and my soul and not a second goes by that I don't want to spend with you. I feel fortunate to have shared this amazing journey with you and hope that God continues to bless us with more love each day. With you, I feel invincible, like a bird high up in the soaring sky; our love has no limit, no boundaries, as if we are two bodies inhabiting one soul. I want you to know that I chose you once, and I would choose you again, without a doubt, without reservation. I declare that my love for you is as deep as the ocean and I will fall in love with you every single day for the rest of my life.

You are probably wondering where I am right now. As soon as you finish reading this, I will be right outside waiting for you to join me, so that we can continue our journey of love together hand in hand, side by side from here all the way to Jannah...

With all my love,
Omar.

I stood captivated by this amazing letter as a teardrop fell onto to it, blurring some of the writing. He never ceased to amaze me, be it through actions or through words. At once I opened the door, unable to be away from him any longer. I searched for him as I walked down our hallway, to discover him waiting patiently in the warmth of our lounge; he appeared anxious. I looked at him and then the letter in my hand and, ran into his open arms, locking mine around his neck in an embrace so tight I almost stopped breathing. Sobbing, I said, 'I am so sorry, Omar, I am so sorry, please forgive me.'

He held me tighter, looked into my eyes and said, 'You have nothing to be sorry for.' We sat together a while; I felt safe and secure, wrapped up in the comfort of his arms as he caressed my hair. 'Saira, did you like the letter?' he asked.

I smiled and answered, 'You're quite the poet, aren't you? I loved it.' We were sitting in front of the open fireplace snug, warm and content. He told me that he had returned just after midnight to find me fast asleep and had carried me into bed. I held his gentle, soft hands and he took them up to his face and kissed them, leaving another imprint of our love for me to cherish. We sat in silence a while, as my mind drifted into another place, only this one was a happy place, a vision of me and Omar in our little apartment, filled with love and care for each other. Two things I had become positive about: I had fallen irrevocably and unimaginably in love with him. Secondly, not only did he nurture my soul but he had now become the sole owner of my mind, heart and body. He reinforced the fruit of patience, and the notion that what awaits you is always sweeter than the bitterness of longing.

Just then Omar received a phone call. He needed to leave imminently to attend to a work-related emergency. 'Saira, I have to leave. I'm sorry, but I really need to sort this out. Will you be all right?' he asked.

'Yes, of course. I will be right here when you get back,' I told him and he smiled, taking my breath away with that magical sparkle in his eyes.

Just then there was a gentle knocking at the door. I figured Omar must have forgotten his laptop that was still on the dinner table, so I grabbed it and walked to the door, holding it out for him. Only the person standing there, to my bewilderment, was Tara. 'Hello, Saira,' she said in a timid voice. I began to close the door at once, furious at the mere sight of her. 'No, please stop,' she said assertively, placing her hand on the door.

'I only answered the door as I thought that you were Omar. I have nothing to say to you,' I told her firmly.

'Saira, your anger is completely justified, but I promise I have not come here to cause any trouble. I only want five minutes of your time, please.'

There appeared to be something genuine about her manner, almost bordering on sincerity, so I invited her in and told her, 'You have five minutes. I don't want Omar to find you here.'

'Thank you, Saira,' she replied, and she walked in looking around in awe. We sat in silence for a moment on opposite sides of the sofa with a tension that seemed to overtake the entire room. 'Saira, I assure you that I have not come here to cause you any harm. It's just... yesterday, seeing you both and the love that he has for you has given me a chance to reflect, and Omar was right – I need to move forward,' she began.

'Tara, I don't want to hear anything against my husband,' I said firmly.

'Saira, please,' she said, choking back tears. 'I came to return something, something that is rightfully yours.' I looked at her in dismay. I felt fear overtake me, as Tara held out something in the palm of her hand, which she then gently placed into mine. I looked, speechless, at the diamond encrusted ring, and the fear I felt earlier now heightened as I realised this was an engagement ring. I looked at Tara, confused, as I tried to comprehend this revelation. 'Saira, you are the rightful owner of this ring, you deserve to be Omar's wife in every way possible, and I want to return this to you so that I can move forward,' she said, as a thousand questions gathered in my mind to which I needed answers right away.

'What are you trying to imply, Tara?' I demanded, heartbroken.

'Saira, Omar and I were engaged to marry upon his return to the UK, but he met you and called off our engagement, and it broke my heart. But, please believe me, Omar only agreed to this alliance due to emotional blackmail, which I hold my father solely responsible for. I know that Omar will never divulge any of this to you for fear of losing you. He has a heart of gold, and I am truly sorry for everything that happened yesterday.'

She walked out, leaving me holding the ring in my hand, which provoked more questions. Part of me felt guilty for entering Omar's settled life, while another part was sad at Tara's heartbreak, although none of this lessened the love he had for me and that I had for him, and nothing would change what destiny had bound together – neither me, Omar or Tara. I recalled Omar telling me about the personal vendetta Chacha had against him and everything began to appear crystal clear now. That moment I decided I would honour the many sacrifices Omar had made for me, as it was because of his commitment to me that today Chacha had gone against him. In turn I decided to bury this revelation forever, and submit myself, and my life, to Omar. I vowed to accept pain, grief and happiness as long as it was with him. My love for him had become pure in the truest sense and my obligation was to embrace my life with him fully and completely, and I eagerly waited in anticipation.

Upon his return he swept me up into his arms at once. I looked into his deep eyes, taking his hand into mine, and made a declaration to him that I never imagined I would.

'Omar, I love you with all my heart, you have held me together through everything,' I proclaimed. He appeared shocked and bewildered more than anything. 'I'm sorry that it's taken so long for me to accept our marriage. You have done so much for me, and I have been so selfish and so absorbed in my own grief that I have failed to see what has been right in front of me all along,' I continued.

He pulled me into his chest, locking his arms around me once again in a heartfelt embrace. 'Saira, I truly feel that we have a connection, it's a bond so strong it can withstand any storm, any form of turbulence, till death do us part.' I looked into his eyes and our hands intertwined, almost as if we were two bodies inhabiting one soul. I laid my head on his supportive shoulder, inhaling that aroma I adored so much: a little of the ocean and light sandalwood with a mixture of amber; it took my breath away leaving me in awe every time.

He held my face with his soft hands and said, 'You know there is no way we will ever forget Ammu. She will always remain cherished in our memories and in our hearts, but you need to stop blaming yourself for what happened. You did everything that you could for her and she knows that. If she were here today she would want you to be happy and to continue living your life, not to be sad and unhappy.'

He was definitely correct; if Ammu was with us she would be unhappy and displeased that I had stopped living. 'You're right, as always,' I agreed, choking back tears.

'No, don't do that again,' he said, standing up and walking out of the room. He returned a few seconds later carrying a tiny box in which I kept small items of jewellery. He sat beside me, opening up the box, and then with his finger rubbed a teardrop off my cheek and placed it inside the box. I couldn't help but let out a small laugh, asking Omar what he was doing. 'I am locking away this tear forever, so that sadness never befalls you again,' he said softly. 'I have captured all your tears in this box and will never return them.' He closed the lid and I smiled and rested my head on his warm chest. I felt in a state of elation, a happiness that I had not experienced in a very long time. This was a moment that belonged to us only, a moment of love to be cherished and treasured. He had taught me that love was living the similarities and embracing the differences; together we made perfect the imperfect.

I held on to him as tight as I could and asked, 'You must think about Ammu sometimes too, I guess.'

'I think about her all the time, in fact – she reminded me of my own parents. And you know what I loved about her the most? The love for life that she had and her strong spirit,' he said looking into my eyes. I knew deep down that if she were here today she would be proud and definitely approve of Omar, as she had adored him as much as I did. Omar pulled my face up so I was able to look at him and said, 'Shall we have some breakfast now?'

'Of course, it's almost time for lunch,' I gasped, noting that it was midday already.

'Let me cook breakfast today, Saira,' he said. I laughed and recalled the previous time he had attempted to make egg bread and ginger tea and in the process had managed to set off the smoke alarm twice and burnt the bread. He soon joined in with my laughter as I figured he must have recalled the same event.

'How about I make the breakfast,' I told him, smiling.

'Just in case I attempt to burn everything and beyond,' he joked.

It was Sunday; I liked Sundays as Omar would be home and more importantly with me the entire day. The day was still cold with patches of mild sunshine, which reminded me of my native land. I was finally beginning to feel content with life here, almost as if I had found a new hope, a new absolution to live and to want to live. We sat together for breakfast in front of our open fireplace. I looked at him and smiled, feeling fortunate to have a soulmate who loved unconditionally and selflessly. One who always saw past the differences; perhaps he had been the solace that God had prepared for me and chose to disclose to me at a time when I was able to embrace it wholeheartedly. We spent the afternoon immersed in conversation about our native land. I shared with him stories about my Abbuji and my childhood spent in Jahed Pur, which he knew very little about. I then disclosed to him the part of my identity that he had never met: my passion for teaching and how greatly I missed it.

'That is the Saira I am very excited to get to know, the life of Jahed Pur,' he said, smiling.

'Have you spoken to Layla? How are they all?' I asked.

'They are very well and keen for us to visit soon,' he replied. 'I keep meaning to ask you, whatever happened to Khushi – she never returned,' I asked.

'Yes, of course, she chose to work in another house closer to her maternal village,' he replied, taking me back to the open blue skies of Gobind Pur and the smell of the damp monsoon soil. I sat back into the sofa, leaning on his shoulder whilst my mind travelled back into the season of Bashonto. I couldn't help but to think about the numerous colourful fun fairs I had attended with Sumayah devouring tangy, spicy hog plum chutneys; I still missed her and longed to see her. After Ammu she was the only other person I thought of as family. 'What's on your mind?' Omar said, caressing my hair.

'I was thinking about Sumayah, actually,' I replied.

'Has she been in touch with you?'

'Oh no, I doubt she even knows that I now live here permanently, and besides, she won't want to upset her father, and rightly so,' I told him.

He suddenly looked into my eyes. 'I forgot to mention something.' I sat up to listen attentively. 'I received a message from Chacha apologising for the incident at the party,' he said hesitantly.

I smiled and said, 'Omar, that's great news.' He appeared perplexed, which I thought may have been connected to Tara's earlier visit. I took his hand in mine and explained. 'This means there is a chance of reconciliation – after all, he is your family.'

Omar seemed disheartened by my suggestion and unapologetically replied, 'No, Saira I won't ever allow a repetition of that party. I have accepted his apology and resolved the matter.' I understood all too well the emotion of betrayal, so did not push the matter any further, sitting back into his embrace. He made this moment sweeter with his presence, and I thanked God for this life and for Omar.

Later that night I was tucked up in bed next to Omar as he slept peacefully; I caressed his angelic face indulging in that scent. I almost felt euphoric and was finally able to think of Ammuji and smile; at long last I had conquered the sadness within me. I climbed out of bed and opened my closet quietly. I carefully took out her shawl and wrapped it around me as tightly as I possibly could, and then brought out my Abbuji's prayer mat, placing it on the floor. I sat down in submission – in prayer. I prayed to the Almighty to take care of them, whispering, 'Thank you Ammuji and Abbuji.' I wanted to thank them for giving me life and for nurturing that life. For helping me to grow, to walk, to learn, to talk, and to fall and stand, for teaching me to be kind, caring and generous. I wished to tell them how they had shaped my life with principles and values that I now held in such high esteem. They taught me about the most beautiful things in life such as love, happiness and unity. I longed to thank them for teaching me to stand strong against the storm and for allowing me to follow my dreams. I wanted to tell Ammuji, 'Thank you for standing by my decision, although the consequence for you proved to be dire.' I wanted to embrace my Abbuji and let him know how much I loved him, and to thank him for allowing me the same opportunities as a son. My brave mother, who had stood against our entire village just so she could stand beside me, had praised me while others slandered and laid blame. She stood strong as my shield all the while protecting me from the horrid wrath of the villagers. 'Abbuji and Ammuji, you have taught me everything I know and I promise that I will never ever forget or forsake the values and principles that you have instilled in me,' I said defiantly.

I wanted to free my captive soul from this pain, and forever hand over my Abbuji and Ammuji to God Almighty. 'Ammu, I'm so sorry I couldn't do more for you, I'm sorry you fell prey to bad words because of my ill-fated actions, I'm sorry that you lost your home and your precious memories. I hope that you are both together hand in hand, side by side in Jannah.' And then I whispered, 'I love you both with every beat of my heart.' I sat in silence listening to the ticking of the alarm clock while I began to feel lighter emotionally and mentally. I thought about a saying I had heard: 'Not everyone you lose is a loss', and pondered whether there was an element of truth in that. I looked over to Omar and recalled something Ammu had once told me about an unmarried girl in our village who had been courting one of the young boys that lived nearby. She told her to save all her love for her future husband; now I was fully able to comprehend her message. All the love I had I was investing in the bond between me and Omar, which was pure and deep like the ocean and gave me purpose. A feeling deep down told me that Ammu and Abbu would have been proud of our decision to marry; I knew Ammu was fond of him as much as Abbuji would have been. I got back into bed and snuggled up as close as I could to Omar and recalled my mother's wise words: 'When the right person comes along you will know, Saira.' As ever, she was absolutely correct.

It was daylight when I woke a few hours later. I climbed out of bed and opened the curtains to discover that the sun was shining. I figured Omar had left for work as it was Monday, and that was usually a busy day for him with back-to-back property viewings. I heard the sound of tapping as I walked into our lounge, and was surprised to find Omar still at home.

'Good morning, did you sleep well?' he asked, taking my hand into his.

'Yes, I did, thank you,' I replied. 'I thought you would have already gone to work.'

'I just need to complete some paperwork and then you have the house all to yourself.' He laughed.

'I'll make you a sandwich before you go,' I told him and walked into the kitchen. I peeped out through the small window and watched as parents dropped off their children at pre-school; this always made me smile, as it reminded me of my days of teaching and the amazing things the children used to do and say. I sat next to Omar as he ate. It was ironic to talk about having the house all to myself; in truth, I had nothing meaningful to do in this house or in this country, and had it not been for Omar's continuous effort and encouragement I would never have ventured outside these four walls. In countless ways he made me feel alive again, and gave me strength and courage to continue, to smile and to live. He raised me up, and on his shoulders I could stand on mountains and walk the stormy seas. He raised me up to be more than I could otherwise ever be. Admittedly, at first I was dejected by the move to London. However, I now realised that it was necessary for me to gain a new perspective. Consequently, after a few months of sitting aimlessly in this apartment while Omar worked, perspective was what I had achieved. The walks that he had sent me on – some for milk, some for stamps – had all enabled me to reflect and evaluate, and today I felt finally able to move forward.

'So, what's on the itinerary for today?' he asked, but I was still preoccupied with thoughts. He nudged me, saying, 'Saira?'

'Yes,' I answered, startled.

He put his arm around me, and I sat back to rest on his warm shoulder. 'Do you want me to rearrange my viewings? I can go in a little later.'

'Absolutely not, you have your day planned and there is no reason to change it. Besides, I want the house to myself,' I told him, handing him his coat.

'Are you sure you will be all right?' he asked, caressing my face. I nodded, walking him to the door. After he had gone, I stared into our small, warm, cosy little abode and began to clean and tidy up, mostly to occupy my mind; these actions were reminiscent of my days as a maid back in Omar's house in Gobind Pur. It was ironic that back then I relied upon Ammu for almost everything in my life, and today it seemed that she had assigned her role to Omar. Most days I would wait impatiently for his return as he had instilled me with confidence and filled my life with a much-needed love, reviving in me the will to continue.

I decided that today for the very first time I would independently take a walk without Omar having to create a scenario around it. Today I fully embraced the cold windy weather, the polar opposite to my beloved humid native land. I smiled at my neighbour who was walking into her house with shopping bags. I had been living here a few months now and was not even on first name terms with my neighbours; this realisation astounded me. Since my arrival here I had been purposefully avoiding all human contact unless it had been declared a matter of urgency.

I recalled walking down the riverbank of Jahed Pur with Sumayah, laughing and chatting in the blazing heat. I remembered the feel of the dry mud under the soles of my feet and the aroma of the fresh vegetables we would meander past, back when I had been happy, content, and had a profound purpose to life. This was almost an emblematic reflection of my being now; I saw myself in a moving car. I appeared aged and perished, and more importantly there was a lack of something – a purpose, a direction – something to call my own other than Omar. I continued walking in search of something meaningful when I noticed a group of parents gathered outside a bus painted with the colours of the rainbow; a few minutes later a smiling lady opened the door and one by one each parent collected their child. All of a sudden the street was filled with laughter and children singing and dancing while they descended from the play bus. I smiled as I walked past; I heard parents asking their children what they had done that day. Some replied singing, some said painting, some said jumping and various other playful activities. Somehow seeing this play bus ignited my passion to want to return to teaching, providing me with a new-found purpose to life, which I wanted to pursue almost immediately.

Chapter 21 – Something Old, Something New

I returned home, letting loose my wavy tresses which Omar had become so fond of, and began to make preparations for dinner. Today I anxiously awaited his return, excited to tell him my news. I looked in the mirror at my hair, recalling those humid, lazy afternoons that Ammu and I used to spend together beside our stream. She would massage my hair with black seed oil, which, back in our village, women believed revitalised the hair, making it shiny and silky smooth. When Sumayah arrived Ammu would massage her hair, much to her annoyance, because she disliked the oil's distinct aroma. I smiled inwardly; I knew Ammu was secretly aware of how much I enjoyed those massages although I protested against them almost every time. Sumayah remained in my thoughts – my mind's way of wanting something or someone who had been close to Ammuji, and in this case she fell into that category almost perfectly.

I had begun to watch television here, although I did not find it amusing enough to enjoy. I looked out through the window as the day slowly began to turn into night. That was one of the things I missed most about my native land: the melodious call to prayer. I sat counting the blessings in my life, the foremost one being Omar. The very thought of him made me smile; I looked at the necklace around my neck, the very first item he had gifted me. We had married under such unfortunate circumstances that I had made it very clear to him I did not want a ring, which he had accepted. The gold necklace shone as I looked at it with adoration and read 'Saira and Omar Till Jannah', and smiled contentedly.

I began to dust the aromatic display of candles on our fireplace; there was lavender, sandalwood, magnolia. Just then I heard the door open and close, followed by the sound of Omar's footsteps. He appeared tired and I joined him in the lounge to find him slouched over the sofa; a part of me felt guilty about the way he had spent the previous night.

'Are you not feeling well,' I asked him, gently placing my hand on his warm forehead.

'Hey, I was just wondering where you where,' he said, smiling and shuffling over a little allowing me to sit next to him.

'I'm sorry, you're so tired because of me.'

'That is a small price to pay – for that smile I would do anything,' he replied. Once again, he made me feel unworthy of him and his love; he was gracious and thoughtful. This time I managed to hold back my tears of happiness, disguising them with a smile.

'Are you hungry?' I asked. Our hands intertwined as he asked me about my day. At once I told him about my walk and just as I expected he was shocked, although he soon pretended to act normally, which gave him away. 'Omar,' I said, and he locked his eyes into mine. 'Are you not surprised that I ventured out of the house?' I asked him, confused.

'I am proud of you,' he said with encouragement. I told him about the play bus I had encountered, as he continued to listen attentively.

I served dinner and reflected on the day's events. It seemed I had found the ultimate solace in his arms. 'I think about her during dinner quite a lot too, Saira,' he said, gently nudging my shoulder. It was completely pointless attempting to hide my emotional state from him, as he had developed the power of being able to read the thoughts in my mind like no other. 'I thought I locked away those tears, so how did they escape?' he said, softly caressing my hair, forcing me to let out a gentle laugh. We sat side by side after dinner drinking ginger and cinnamon tea; this cold, windy weather appeared to sweeten the distinctive bitter taste. We reached the topic of the play bus again.

'Omar, I was thinking, you know seeing that play bus today, and those children. I don't know how to explain it,' I began. 'I think I want to return to teaching,' I blurted out.

'That's great news,' he said.

'I could maybe even work in that play bus,' I told him. 'I appreciate everything that you have done for me, and I also know that if it hadn't been for you then I don't know where I would be today, or even what state I would be in,' I said looking into his deep eyes. 'I just think I need something a little more meaningful.'

'Saira, that's a very good idea,' he told me. 'Is cooking and cleaning for me not meaningful enough for you then?' He laughed.

I smiled and said, 'Every day with you is meaningful, and I hope to continue cooking and cleaning for you till we're seventy, but I just need to find the part of myself that's perhaps lost somewhere.' In remembered pain the expression on my face weakened as I felt the build-up of moisture in my eyes again. 'If it wasn't for you then I would have been stoned and taken back to…'

Before allowing me to finish my sentence he immediately placed his hand over my lips and whispered, 'Shh. I will protect you with my life, whichever path you choose to walk on I will always be your shadow,' and with the warmth of his hands he wiped away the tears that were decorating my cheekbones.

I found comfort in him to the extent that not only was he my husband but he had also become my soulmate, my confidant, and the one I turned to for almost everything. Our bond had become deep and magnetic with no boundaries to cross. It appeared we had no dark spaces in our relationship to shield each other from. Our journey had begun from the moment that he had rescued me from the swaying of the bamboo bridge in the midst of darkness, until fate decided to bind us in marriage providing me with an everlasting guiding light to my life. We were now together hand in hand nurturing this infinite bond; he had truly become the absolution to my desolation.

'Hey, did I mention Kareem?' he said to me, diverting my attention back to where we were.

'What's happened to him?' I asked with concern.

'No, no, he's okay, he is currently in Bangladesh with his father. It was his father's wish to travel to his native land and stay there for a few weeks,' Omar explained.

'We never did go round for that dinner,' I said.

'They will be back in a few weeks, we can arrange it for then,' he said. Kareem resembled Omar in many ways; he was the epitome of the perfect son so it did not surprise me at all that he had accompanied his sick father all the way to Bangladesh, leaving his business unattended.

I continued to enjoy my evenings spent with Omar, although every day he made a point of suggesting we dine in the smartest restaurants or to shop in the variety of malls that most women back in our village would be captivated by. Materialism held no significance for me, though; I much preferred to enjoy Omar's company and was content with the moments shared in our home. In the mornings I would watch him prepare for a busy day at work, and had even assigned myself the task of choosing a tie that best suited his itinerary for that particular day; I found happiness in those small things. The irony was that although we did not marry in a way that was traditional – we did not even host the lavish feast that most people do according to societal expectations – here I was serving Omar as my husband according to the traditions held by most in our village. The inescapable reality was that in doing this I found joy, peace and serenity. I smiled as I thought of Sumayah and imagined what she might have said if she were to see me like this; I pictured her mischievous loving face and smiled in remembrance.

A few months passed, made up of busy mornings and lazy, love-filled evenings.

The much-detested British winter had arrived bringing with it cold, mist, wind, rain, hail, and even colder mornings and grey skies, with the days short and the nights long. Omar had told me many stories about the snow, about how picturesque it looked as the rooftops and everything else beyond shone, beautifully covered in white. He told me about the gale-force winds and blizzard of December 1990 when many parts of the United Kingdom became covered in almost four metres of snow. This fascinated me and was a sight I eagerly anticipated as I looked out of the window at the grey and cold foggy day, while the inside was filled with warmth from the open fireplace. I missed the warm humid heat of my native land, especially the golden early mornings. I reminisced about the joyous exchanges between villagers in comparison to the hurried gestures of tolerance here, as people were generally far too busy to engage in anything more than a smile if even that. I pictured little Jamal's angelic face as he dived into the water, splashing all the other children. Gradually I was becoming accustomed to this cold weather as well as my new environment, which Omar helped me with. I was even on first name terms with my neighbours, who we had hosted for dinner, and just like Omar they too had enjoyed curried papaya, in turn complimenting my culinary skills.

It was early evening as Omar returned from work one gloomy day; it was almost dark now. 'Assalamualaikum,' he said, walking into the lounge. I smiled and enquired about his day. He took off his hat and his short curly hair stood up with static, making me laugh. He sat next to me, and I held his cold hands trying to warm them up.

'You look cold and tired,' I told him and he laughed.

'Is it ever warm in this country?' I said humorously. I listened as he talked about his day; his business was doing extremely well, allowing him to employ another worker, which lightened his burden, and he had begun to appear less tense and overworked. He informed me about Kareem's return from Bangladesh, and I was ecstatic to hear this news. 'How come he stayed that long?' I asked. Omar was unsure why, and said that Kareem wanted to host a dinner for us at his house.

'Think about what day you would like to go,' he said, resting his tired head on my shoulder.

'You need to take some time off work,' I told him, and he laughed. 'Omar, you work way too hard,' I protested, which was one of the things I admired most about him.

Not a day passed when I did not think of Ammu, only now I was able to remember her with the light of joy as opposed to the darkness of pain. I guess I had finally let go of that inescapable pain I had been holding captive inside. I looked over at Omar; how composed and content he was with his life. He had not had the blessing of being raised by his parents and one could only imagine the devastation and sadness he must have suffered throughout his life. Yet he had turned into the most remarkable man I had ever known – the love of my life. He caught me looking at him. Inevitably my thoughts were transparent to him and he smiled knowingly, bringing me out of my daze. I did not possess the words to praise him; all I was positive about was that he was truly a godsend for me: an angel sent from the heavens.

We were sitting opposite the fireplace after dinner as he played with my hair. 'Do you want to go tomorrow to Kareem's?' I asked.

'Sure, I will let him know,' he replied. Kareem later confirmed the arrangement by text message. The next day was Friday, which made me feel happy, as the weekend was approaching and that meant more time with Omar. I concealed my loneliness from him during the week as I did not want to become a hindrance in his work. We sat together, and I told him about the voluntary work I had arranged for myself. 'Are you sure you want to do this?' he asked. I explained to him that I would be in the play bus for a few hours every morning and it was something that I was looking forward to. My rationale was that teaching was a little different in this country so the voluntary work would provide me with a starting point, as if I was setting myself some expectations and goals. I was grateful that he allowed me the space to grow and develop in the form I deemed best, without hindrance. He elevated me and allowed me to become the best version of myself that I could be.

The next day Omar arrived from work a little earlier than expected, just as I walked out of our room all ready to leave. He stared at me, looking slightly baffled. 'What's wrong,' I asked him. He smiled and walked me over to stand directly in front of the mirror, standing beside me as the warmth from his body radiated towards mine. 'What is it?' I asked in confusion, turning around to face him.

'Absolutely nothing, because your beauty is beyond my comprehension,' he said to me.

I smiled and mocked him. 'You're biased.'

He turned me around to look directly into the mirror once again and said, 'Look, see for yourself, beauty lies in the eyes of the beholder.' For a moment I stared into the reflection. I wore a long floor-sweeping dress, the colour of plum and made of a soft chiffon fabric. The dress was beautiful and simple, decorated with an intricate line of silver beads at the neck. My make-up was simple, yet my face glowed like never before.

I looked towards him and said, 'You beautify me,' to which he just laughed.

This dinner had been long awaited. I recalled the first time Kareem had asked to host us, which had been months ago, and I had declined many times out of self-isolation. A part of me felt guilty as Kareem had always treated both me and Omar with such kindness and generosity. It was just after dark now and we had arrived at Kareem's house as he lived nearby. Their house was large, larger than what was required for two people. He greeted us at the door with a gigantic smile across his face, welcoming us into the house through the wide hallway and into the front reception room, which again was larger than our little apartment.

'Omar, Bhabi please come inside,' he said joyfully. They shook hands and for a moment it seemed that they could be biological brothers.

'Kareem, how are you and your father?' I asked. He replied that they were both very well; his father was currently resting upstairs. There was something different about him, something unidentifiable, as if he was happier and more content. Omar and Kareem chatted together, mainly about his trip, and I listened attentively.

'I have to say, Omar, that it's so nice to see you guys together and smiling. I pray that God keeps you like this for eternity,' he said, and I glowed inside with happiness.

'I hope so,' Omar added, looking in my direction.

'Do you want a hand with dinner, Kareem?' I said to him, standing up and starting to walk towards the kitchen.

'No, Bhabi, it's fine,' he said, startled.

'I absolutely don't mind,' I assured him.

'Kareem, you would be pleasantly surprised with Saira's culinary skills,' Omar added in encouragement.

'Okay, guys, so there is a reason why I don't need help,' he muttered. Omar and I were perplexed. 'I have an announcement to make,' he continued now, his face beaming with delight. Omar and I looked at each other in suspense. He then disclosed that his fiancée was in the kitchen helping him with dinner preparation.

'You're engaged – that's brilliant news,' I blurted out in excitement. Omar congratulated him, standing up at once to give him a hug of approval. He told us that he was very excited to introduce her to us today, which just made this evening even more memorable and special.

'How did this all happen so quickly, Kareem? You are a dark horse,' Omar joked with him. He explained how, for some time now, his father had expressed a desire to see him betrothed and settled in life. While they were visiting Bangladesh he began to receive many proposals, one of which he had decided to pursue further. He then got to know the lady and chose to extend his trip, and then they became engaged. He told us that she was from a small village near his, and that she was also willing to undertake some of the caring responsibilities for his father, which Kareem was delighted about. This truly captivated me, and I felt overjoyed as did Omar. Kareem added that his father was not coping well with the village heat and consequently they had postponed the wedding. He then applied for a fiancée visa, which miraculously was accepted on the grounds of his father's ill health, and the three of them had travelled back to the UK together.

'Oh, Kareem, what wonderful news, and now you have a wedding to plan,' I said to him.

'I would like for both of you to be involved as well,' he said kindly.

'Goes without saying. We can also tell her all your bad points in case she wants to rethink her decision.' Omar teased him, and we all began to laugh.

'Shall we sit at the table,' he said, and we followed his lead. I sat next to Omar and Kareem walked into the kitchen. He returned to the room saying, 'Guys, this is my fiancée.' I saw a young girl who hesitantly walked behind him; she was dressed in a very pretty emerald green floor-length kameez, with matching bangles and a green hijab with small silver stones scattered all over her head.

She raised her head slightly, still looking down to the floor, and in a very timid voice greeted us both saying, 'Assalamualaikum.'

I stared at her face while a rainbow of emotions overtook me, paralysing both my mind and my body; first shock, then horror, followed by pain, grief, sorrow and anger. My suspicion was confirmed: as I observed her walk into the room I had noted that her posture resembled that of Sumayah. I continued to stare at her face and whispered, 'Sumayah,' as Omar turned to look at me, holding my hand beneath the table, subliminally asking me to compose myself. I was in disbelief at the sight of her right here in front of me. That round face, big, beautiful eyes and small frame I would have recognised anywhere. Omar squeezed my hand, trying to tell me everything was going to be fine. My eyes were welling up and I battled to conceal the expression upon my face.

Kareem was standing close to her, his face radiating joy as he said, 'Sumayah, this is Omar and Bhabi, almost like family to me.' She looked up at us both and my eyes met hers. She then looked at me and then Omar and then back down to the floor again. I witnessed the same rainbow of emotions overtake her as she looked up at me for a third time in confirmation. Part of me wanted to embrace her and ensure that she was well, while another part felt betrayed as I recalled past events.

'How are you, Sumayah?' said Omar, attempting to keep it all together for us both.

'I am very well, thank you,' Sumayah answered hesitantly.

'Shall we eat now?' said Kareem, and they both walked back into the kitchen.

'Omar, I can't breathe,' I told him as panic began to set in.

'It's okay, take some deep breaths, you will be fine. I am here with you,' he assured me, holding my hand tightly. I began to take deep breaths. 'I promise we won't stay long.' Just then Kareem and Sumayah walked back in, carrying what seemed to be a variety of different dishes reminiscent of the culture of my native land.

'Please, guys, try a little of everything,' he said.

'Saira, what would you like to try first?' Omar asked me in a soft voice.

Before I could answer, Sumayah said, 'Please try this papaya chutney first,' placing a few spoonfuls onto my plate. She looked into my eyes apologetically. She knew all too well that I was fond of papaya.

'Thank you,' I replied submissively. Both of us remained quiet throughout dinner as Omar and Kareem talked, mainly about the climate in Bangladesh. I was distressed, and Omar nudged my hand, encouraging me to eat. I noticed Sumayah look at me time and time again, almost as if she had so much to divulge but something was holding her back. I began to feel as if time had stood still.

Dinner and the serving of tea and desserts finally came to an end, marking the end of my agony. However, my anxiety seemed to heighten and I felt a build-up of moisture between the palms of our hands. Omar conjured up an excuse, saying he needed to prepare a work-related report for first thing in the morning so we could be excused immediately. We thanked Kareem for his wonderful hospitality and once again congratulated him. Just as I was about to open the door to leave, I noticed Sumayah standing there. Placing my hand on her shoulder I said, 'Thank you for a lovely dinner, Sumayah.'

She momentarily held my hand and whispered, 'Saira,' as I walked out, choking back the uncontrollable tears. The touch of her hand had brought forth a paradox of memories that I had fought within my inner being, not having been able to lock them away somewhere as deep and dark as the depths of the ocean. This box of memories was one I did not want to open. Most of all I did not want to grieve anymore, because I had found Omar who was my solace for all the things I had lost and grieved for.

I just about managed to climb into the car as Omar followed. My breathing began to escalate along with my pounding heart. 'I can't breathe, Omar,' I said again, sobbing uncontrollably.

He pulled me into his chest, embracing me with both arms. 'Just breathe nice and gently. I promise you it will be fine,' he said holding my face. I looked into his big brown eyes and began to breathe slow and deep.

'I don't know what happened to me in there. Everything just came flooding back and it hurts really bad, I'm so sorry,' I continued.

'It's okay, shh,' he said, placing his finger slightly over my lips. 'I don't want you to cry anymore, I'm here with you and I promise I won't let anyone hurt you. We're going home and we are going to put this evening behind us just like we did with everything else,' he said.

We reached home, and he sat me down in our usual spot beside the warmth of the fire. I felt safe here, shielded in his arms. We sat in silence as he gently held me. 'Omar, I never mentioned this to you, but before I arrived here I sent for Sumayah,' I said quietly, and he listened with undivided attention. 'My last day in the village, I sent Abdullah to collect Sumayah just so I could see her one final time and bid her goodbye. Only she never came because her father had forbidden her.' He appeared shocked. I explained how deeply hurt and betrayed I had felt. 'You know me and Sumayah grew up together, we were almost like sisters, we were inseparable, and to think that she never came to see me one final time. That was unimaginable pain,' I whispered in tears. I held on to his supportive shoulders.

'Saira, please don't upset yourself anymore. I wish I could erase this evening out of our memory,' he said. My mind took me back to those days when I was so absorbed with pain and sadness, and Omar had brought light back into my life with great struggle and difficulty. I felt afraid that I would regress into that dark and sad place once again where everything hurt and my heart ached with inconsolable pain.

'Omar, I'm really scared. I don't want to turn into that person I was a few months ago. I don't want to put you through all that again,' I told him, frightened.

'I'll never let you go back there, I promise. We have come this far and we will deal with this together, just as we have with everything else.'

I felt unsettled, as if something unresolved had reared its head again causing waves in still waters. This was something I knew I had to resolve and perhaps that was the reason fate had once again orchestrated for me and Sumayah to meet in this mysterious way. I stood near the window staring out into the pitch dark, cold, windy night, reflecting on the turbulence of the evening. Later I lay next to him as he caressed my hair, telling me to rest and sleep, but this was the furthest thing from my mind. I was grateful that he was beside me, strong and courageous and ready to triumph every battle I had to contend with. Wide awake I contemplated sleep for a short while and then fought with an unsettled mind that refused to subside. The only thing in my mind was Sumayah. I could not help but think of her sad face. I had been hurt by her actions, but I found myself slowly succumbing to the memory of our lifelong friendship, and a love I was unable to deny. I found myself wondering if she was okay and whether she was happy with Kareem; the sadness I had witnessed on her face made me doubt that.

I must have only managed to sleep for a few hours before waking to the serene sight of Omar who was deep in peaceful sleep with my hand locked into his. I smiled at his beautiful face, dwelling in his scent. Gently I released my hand from his and climbed out of bed, peering outside to find that it was still dark and foggy – another typical cold day; mornings such as these made me long for the intense heat of my beloved village. To escape the morning cold I got back into bed, curling up next to him and burying myself in his chest. 'How did you sleep?' he asked.

'Beautifully,' I replied, and he smiled. A large part of me still couldn't believe that I had encountered Sumayah in this way. I struggled to comprehend what I had witnessed. Why did I have to meet her now, when I had only just settled into my life here, and had finally managed to find happiness? I questioned. Seeing Sumayah distorted my entire perspective that Omar and I had worked so hard to alter from a path of self-destruction. Daylight gradually began to descend into our room.

'What do you fancy doing today?' he asked. 'Saira?' he said a second time.

I turned to look at him and replied, 'I'll prepare us some breakfast,' and walked into the kitchen. I thought of Ammuji; today I missed her deeply and needed her guidance. I cared for Sumayah, although I cared more for Omar and my bond with him, and seeing Sumayah had sent me into an internal battle that would cause me and Omar nothing but distress. I served us both breakfast, and we sat together in silence. I had envisaged a wonderful weekend with Omar, but this incident had displaced everything and beyond.

'You're not eating anything, Saira,' he said to me; I was oblivious to the fact that I had been sitting staring at my plate for some time now.

'Yes, I am,' I reassured him, and began to busy myself with cleaning up the dishes and vigorously wiping clean the table. 'I'm sorry, Omar,' I cried. 'We had finally worked everything out and things were going so well, and then seeing Sumayah just turned everything upside down and I feel so lost.'

'Hey, it's okay. I'm here with you and I will never let you feel lost,' he said, looking into my eyes. 'I promise you everything will be fine. Do you trust me?' he said.

'I trust you with my life.'

'Then believe me when I tell you that it's going to be fine,' he assured me. Wrapped up in his arms I came to the conclusion that no matter what happened, I would not allow our bond to be jeopardised. I decided I would put Omar first in the way that he had been prioritising me and my needs, with nothing but unconditional love.

'I'm being silly. Of course it's going to be okay – I have you beside me,' I told him. 'I won't let this break me, and I won't allow it to come between me and you.'

'So you won't burn anymore sandalwood today?' he asked.

I was confused. 'What do you mean?'

'Then I will feel assured that you're all right,' he explained.

I smiled. 'No, there's no need for sandalwood anymore.' I should have known that the early morning aroma of sandalwood incense would have informed him of my aroused state of mind; he knew I only did that in times of stress, and I silently vowed to remain undeterred and strong for us both.

We decided to spend the day watching movies beginning with *The Lion King*, one of our all-time favourites; watching this film always brought a smile to my face. I curled up next to Omar, resting upon his shoulders as he played with my hair. I must have heard his telephone ring at least a dozen times but most of the calls he disconnected, much to my surprise.

'Is it work, Omar?' I enquired.

'Yes, it's okay, nothing too urgent,' he said. The phone rang again and Omar held it up, appearing to contemplate whether or not he should take the call.

'Answer it,' I said to him.

'I'll be right back,' he told me, taking the phone to our bedroom. I continued watching the film. Half an hour later Omar was still on the phone, making me wonder what the emergency was. To put my mind at rest I walked towards our room; the door was wide open and he was standing facing the window, sounding irate as he spoke.

'Kareem, I don't feel there is anything to discuss. We are very happy you're marrying Sumayah and we have no issues with that,' I just about heard him say in a firm tone of voice. My heart began to palpitate, raising a dozen questions all at once. I stood still, pondering what discussion Kareem had wanted to have and why. Suddenly Omar was standing right in front of me, and I looked up directly into his eyes.

'Was that Kareem?' I asked.

'Yes, I took the call in here as I did not want to worry you.' The panic on my face must have given me away. 'Saira, this is why I have been ignoring his calls. I don't want this to continue upsetting you. I am happy to reduce contact with him,' he told me.

'Omar, it's not going to go away. It's all come back again,' I said in distress.

'Come here, sit down,' he said.

I managed to compose myself. 'What were you talking about with him?'

'It's nothing, Saira, it's not important,' he replied. I looked into his worried eyes and his creased forehead.

'Please, Omar, tell me,' I pleaded. He informed me that Kareem and Sumayah had asked for us to go round to their house as they had something urgent to discuss.

'Is she okay?' I asked.

'Yes, Saira, they are both fine, only he won't tell me over the phone what the issue is,' he explained.

'I think we should go, Omar.'

'Saira, do you really think that going there will resolve anything?' he said. I was lost in deep thought, contemplating the fact that if we did not go I would probably regret it at a later date, either way subjecting myself to further agony. 'Are you sure about this?' he asked.

'I am, if you are,' I said to him.

'I only want you to be happy,' he said, kissing my hand gently.

'Thank you,' I replied, and we left for Kareem's house with a mystery to unfold.

We arrived at the house, both of us anxious and slightly tense. Kareem and Sumayah greeted us with big smiles, although there was an awkward silence as the four of us sat down in their front room. Sumayah looked towards me and smiled, gesturing me closer towards her.

'I want to first thank you guys for coming,' said a nervous Kareem. I looked at them both and then looked away, while Omar sat looking subdued. 'You are probably wondering why I have summoned you in this manner,' he said. 'Bhabi, firstly I would like to apologise to you. Sumayah has told me everything – that you two are from the same village, almost sisters in fact.' I stared at them in disbelief.

'Kareem, let's not bring everything up,' said Omar.

'Omar, it's okay,' I reassured him, as Sumayah clutched on to me.

'I am so sorry for everything, Saira. I have missed you so much,' she cried out, putting her arms around my neck. Seeing Sumayah in this state of distress invoked in me the love that I had for our lifelong friendship and my mind finally surrendered to the pleas of my heart; I placed my arms around Sumayah in return to comfort her. Kareem and Omar quietly left the room, which I figured was to allow us time to reconcile. Sumayah and I sat close for a short while, sobbing, as I reflected on my painful journey, and thinking about Ammuji only seemed to elevate the pain from within.

'No more tears,' I said to Sumayah, forcing out a smile.

Sumayah composed herself and looked at me. 'I'm so sorry for everything. I should never have stayed away from you, Saira. I couldn't even be there for you when Ammuji passed away. I couldn't even bid you goodbye when you left to come here. I have told Abbuji that I have met you here and that I will see you every day.'

'You shouldn't have, Sumayah. I don't want to cause any problems for you both.'

'You have never caused me any problems, Saira. I have wronged you in many ways. I should have stood by you when our whole village stood against you,' she said. 'That is why I decided to reveal everything to Kareem. Can you find it in your heart to forgive me?' she cried.

'Sumayah, don't be silly, there is nothing to forgive,' I said, hugging her. We sat and talked for a while.

'You're still so beautiful, Saira,' she said.

'Don't be silly,' I replied.

'You and Omar are perfect together. I saw the way he looks at you – he adores you,' she said.

I smiled. 'Yes, I am very lucky to have him in my life. He has taken care of me well.'

'That time when you sent Abdullah I wanted to see you, but Abbuji began to curse me really bad, and…'

'Sumayah, it's okay, that time has gone now,' I reassured her. 'Thanks to God and Omar I am very happy and content here,' I told her.

'Will you do one thing for me, Saira?' I nodded. 'Will you help to arrange my wedding?' she pleaded.

'Yes, of course I will.' Just then there was a knock on the door, and Kareem and Omar came in with tea and snacks.

Omar sat right beside me, whispering, 'Are you all right?' I nodded and smiled.

'I really hope the four of us can put everything behind us and move forward,' said Kareem.

'We had better leave,' said Omar, looking at them.

'Saira,' said Sumayah, 'will you and Omar give me away?' I stared at her, astonished by her question, and then looked at Omar who seemed as shocked as I was. 'Only if that's all right with you both,' she added.

'We would love to, Sumayah,' I told her and Omar smiled.

We reached home as the light of the day turned into darkness; it had been another eventful day. The sky was now dark with very few stars; I recalled the blue skies of my beloved land. 'Tea is ready, Saira,' Omar said from behind me, and I sat next to him inhaling the fragrant aroma of ginger and cinnamon.

'Thank you for today,' I told him.

He looked into my eyes. 'Thank you for this life.' I cuddled close to him, a place where I felt safe, found love and life, and a place that shielded me from everything that hurt. I felt alive and content. I no longer felt perished or emaciated and no longer feared society or its consequences; he had taught me to live on the terms and conditions that best suited me and I cherished every moment beside him. He allowed me to become the definition of myself that I wanted to be. With

Omar, every joy was exhilaration and everything sad felt lighter.

Additionally I was overjoyed with the return of Sumayah into my life; it was as if I had never been away from her. We were almost the same people we had been back in the village, laughing and giggling at everything; I had been reunited with my sister again. We often sat together and talked about Ammuji, which made me sad, although I was glad to have Sumayah to share those moments with. I reflected how God truly works in mysterious ways. Even though I had lost Ammuji, and the pain of that ache was present in my heart every day, I had gained Omar, who I could not imagine being without, and now Sumayah, the sister and best friend that I had lost and was reunited with once again.

The next few months were busy. I commenced my voluntary work in the play bus a few hours each day with the intention of returning to education and teaching once again, which Omar was delighted with. I met with Sumayah almost every day as we planned her dream wedding. We joked about how she had always wanted to marry somebody from the UK. She had found true love, it appeared, as every time I met with her she had a different story to tell about how Kareem had brought her gifts and showered her with her favourite flowers and chocolates.

'I love this colour, Sumayah,' I gushed as we looked at colour schemes for her bridal outfit; we were both enchanted by a violet and cream-coloured three-piece gown. The wedding was now only six weeks away and everything was almost organised and set in place. I had had a busy morning at the play bus and then went to visit Sumayah. 'Right, that's finalised. I will place this order for you tomorrow, unless you want to go for a more traditional colour,' I said.

'No, I really like this one,' she asserted. It was almost 6 p.m. and I wanted to return home, as Omar would have finished work for the day, too.

'Sumayah, I will have to leave now,' I said, hurriedly collecting my bag and putting the collection of bridal magazines away neatly.

'Are you that anxious to see him?' she joked and I laughed. It was ironic that we were both living in an unknown country so far away from our native land, yet somehow we were content and had found solace within our lives.

I arrived home, immediately immersing myself in his aroma through our small hallway, and purposefully inhaled some more. 'You're back,' he said, smiling as he took my bag and coat. I wrapped my arms around his neck, locking my body into his. He smiled. 'What's this?'

'I missed you today,' I said.

'While you were busy planning a wedding.' He laughed. We sat in our favourite place and I laid my head on his shoulder to rest. We talked about my day followed by his. 'I have a surprise for you,' he said. 'Well, it's more of a suggestion,' he added. I listened eagerly. 'You know those new water wells I started? They need completing. So I was thinking of overseeing the work myself to ensure that the most needy villagers have access. So would you like to accompany me to Bangladesh for a few weeks – after Sumayah's wedding, of course.'

'Oh my, really?' I screeched.

'Is that a yes?' he asked humorously.

'Omar, that would be amazing,' I said captivated.

'Yes indeed.' He smiled and then kissed both my hands with his soft lips.

I lay back in his arms, contemplating the breathtaking beauty of my life, and as the saying goes, it's not the destination: what matters is the journey. I still thought about my beloved parents every day, although now with joy. Omar had completed my life in every way possible, bestowing it with love, peace and tranquillity. I felt blessed to have him by my side and he sweetened every moment I spent with him. I had lost many things on this tumultuous journey, only to realise that God replaces as much as you lose. I had finally begun to live with happiness and contentment, and eagerly anticipated the wedding of my beloved sister Sumayah followed by a return trip to my native land – its open blue sky, the feel of the soft wet mud beneath my feet, the sound of the water, the aroma of the open village air, and most importantly, having the most precious blessing of my life beside me…

The End

23285769R00163

Printed in Great Britain
by Amazon